RADIO FREE OLYMPIA

RADIO FREE
OLYMPIA

a novel

JEFFREY DUNN

IZZARD INK
PUBLISHING

IZZARD INK PUBLISHING
PO Box 522251
Salt Lake City, Utah 84152
www.izzardink.com

Library of Congress Cataloging-in-Publication Data

Names: Dunn, Jeffrey, 1956- author.
Title: Radio free olympia / a novel by Jeffrey Dunn.
Description: First edition. | Salt Lake City, Utah : Izzard Ink Publishing, [2023]
Identifiers: LCCN 2023015421 (print) | LCCN 2023015422 (ebook) |
ISBN 9781642280944 (hardback) | ISBN 9781642280951 (paperback) |
ISBN 9781642280968 (ebook)
Subjects: LCGFT: Novels.
Classification: LCC PS3604.U5586 R34 2023 (print) | LCC PS3604.U5586
(ebook) | DDC 813/.6—dc23/eng/20230516
LC record available at https://lccn.loc.gov/2023015421
LC ebook record available at https://lccn.loc.gov/2023015422

Designed by Daniel Lagin
Cover Design by Andrea Ho
Cover Images: shutterstock.com/Dmitriy Samorodinov
First Edition

Contact the author at info@izzardink.com or inchitensee@gmail.com
Hardback ISBN: 978-1-64228-094-4
Paperback ISBN: 978-1-64228-095-1
eBook ISBN: 978-1-64228-096-8

for my son Wilson
and
the Olympic Peninsula
Folk

RADIO FREE OLYMPIA'S OLYMPIC PENINSULA

CONTENTS

BOOK ONE
PETR'S BEGINNING

BOOK TWO
BAIE'S BEGINNING

BOOK THREE
BOOMER AND THE FAIRIES

BOOK FOUR
WILDSISTERS

BOOK FIVE
PASTURE POODLE AND THE LOST CHILDREN

BOOK SIX
STRANGERS

BOOK SEVEN
DOG SALMON BROTHER
AND THE WHISKY JACKS

BOOK EIGHT
TRESPASS

BOOK NINE
KUSHTAKAS AND SALMON WINGS

BOOK TEN
BURNING FOR YOU BURNING FOR ME

BOOK ELEVEN
SHE ONCE AND SHE ONCE MORE

BOOK TWELVE
ONLY OLD JOHN KNOWS

BOOK THIRTEEN
SHOT THROUGH

BOOK FOURTEEN
INTO THE DEEP BLACK

BOOK FIFTEEN
CONFLUENCES

PREFACE

first moved to Washington State's Olympic Peninsula during the summer of 1993. My enchanted wife, one-and-a-half-year-old wild child, and I left the industrial grit of Pittsburgh, PA, for the sodden slash of Elma, WA. We rented a quintessential logger special: Doug-fir frame, Doug-fir siding, no insulation.

> my very first night
> from the front porch listening:
> an ocean of frogs

Seriously, an ocean of frogs? But hear me out. Standing on that north-facing porch, I was overwhelmed by the volume and the resonance and the UTTER UBIQUITOUSNESS of those frogs. How shall I compare thee? To a symphony of leaf blowers? Kitchen appliances? Jet engines?

No? Then maybe we can settle on an ocean. Think of the way heavy surf sounds: its volume, its resonance, and its utter ubiquitousness—that sort of sound. That's what the frog chorus felt like for me on my first Olympic Peninsula night: completely natural yet thoroughly unnerving and destabilizing and overwhelming.

And as my little family and I found our way, I grew to realize that this was no place for me, at least if I were to be all that I was intended to be: a proselytizing European Christian in manifest destiny America. I also had a suspicion that the whole "dominion over the fish of the sea, and over the fowl of the air, and over every living thing that moveth upon the earth" simply wasn't going to fly, swim, or tunnel. No, not all.

But why? Could it have been the whole dominion thing?

Try wading into a Pacific Ocean current.

Try standing, much less walking, in a Pacific gale.

Try staying dry in Elma, WA's fifty inches of rain between November and March, just thirty inches south of the Olympic Mountains' eighty.

Try going off trail on the Olympic Peninsula without getting completely entangled and utterly exhausted in the undergrowth, stung by devil's club and nettles, and stalked by the bear or cougar that you can't possibly see ten feet in front of you.

Try finding somewhere that doesn't have fungal slippery jacks, panthers, fairy bonnets, oysters, fly agarics, all manner of russulas, red- and orange- and green- and yellow-tipped corals, in addition to slime molds, ghost plants, mildews, and the slime trails made by six-inch banana slugs. On the Olympic Peninsula, the kingdom of decomposition rules.

DOMINION? . . . not bloody likely.

Which brings us to *Radio Free Olympia,* a novel I started five years after I first encountered an ocean of frogs. Back then my idea was to write about a pirate radio station (an unlicensed, highly portable radio transmitter) that broadcasts voices from the Olympic Mountains. Some voices were to be natural and others not so natural. Seemed interesting, right?

And it didn't stop there. I also wanted to add a poetry journal kept by the spiritualist proprietor of a women's roadhouse on the Humptulips River, a place I named Wildsisters. I figured that somewhere along the way the pirate radio broadcasts and poetry journal would cross paths and maybe even marry. Who knew? It was a novel after all.

In planning the first draft, my aim was to be an open channel to all things Olympic Peninsula: explorers and natives, loggers and Wobblies, the Wild Man of the Wynoochee John Tornow, the Iron Man of the Hoh Bernard "John" Huelsdonk, the character from Native folklore named Sxwayo'klu (Basket Woman), the otter people from Native folklore known as the Kushtakas, and so on.

So when I got into writing the pirate radio broadcasts, the open channel idea got out of control. In addition to the characters from history and folklore, Raven stopped by and told me about being young and dumb and flying too close to the sun—you know, the Icarus thing. Then a little later he talked up his friends and acquaintances, like Coyote, Mole, Dog Salmon Brother, and Silver Salmon Sister, and before I knew it, Raven dubbed himself master of ceremonies and took over the whole caw-caw-phony.

But that's only the half of it. When I started writing the poetry journal, White Otter showed up and pushed Raven aside. In fact, White Otter rolled right in like a Pacific swell, and let me tell you, she didn't come alone. Oh no, in her wake she brought Orca, Gray Whale, Cormorant, Gull, Razor Clam, and, oh yes, Candlefish, who is a light unto our world.

And there was more. As I wrote, I remember thinking, say, this is a lot like *Huckleberry Finn*. And isn't that an echo from *The Red Badge of Courage*? And goodness me, this seems a lot like "Prufrock." And *Portrait of an Artist*. And, oh my God, the Bible, it's practically everywhere. And what's all this fuss over a shower of kelp? I'll be damned if these salty greens don't remind me of Saint Thérèse de Lisieux's shower of fragrant roses. And before long, I began to think that this, that, and everything else was some whimsical return from the literary repressed.

Finally after ten years, the great caw-caw-phony stopped, and with first draft in hand, I remember having a good bit of faith in the concept, but not so much in the execution. I mean, if I felt overwhelmed, what would readers think? It was clear to me that *Radio Free Olympia* wasn't ready to be my first novel, so I put the draft in a drawer and pushed it closed.

Ten years later our wild child passed, and I coped in various ways. First, I grieved with my enchanted wife and precious second child. I also tried to remember that life is for the living and stayed the course teaching high school English. I even started writing something completely new that turned out to be a number of surreal stories. My aim was to push the boundaries set forth by Richard Brautigan's *Trout Fishing in America*. When I finished, I thought I had something and self-published these pieces as *Dream Fishing the Little Spokane*. *Kirkus Reviews* called it "melancholic, irreverent, and untamed."

Which brings us back again to *Radio Free Olympia*.

Because I thought *Dream Fishing the Little Spokane* was successful in both concept and execution, I found the confidence to tear into my old scribbles. As a result, I radically rewrote the first hundred pages, tossing out half of the old and writing a whole lot of new. After that I went to work and revised the entire 450 pages. I tried to make each sentence so interesting that you'd go onto the next and the next and the next. And because *Radio Free Olympia* was so complex, I spent a good bit of time revising transitional words, sentences, paragraphs, and even chapters.

As I revised, I realized that *Radio Free Olympia* would only work if I quit thinking of it as a traditional novel. I mean to say (and this is where I'm going to get into some serious literary shit, the place where regular readers go to die) that *Radio Free Olympia* wasn't truly FREE until the channel was WIDE OPEN.

Too metaphysical? Too vague? Fair enough, so let's continue by noting that most readers call anything that's long-form fiction a novel. And that's true, of course, until it isn't, because if we go to the land where literary scholars play, we learn that not all long-form fiction is a novel.

Just to be clear, literary scholars define the novel by often citing Ian Watt's *Rise of the Novel* (1957), and if I may paraphrase, Mr. Watt's definition boils down to *long-form fiction that records a consciousness moving through a particular time and place—all of which a middle-class reader will recognize as real.* Egregiously reductive, yes, but for my purposes, which is to provide a preface for this piece of long-form fiction, I think it will do.

And it's not like there aren't a bunch of novels that break this definition. Literary scholars call these antinovels, and regular readers just call them hard. Examples abound, so to name a few, there are William Faulkner's *As I Lay Dying* with its multiple points of view done in different voices; or Kurt Vonnegut's *Slaughterhouse Five*, which is "unstuck in time"; or Chinua Achebe's *Things Fall Apart*, which sets the Igbo culture against the European (middle-class) culture; or James Joyce's *Ulysses*, where the words arise from a place, Dublin, in multiple and sometimes unreliable forms.

Okay then, so *Radio Free Olympia* isn't a regular novel. It's got all these voices. It jumps from place to place. And the Olympic Peninsula is set against North American (middle class) culture. So how in the hell should it be read?

A good question, and here is my best answer. No antinovel (actually, in this case I prefer novel of place) is without a way to read it, and this is because a writer provides threads to follow. The problem is that *Radio Free Olympia* doesn't follow the thread of a single consciousness. Instead, four of its threads are different points of view done in different voices, and the final thread arises from a place, the Olympic Peninsula itself. Keep that in mind, and *Radio Free Olympia* can be a joy to read. And with that in mind, here is an outline of those five threads.

1. Petr (pət-ər, from *petr*oleum) Bauer, the focus of every odd-numbered "book," is cast adrift in a 55-gallon petroleum drum and found by the reclusive, down-and-out logger Bear Bauer. Because he has cut ties with society, Bear feels no compunction in taking in the infant. Soon after, Bear gives infant-Petr a transistor radio for a mother, the broadcasts becoming Petr's mother tongue and the foundation for his later Olympic pirate radio broadcasts.

2. Raven interjects his own story into every odd-numbered "book," and as you read, you'll find that Raven's story is in the same place heading toward the same time as Petr's. I think knowing this relieves a little bit of narrative anxiety, the sort that comes about when you think all these words lead in different directions. It also helps to know that Raven sees Petr from a bird's-eye view and is able to provide useful transitions along the way.

3. Baie (bay, from the French for berry), the author of the poetry journal that comprises the even-numbered "books," has returned home after a failed French postulancy (prenoviate in a monastery) and her parents' deaths. Once home, she takes over her parents' wild cranberry farm and teams up with her battered yet resourceful friend Dori to turn the cranberry barn into Wildsisters, an all-women's roadhouse. From there, Baie and Dori collect a band of wildsisters and kick their collective human drama into the spiritual realm.

4. White Otter brings her own stories of environmental purity and degradation to Baie's even-numbered "books," and as you read, you'll find that White Otter and Baie talk the same spiritual language. I think knowing this relieves some existential anxiety, the sort that comes about when you're stripping wallpaper and are afraid there won't be a wall. But no worries, because there's definitely a wall in *Radio Free*

Olympia, and if you want to know what and where that proverbial wall is, White Otter is the character to ask.

5. Finally, the Olympic Peninsula is the source from which all words arise. The novel's words refer, of course, to a place (the Aristotelian *mimesis* sort of thing), but I want more—I want the place to speak for itself (the Joycean *mother tongue of place* sort of thing). To accomplish this, the Olympic Peninsula speaks mostly in English, sometimes in French and Salish, and draws from its lexical wealth: logger, labor, and sewing slang (I have included a glossary), Christianity (especially Roman Catholic) and the Bible, tribal history and folklore, European settler history, Western literature, plant and animal biology, geography, geology, radio tech jargon, and drug subculture slang. The intended effect is to focus and amplify setting while at the same time diversifying character.

Which brings us full circle, back to that first night on my north-facing porch, the place where an Olympic Peninsula chorus of frogs went to work on me, work I greatly appreciate, work that made me a better person.

And my hope is that while reading *Radio Free Olympia*, you will enjoy following Petr and Baie's exploits. You will take delight in all Raven and White Otter have to say. You will be transported to the Olympic Peninsula, a place that refuses anyone's dominion, creates a space for our imagination, and provides the possibility that maybe, just maybe, if we let it, our planet will change us for the better.

IF

If Raven soared beyond the red huckleberry sun
If Coyote chased his echo 'round and 'round and 'round
If White Otter rocked in the surf, a cradle
If torn flesh hit Orca's pulsing mainline
If Gray Whale sang, calved, sang again
If Mole beckoned, dangling a bleeding heart blossom
If Gull winked, the twinkle an ironic starlight
If Candlefish burned a Pentecostal bright
If Boomer planned an eclipse, dark, darker
If Cormorant cursed the whole works
If stigmata returned, this time running kelp-forest green

BOOK ONE

PETR'S BEGINNING

IN HIS BEGINNING

In His beginning He cast a six-sided die. Yes, He's a gambler, despite His all-knowingness, despite the fix being in. And although He knew the end result, He couldn't SEE, so He flipped on the switch. He heard a buzz and saw the flicker of a fluorescent bulb, yellow through the cigarette-dirty glass, nothing to be done, the ballast going. And there was the tumbling and the coming to rest—the first throw.

And He cast again, and the result was a rumple of dirty clothes strewn about His bedbug floor. Later someone, certainly not He, called the rumple Olympia. And there was the tumbling and the coming to rest—the second throw.

And He cast another time and knocked over His scotch and water. The volatile spill bounded the rumple on three sides and trickled across the fourth. Some other nameless ones called one puddle Pacific, another Juan de Fuca, the last Hood Canal, and the trickle Chehalis. And there was the tumbling and the coming to rest—the third throw.

And He cast again (yes, you're starting to wonder, I've heard this all before; where exactly are "the plants bearing seed according to their kinds" and all that?) and up came the Sitka spruce, salal, the slippery jack. And there was the tumbling and the coming to rest—the fourth throw.

And now He was feeling an edge, so He decided to play the rush. He was going all the way to the river and casting to crack the nut. As a result, gray whales struck out from coastal nurseries and orcas breached into the crystal-line air. Spadefooted moles tunneled for worms and bulbs, and amorous fishers scent-marked down fir trunks and across the forest floor. Close-to-the-bone humans hunkered down about their sparking fire and sharpened stone points and edges. And there was the tumbling and the coming to rest—the fifth throw.

And He cast a final time, the die showing only six numbers, the die possessing a mere six sides. As a result, we Old Growth Folk became speech and spirit incarnate. White Otter took to her kelp beds, and I, Raven, found a red cedar perch on which to fluff my iridescent feathers. And there was the tumbling and the coming to rest—the sixth throw.

Then He stopped short of a seventh throw. He knew He had underplayed and won. He was no pigeon. He was He after all, and He knew when to tap out. And He rested from all the gambling and decided to cash in His luck, collect the story whose cataclysm He already knew, but I don't know, and neither do you.

THE INFANT

Someone had swaddled the infant in a thin cotton blanket. Someone then repackaged the newborn in an army surplus blanket, one made of wool, the kind soldiers wrap about themselves, down in a foxhole, a mortar shell bursting close by.

That someone later put the bundle in a fifty-five-gallon petroleum drum. Then that someone shoved the babe out into the Pacific. At least for that moment, that someone had lost interest in childcare. That someone must have decided to do something else.

No one knew how the oil drum got out to sea, was it dropped off a dock or was it shoved off the beach only to be pulled offshore by the tide and the wind? Suffice it to say that the drum did not take on water and sink. The drum didn't become the infant's coffin. It didn't become a dumpster where Dungeness crabs crawled in for their next meal.

Instead, the Pacific currents, tides, and winds conspired to deposit the oil drum onto a solid strand. The infant, all cotton-swaddled and wool-packaged, remained safe and warm, all the while looking through where the lid had been, all the while gazing up at the stars. The ocean's hand had ceased to rock. A single raven's one, two, then three knocks came down from a Sitka spruce along the forest's edge.

Fact was the infant was like damaged goods in a discount grocery store. Nameless and unbaptized, who was going to take it home and put it on the shelf among the name brands? Who was going to have faith that someday it would come to something?

A planet, probably Venus, shone like a mother's earring. The light caught the infant's eye. The infant stirred against its packaging, and a bubble of saliva formed on its lips. The bubble popped.

SHI SHI BEACH

Although the infant didn't yet have a name, the beach upon which the newborn had been deposited sure did. Long ago the Makah people named this strip of sand Shi Shi (shai shai). Some say that *shi shi* is Makah for surf beach. Others say smelt beach. The truth is we here on the Olympic Peninsula don't concern ourselves much with the something-lost, something-gained of translation. The truth is we call this stretch of sand Shi Shi.

And because people and landscapes become inextricably intertwined, the Makah became a native people not only around Shi Shi Beach but also throughout the entire northwest corner of the Olympic Peninsula. The Makah traditionally ate whale, harbor seal, porpoise, salmon, halibut, and all manner of bottom fish. Seal blubber was rendered into an oil eaten at every meal.

Five permanent villages, Waatch, Sooes, Deah, Ozette, and Bahaada, were constructed of red cedar plank longhouses. Kidickabit, Archawat, Hoko, Tatoosh Island, Ozette River, and Ozette Lake were summer camps established for food gathering.

The Makah were particularly adept at red cedar canoe building. Each canoe had a special purpose. Some canoes were built for waging war. The Makah had a particularly fierce reputation among other native peoples.

Other canoes were built for halibut or salmon fishing. The largest were built for whale and seal hunting or cargo transporting.

All of this is to say that Shi Shi Beach, the very sands upon which the infant was deposited in a fifty-five-gallon petroleum drum, has a long human history, one that greatly precedes European invasion, one that I, Raven, have been watching over for a very long time.

BEAR BAUER

Although the infant didn't yet have a name, the old man who came upon the infant in 1965 did. The old man had matted hair like a feral dog. He had a single worn-tombstone tooth and a ten days' growth. He wore a faded olive M-51 military jacket with a tear under the right arm. And he had a birth certificate, a document he had never seen, but nevertheless, one that was filed in the Grays Harbor County Public Records Department. Once in 1928, some record keeper had written a name, Lancelot Aloysius Bauer, in childish cursive. His mates called him Bear.

Born in a logging camp, Bear grew up in various bunk houses and one-room schools. He was introduced to tragedy early, his mother dying on a mess hall table, his younger brother stillborn like a slab of beef liver ready for onions. His father, a choker on a logging gang, had his head taken clean off when a yarding cable snapped, whipcracking through the godforsaken air. "Oh, shit." Silence. "Shit."

From that point forward various cookhouse mavens kept an eye on child-Bear by keeping his little hands useful. Before breakfast he was put to work making sandwiches. First, he lined up the bread in three automobile assembly line rows. On the first row he spread a generous layer of grape jelly, a Chevrolet Six of a sandwich. On the second row he peeled off sliced bologna, a Pontiac Straight Eight of a sandwich. And on the third row he laid down thick slabs of ham, a Cadillac V-16 of a sandwich.

Once the middles were topped with a second slice of bread, the loggers, all bleary-eyed with the previous night's sleep, would pass under the sign nailed above the cookhouse door:

TAKE ALL YOU WANT
AND
EAT ALL YOU TAKE

And once inside the cookhouse, the loggers would help themselves to sausages, ham, bacon, eggs, French toast, hotcakes, hash browns, toast, rolls, juice, and coffee. As per both custom and contract, the loggers ate their fill, and once fully satisfied, they would pick up a sandwich from each of child-Bear's production lines, pass back under the sign, and pile into a crummy, in this case a dilapidated school bus commandeered to transport men to the job site. As the crummy pulled out of camp, child-Bear always felt himself a worker on America's bean-can line awaiting the call of the four-four; the four long and four short blasts blown on a steam donkey whistle when a logger was hurt.

Not surprisingly, Bear grew up fast. Soon enough he piled into a crummy and headed out with a big-boy logging crew. The hooktender—he was the man in charge on the logging site—started him out as a whistle punk. Not-so-child-Bear's job was to yell commands back and forth between the choke setter and the donkey puncher, who ran the engine that pulled logs to the collection area. He learned to spit the tobacco called snus, so that even when the Pacific blew a gale in his face, he never stained his flannel shirt.

And because Bear proved reliable, the hooktender quickly assigned him to choke setting, the passing of a short steel cable from the choker hook around a log and back again. Once set, young Bear would yell up to the whistle punk who yelled to the donkey puncher to engage the donkey engine's drive. The main bull line cable then began to wind on a spool, which cinched the choker cable tight around the log. Finally, as the spool continued to wind, the log was pulled back toward the donkey to be yarded for shipment out.

As he matured, Bear proved to be nimble at choke setting among cut timber. He was adept at moving from log to ground and back to log, and when the logs were close enough, simply from log to log. He also proved to be bull-line strong. He could sling rigging from sunup to sundown, only resting between turns, the time between one choke set and the next.

Back in the bunkhouse, loggers chipped their teeth on stories, and one of those stories was about Bear and the mountain goats. "Now, y' got t'understand that mountain goats ain't native t' these here mountains. Bunch o' hunter dudes in chokebores from Alaska and British Columbia brought 'em here. You seen them goats up on the ridge? Why, they hop 'round up there on them rocks like rabbits. Cougars cain't get at 'em. People cain't neither, unless y' got a rifle.

"Now, I seen young Bear down in a jackpot o' logs and a bunch o' goats up on the ridge watchin' 'im. I'll swear I seen 'em watch young Bear bounce 'round on them logs. They's tryin' t' fig'r out if he was one o' them. I jus' bet that if Bear went up that mountain he could o' joined up with 'em. We never would o' seen 'im ag'in. Ain't that just the truth, young Bear? We'd've never seen y'ag'in."

Once Bear's chest filled out, the hooktender moved him up onto the landing bucking logs, and once Bear proved to be a capable sawyer, the hooktender moved him down in the timber felling Doug-fir, western hemlock, and red cedar. As a full-fledged member of the logging crew, Bear also became entitled to head out on weekends with the other timber beasts. Most often they blew off steam in Forks and sometimes blew up the engine in Port Angeles or Aberdeen. There Bear tossed down boilermakers and was introduced to the Industrial Workers of the World. There he learned about fellow workers fighting a class war against the scabs and scissorbills whose aim it was to steal his job. He learned about Jerusalem Slim, whose dad was a woodworker and who was nailed to a sawlog because he upset the money changers' table. And he learned about the Jesus of the Lumberjacks, Jimmy Rowan, who wrote "The IWW in the Lumber Industry," first published in the Lumberworkers Industrial Union #500, Seattle, WA, 1920.

If a saw mill worker is submissive and subordinates his manhood and sacrifices his independence to the will of the company, he is rewarded by a life of grinding poverty, hopeless drudgery and a condition of economic dependence and insecurity. If he asserts his manhood, he faces discharge and the blacklist which, if he is a married man, means the breaking up of his home, and separation from wife and children.

Bear had never known any place but the camp and the woods, and in these places, anything but a square deal resulted in rough justice. To learn that there was a wider world where this arrangement did not win the day troubled him to distraction; these new ideas fed like wild yeast on the home-brew in his skull.

No sooner had Bear learned that being a logger was a bitch and a whip-saw, he pledged the IWW. He was no different from most young bucks; he wanted to join together to overthrow the current unjust order. And follow-ing the algebra of the timber industry laid out by Jimmy Rowan, Bear soon found himself on the blacklist, which is to say, Bear's cherished IWW mem-bership made him damn near unemployable.

As a result, Bear was taken on by only the most desperate gyppo loggers. These small-time outfits logged tiny parcels of culls, timber not worth cut-ting. The work was hard. The work was scarce. And over time the work ate at him like a wood-rotting fungus. "Now, Jake, take it easy when y'get t'cuttin' on that tree. I'm guessin' it's got a blind conk." "Yep, I got a feeling this tree's an outlaw." "You got that right, Jake. This whole stand's full o' deadfall an' widowmakers. Once a tree gets all rotten and conky, ain't nobody can tell what it's goin' t' do."

No longer welcome in company logging camps and intolerant of any-thing approaching town life, Bear struggled to find a place to lay his head. He found he needed to get creative, and to that end, he chose a spot east of Shi Shi Beach, north of Olympic National Park, south of the Makah Reser-vation, and well west of Highway 101. This spot was situated on company land, logged ten to fifteen years ago, and only accessible on a derelict one-lane logging road. Because Bear knew that such land, like himself, was of little interest, he could live for a good long while outside a number of laws.

He salvaged his shack from a ghost town of an old logging camp. Once upon a time, loggers lived in bunkhouses pulled about on narrow-gauge log-ging railroads. As logging camps became more permanent and then became not at all, abandoned sites were quickly overgrown with moss, blackberry, fireweed, and fern. As the saying goes, one man's trash is another man's trea-sure, and Bear enlisted a fellow Wobbly, one who had started up his own hauling business, to help him resituate his treasure. Together, they hitched a creaky, abandoned bunkhouse to a come-along and pulled it, old groaning, rusty railroad wheels and all, onto a flatbed trailer. Bear then directed his buddy to the spot where the old bunkhouse was laid to rest. No longer a hog at the cookhouse door, Bear planned to live out, in this place and from this point forward, what he suspected would be the short of his life.

NAMING THE FOUNDLING

Around here, Captain James Cook named a place Cape Flattery because "there appeared to be a small opening which flattered us with the hopes of finding an harbour." Also around here, the Salish named the tallest glacier-covered crag Sunh-a-do, the Spanish named it Cerro Nevado de Santa Rosalia, and the English settled on the anglicized-from-Greek Mount Olympus.

Unlike capes and mountains, most children hear their names before coming into the world. Little hotdogs that they are, some infants already have a brand. Some even have a variety and a serial number. A few newborns, especially ones cast off at birth, may not hear their names through the mother-flesh and amnion-deep.

Of course, Lancelot Aloysius Bauer, better known as Bear, hadn't heard our infant's name, so it was fortunate that when Bear peered down into the oil drum, he gathered up the contents, looked over the fifty-five-gallon drum, read the word "Petroleum," parsed out the name Petr (pət-ər), and tentatively growled "Petr" to a low-hanging glaucous-winged gull. Then more emphatically he growled "Petr" to a razor clam squirting a few feet away. And finally marking his territory, he growled "Petr Bauer" up to me, Raven, sitting on a Sitka spruce branch.

How serendipitous, wouldn't you say? Fact is I like biding my time along Shi Shi Beach because I never know when something shiny and new might come ashore. And so on that particular day, the shiny new thing turned out to be you, Petr Bauer, and may I say, it was a pleasure to meet you.

HUCK FINN AS A YOUNG AMBROSIA BEETLE

Bear decided to take the newly named Petr fresh off the beach and deliver him to his shack. Once the two were safely inside, he cradled the infant in his left arm like a precious venison ham.

And what came next should come as no surprise because Bear held firmly to the timber beast code: when it comes to necessities, food was third only to air and water, and since there was no shortage of air and water on the Olympic Peninsula, food immediately jumped to number one. The timber beast code also maintained that a friend always opened the cookhouse door to another friend. Being that this friend was an infant, Bear looked down and asked, "What'll it be, bud, milk or milk? Well, milk it is, then," and Bear busied himself with improvising.

Problem #1: Bear hated being dependent on anyone or anything to get his life done, and as a result he hated modern convenience. From there it followed that he refused to have an electrical connection to power such things as lights and a refrigerator, so preserving fresh milk was a problem.

Solution #1: Bear canned, pickled, smoked, or dried any excess food, and luckily for Petr, Bear kept a canister of powdered milk on the hand. In no time Bear combined some dry milk powder with spring water in an old clay jug, stuck his thumb on top, and shook like a logger rolling a floating log with his feet.

Problem #2: Bear needed to get the milk from the jug into Petr, but he didn't keep a box of bottle nipples around. Luckily, he remembered reading *The Adventures of Huckleberry Finn*. No, Bear wasn't much of a reader, he much preferred wrestling the world to reading some words, but when he did read, he didn't so much sound out the letters as make moving pictures, and what he pictured from *Huck Finn* was Huck finding a milk bottle stuffed with a rag for a baby to suck.

Solution #2: because he saved his empty bourbon bottles, Bear poured the mixture into a pint bottle, grabbed a loose sock, and stuffed it home. To be sure, it was a crude fix, but lickety-split, Petr latched onto the milk-soaked rag like an ambrosia beetle on tree fungus, drained the bottle, burped, and fell fast asleep.

With a just-satisfied baby in tow, Bear looked about his shack and felt a decidedly foreign sensation: shame. Embarrassment? He really didn't see the value. Remorse? It really felt like a luxury he couldn't afford. But looking into this peacefully sleeping, innocent face, Bear felt a twinge of humiliation. True, he had collected everything he owned from beachcombing and camp-site trolling. True, his old knives, forks, and spoons had come ashore after many an Olympic storm. True, his old cast-iron skillet, enamel plate, and tin cup had been found in a long-abandoned hunter's camp. And true, his old bedding had been lifted by the wind out of someone's pickup and deposited in the middle of the road as sometimes happens between the time the evic-tion notice is served and the sheriff comes knocking at the door.

But that face. That innocent face. Bear couldn't help but feel that it was time to make his shack a home, and because necessity is the mother of inven-tion, he snatched an old tattered hickory shirt off the clothes pile and arranged the shirt in his firewood holder, a sliced-in-half, ten-gallon steel drum. Then after nesting Petr in the softness of the old shirt, Bear awkwardly logger-squatted and gently rocked the steel half-moon, which just happened to be below where I, Raven, was sitting outside on a Doug-fir branch.

Pretty bucolic scene, wouldn't you say? You see, I followed this shiny new Petr from Shi Shi Beach to inside Bear's shack. It's really not so far as the raven flies. And, hey, I'm proud that I was the first to say, "Welcome home, foundling Petr. Welcome home."

BAPTISM

We on the Olympic Peninsula don't do baptism with water. Of course, it's not because we have a shortage. Oh, no, if water is the necessary ingredient, then every day here is a baptism.

But that's not to say that Petr was never baptized. It's just to say that Petr was baptized in the regular Olympic Peninsula way, something that happens often, in fact, nightly in certain seasons. You might even say Petr's baptisms were somewhat orthodox, a full immersion really, but in Petr's case, his full immersion was deep in the sharp trill of countless Pacific treefrogs and the soft cluck of red-legged frogs, a total submersion in a hymn of amphibian rapture.

And it's not that we don't have churches on the Olympic Peninsula. The truth is I quite like sitting on the bell scaffold of the Quileute Indian Shaker Church. I especially like to perch there when the sun's energy begins to wane in the west.

I also like listening when the old Shaker stops by every night and rings the bell. I'm not much of a Bible reader, and neither are these Shakers, but we here on the Olympic Peninsula really like to listen.

MOTHER TONGUE

As a father Bear was fairly thoughtless, but he wasn't heartless. Having no recollection of his own father's voice, Bear's attitude toward Petr was summed up in the words, "Yep, Petr, we got the whole out-o'-doors to piss in," words he often offered up while stoking the fire or frying up razor clams and chanterelles.

But Bear did remember his mother's voice before falling off to sleep every night. He didn't recollect any conversations or even specific words, but he did remember her voice's color and cadence, so much so that every twilight he wove his remembrance with the sounds of the forest, the two becoming one in a single serenade.

And because the heart is an empathic organ, Bear was troubled by the similarities between Petr's and his own childhood experience. As Bear saw it, Petr most assuredly, though unverifiably, had no memory of his dear mother's voice. Over time this intimation gnawed at Bear like an engraver beetle. The intimation furrowed out an elegant pattern between his cortex and skull. It left behind galleries of regret, desolate crypts of remorse.

As a result, Bear decided to fill this void, and toward this end he used something that had recently come his way. The story goes that while beachcombing, Bear came across a number of Japanese glass fishing floats, commodities that were becoming valuable with West Coast urban decorators. To take advantage of this windfall, Bear took the glass floats out to U.S. 101 to sell, and once there he came across an unattended backpack, another piece of luck he figured bounced off the back of a pickup. He looked up the road. He looked down the road. He looked into the woods toward the ocean, then the other way toward the mountains. And after seeing no one except a Doug-squirrel run up a Sitka spruce and a lone dark-eyed junco disappear into the snowberries, he made the backpack his own.

Inside the backpack Bear found two pair of underwear, a few odd socks, and an unopened tin of snus, not exactly treasures to be sure, but Bear knew as well as the next brush ape that underwear and socks, used or otherwise, were always welcome additions, and who didn't need a fresh dip? He also found a red Realtone TR-1088 Comet transistor radio. Bear recalled turning over the ethereal plastic rectangle in his hand. He recalled feeling, well, what was it? Anticipation? Maybe. A bit of fear? Sure. Attraction? Hmm . . . Naturally he thumbed the on/off/volume dial, and what came was a woman's voice. Truth be told, Bear had never been one to hunt or scavenge for women. Like his mother's voice at night, this one came to him.

And Bear thought it shouldn't be any different for Petr. To make it so, Bear busied himself intently clearing a place on his scarred and spotted table. He removed three bowls clotted with oatmeal and a plate littered with mussel shells and set them in the wash basin. He then set the radio in the open space and let it play what was now the voice of Petr's mother.

". . . OLYP weather tonight is partly cloudy with a low of forty-eight degrees. Tomorrow, after the marine layer burns off, you may be rummaging for your sunglasses. Speaking of sunglasses, remember that our friends at the Driftwood Pharmacy carry a complete line of heading-out-to-the-beach needs. If you can't remember where you put your sunglasses or need some sun block to protect that oh-so-white skin you've been hiding from the world, then stop in and check out what the Driftwood Pharmacy has to offer, a full-service pharmacy meeting the needs of Peninsula families since '56.

"And since you are still up, working the night shift or just having another one of those hot flashes, here's a blast from the past, Buddy Holly and 'Raining in My . . .'."

BUT I DIGRESS, LET ME INTRODUCE MYSELF

I thought you might be wondering about the voice telling this story. You might be curious about the one who hears what is said, witnesses what is done, and sits up in these trees, first this Sitka spruce, then that Doug-fir. You might be someone who prefers that fictional voices, especially those offering a bird's-eye view, be held to full disclosure. So in that spirit, here is my coming of age story.

I, child-Raven, was lucky to soar without peer. I was lucky to be a yearling out among endless todays. I thought no one would notice if I flew too near the sun. I didn't foresee what might come next.

As a result, I left my father below and caught an Olympic Mountain updraft. I circled higher and higher. The sun burned into the black pool of my eye. The air crackled my feathers and drove me into the all-enveloping blue.

Beneath lay a blanket over the forest, deep, an exhale of fog.

Above boiled a turbulence of interference, a cacophony, a chaos of noise.

"...hissssssss...scritch...pop...scritch...hissssssss..."

I couldn't shake the fizzle blooming in my head like forget-me-nots, paintbrush, and avalanche lily. My skull became a tuner, my beak an antenna, and as I received, I lost my compass. Alive with radio waves, my body skipped off the upper atmosphere. Brilliant as magnesium flame and then black as coal, I tumbled back to earth, vibrating.

"...buzzzzzzz...crack...crackle...crack...buzzzzzzz..."

Suddenly I hit the green-black surface of the Hood Canal. My feathers unglued on impact and scattered in the current of the incoming tide. Smelted by the sun, the pool of my eye, now a black diamond, sank down, down, down.

MORE MOTHER TONGUE

When Petr awoke, Bear stood grinning above him. "There y' go, li'l Petr," he said using a grimy thumbnail to dig the sleep out of the corner of the foundling's eye. "I got y'a mum, yes siree. Now I'll go split us some wood." Then the door crashed. Petr blinked.

From that moment forward, Petr was often left alone with his Realtone TR-1088 Comet of a mother. She needed nine volts. She was red. And she had an earphone jack. Petr dreamt to the sound of her back-back-back sports play-by-play. He toddled about in the sound of her coming-up-on-the-hour news patter. He gazed in the new moon night through the window up into the Doug-firs and further to the Milky Way, and as with most children, his mother's voice became his own, the one he used to speak up into the trees and out into the stars.

"Top of the morning, La Push. Life got you down? Can't seem to get that special she frog to answer your call? Well, Slimy Time Dating Service is for you. Slimy Time has thousands of eligible bachelorettes just listening for Mister Right. If you're tired of the swamp scene, just give Slimy Time a call and take their free, no-obligation compatibility profile to match you up with the red-legged darling of your dreams. That's right, just one call can put you on the path to a relationship you've only dreamed about. Stop all that chirping in the dark. Call one, eight hundred, five five G-R-E-E-N. You'll be glad you did.

"And now, for those of you already braving it in the early morning migration, be advised there is a pileup between Spruce and Star . . ."

FAST FORWARD

Young Petr was making breakfast. He stood in the kitchen, all of seventeen years old, beard starting, deodorant innocent, dropping dollops of pancake batter into sizzling grease. Making pancakes made him feel sexy. He hadn't yet met a girl, but when he did, he thought she'd be like pancake batter. He knew he would oh-so-gently put his spoon into her mix and oh-so-slowly stir.

While Petr lifted perfectly browned pancakes from the hot skillet, the percussion of Bear's splitting maul rang among the trees. Over the years, Petr had become accustomed to the rhythm of Bear's maul. Its regular thwack was a tick tock in these wilds, safe, a Big Ben reminding Petr that all was well. Then the sound stopped.

What always came next was Bear's entrance. He always came in like the weather. First came the back-to-back thunder claps: BOOM, the door opening; BOOM, the door closing. Next came the drop of atmospheric pressure: gruff, tired, hungry. But that's not what came next. This time nothing broke the silence. Petr wondered. Then he wondered some more. And finally he went outside, scanned about, and found Bear sitting, wedged between a vine maple's crook. Bear's maul stood upright between his feet, the tool's toe sticking in the ground, the handle supporting his hands, his head resting on this accidental pedestal.

Petr may have been only seventeen, but he knew death when he saw it. He'd helped Bear butcher any number of deer, worked on a few elk, once even on a bear.

The only man he knew had just become a statue.

Petr bit at his left thumbnail. Petr became a statue, too.

WHAT WAS LEFT

Petr didn't stay a statue for long. He found he didn't have what it takes to be a statue. He was too squirrelly to go into being a statue full-time.

Looking at the undelightful body of Bear, Petr wasn't sure what came next. He had no formal education. He had never sat in rows of desks with other children getting the daily question, "Pet . . . r, that's got to be a misprint. Peter Bauer?" He had never answered, "Here," never been institutionally accounted for.

But Petr had learned. He learned in the same way that all Olympic creatures learn, watching and listening to other creatures, especially their own kind, even if his mother was a transistor radio and his father a green bucker when it came to parenting.

Petr remembered being a child, snuggling into the flannel-soft crook of Bear's arm, and listening to Bear read from a cheap Modern Library paperback, one that Bear had collected from a swap meet and stacked with others in one corner of the shack. "But green trees are a different thing. Hist! that sound is the air breathing among the leaves!" and "A bird came down the walk. He did not know I saw. He bit an angle-worm in half and ate the fellow, raw." and "'My good boy!' The Director wheeled sharply round on him. 'Can't you see? Can't you see?'"

When he was older, Petr watched Bear bury what was left from a butchering. Bear said that everything wanted an easy meal, "You don't got t' put a free sign out for stuff on the side o' the road. The side o' the road's just one big party. If y' don't want no party at y'r place, then don' leave it on th' side of the road."

Petr certainly didn't want Bear's leavings to be an easy meal, so off he went to the cedar-gray, moss-shrouded outhouse. He grabbed the door handle and pulled, grating one hinge against the other. Inside was a spade that he lifted free. Outside was a Doug-fir that he set the spade against.

Petr then went to work moving Bear's body. He wedged his hands into Bear's armpits and tried to raise him. He desperately struggled with Bear's deadweight. He hadn't come into his man strength yet, but he lifted enough of Bear to drag and dump him onto their log caddy, a reclaimed wheelbarrow frame with a piece of beachcombed plywood bolted on top. Finally he placed the spade between Bear's legs to keep it from bouncing loose.

The destination was a boggy place where Bear took things to disappear. Here Petr began to dig, cutting through the root tangle and into the moss muddle. As he dug, he remembered that when Bear worked, he often gruffly sang over and over, "Nobody wants t' work too hard. Nobody wants t' work too hard. Nobody wants t' work too hard. Nobody wants . . ."

Soon it began to rain. The steady drizzle ran across Petr's forehead, into his eyes, over his cheeks, off his chin, and into the opened earth. He turned shovelful after shovelful and then stopped. He decided to walk back to their shack and get a few of Bear's things. He decided Bear might need these things wherever Bear was now.

When he returned, Petr rolled Bear off the log caddy and into the shallow grave. Next he dropped in Bear's whipsaw, axe, splitting maul, and chip-edged wedges. Hair greasy wet, Bear's mother-of-pearl eyes stared up at Petr, and then Bear's leavings disappeared under a final shovelful of earth.

Petr said his last, "Nobody wants to work too hard," and walked away. He found walking away from Bear no more and no less difficult than being cast adrift by his mother.

DO YOU KNOW THE WAY TO ABERDEEN?

Petr put on the what-the-hell attitude that so many down-and-out loggers wear and packed a worn duffel bag with a few pairs of socks, some underwear, seventy-two one dollar bills (he got them from Bear's swap meet jar stowed under Bear's bed next to the wood stove), a few pairs of tattered jeans, some flannel shirts, his worn Stihl cap, his Realtone TR-1088 Comet radio, the remaining batteries, and the hand crank charger Bear used to power the batteries. He then ventured out into a cold Pacific rain.

After the long, wet walk out to Highway 101, Petr flashed his thumb. He knew there was always a pickup with an empty bed passing by. "Where y' headin' boy?"

"Aberdeen."

"Got Buster in the front, but y'r welcome to the back. Suit y'rself."

He did.

HITCHING TO ABERDEEN

dead in a cardboard
box on an abandoned roof
trying to change lanes

WELCOME TO ABERDEEN

Around here, Aberdeen is known as a rough town. Back when the newcomers pushed the old-timers into hard times, Aberdeen was known as "The Hellhole of the Pacific" and "The Port of Missing Men."

You might be interested in our local serial killer Billy Gohl. The story starts with Billy up in the Yukon prospecting for gold. He dug a slew of coyote holes which yielded only muck, so he gave up and came to Aberdeen. He tried his hand at bartending, and then he signed on as an official for the Sailor's Union of the Pacific. He saw a better percentage in mining flesh-and-blood sailors than wishful-thinking gold.

The shakedown started when sailors got off their ships and reported to the Sailor's Union Hall on East Heron Street.

"You new 'bout these parts?" said Billy.

"First time," said the sailor.

"First time, huh? How's your family? You keepin' in touch? I'll bet they miss you."

"Don't got none."

"Too bad, too bad. Didn't quite catch your name. I'll check to see if you got any mail on hold."

"Ivar Ingersolson. Don't get mail."

"Right you are. Don't got no mail. Hey, it can be hard 'round here after you get paid. Union's got a little bank here t' keep your pay safe, so it don' get pinched tonight when you're out, if you know what I mean."

"Don' got much, just this pocket watch and my pay. I don' like mindin' my P's and Q's. Don' like owin' nothin' t' no one. Jus' gets me in trouble."

"Don' blame you. Now, if you could step over here and sign this registry. Union needs t' keep track."

What came next was disturbing if you're not from around here, if you don't sleep with one eye open. What came next was a telltale crack, in this case a gunshot, and then came a muffled thud like somebody dropped a sack of flour followed by a sack of potatoes, and then came the sound of somebody dragging off a bale of hay, or maybe not a bale of hay, maybe it was that sailor who just got off his ship, Ivar Ingersolson, maybe he just took a .38 bullet to the back of his skull, a bullet from Billy's Colt single-action revolver.

You might be surprised that Billy wasn't arrested for a long time. It wasn't like folks in town hadn't connected Aberdeen's well-deserved monikers with old Billy Gohl. Fact was when it came to Billy, the Aberdeen Police preferred to look the other way. Business was business as they say.

But one day Billy was arrested. And charged. And found guilty, although the jury recommended leniency. Remember, this was Aberdeen. And sentenced to two life sentences. And spent time in Walla Walla State Pen until he became crazier than the other run-of-the-mill, cold-blooded killers.

It's supposed that before his incarceration, Billy visited a *femme fatale* who gave him more than he bargained for, the great imitator, syphilis, his case of the crazies, and later when the prison doctors diagnosed Billy as a *homme fatale,* he was transferred out of Walla Walla to a mental institution at Sedro Wooley and then to another at Medical Lake. And when Billy's end came, his rotten body and mind were disposed of in an open field on the grounds of the Eastern State Mental Hospital.

ENTERING THE CHILD REDEMPTION CENTER

Petr saw they were rolling into town. He could see this because his sightline was just above the side walls of the truck bed. A sign read

REDUCED SPEED AHEAD

Then he felt the Pacific wind pick up. He could feel this because the trees that broke the wind were gone. Sitting on the truck bed, he felt like he was being repeatedly slapped with a cold, damp rag. He wondered if all of Aberdeen cut like a kickbacked chainsaw.

Petr turned his head. He watched the road pull away in a straight line. The pavement lay on top of silted mudflats. Mildewed and moss-covered wood structures bloomed like fall fungus. If this highway were a river, it would not be an Olympic dead-end slough. Instead, this highway would be a dredged channel.

Petr smelled the sharp sour odors from the pulp mill, and when the truck stopped at a red light on the corner of Heron and G, he grabbed his duffel bag with one hand, put his other hand on the side wall of the truck bed, and vaulted into the street. He waved at the driver who nodded back.

After the light changed, Petr found himself standing on the sidewalk in front of a diner. Across the street a sign on a derelict building read

THE CHILD REDEMPTION CENTER

Petr wondered about the sign. He didn't have experience with social service agencies or with churches. He didn't have experience asking for help. Living with Bear had been just that, living. They lived. Time passed. They lived some more.

So far, nothing about this 1982 version of Aberdeen recommended itself, so Petr looked to the left and looked to the right and then crossed the street. Like a July salmonberry, he was overripe for socialization. He went inside.

THE KEEPER OF THE CHILD REDEMPTION CENTER

The Keeper of the Child Redemption Center was not born in Aberdeen or for that matter on the Olympic Peninsula. He was not a logger. He was not a sailor or a dock worker. He had never been a member of a union. And he certainly had not killed any yet-to-be-determined number of men.

The truth was that the Keeper of the Child Redemption Center had been born in Kansas, a place so unlike Aberdeen and the surrounding timberland that Olympic locals liked to think of themselves as Dorothy from The Wizard of Oz. It was customary when a house was squashed under a blown down tree or a logger was squashed under a freshly felled tree to say, "Toto, I've a feeling we're not in Kansas anymore." It was customary for locals to think of the arbitrary violence of their everyday lives as fairly magical.

Statistically, the Keeper was born in 1932. Historically, this was the start of the Dust Bowl, the year that the first dust storm was recorded, the year that was followed by thirteen of the same. Folks remembered a wall of dirt coming in from the north. The wall went up more than a thousand feet. Who could tell? "Hey, Gus, it's about time for lunch, but I can't see across the road." "Suppose it's time t' put a wet rag over our nose and mouth ag'n." "Whatcha think, Gus? Could be the end times, and this is our last day."

Growing up in Kansas during the Dust Bowl was hard. The Keeper's daddy died of dust pneumonia. Then his older sister (the Keeper was the youngest of two) died. As a result, his mom walked away from their dead farm. Cause of death: buried alive under six feet of dust. She got a waitress job at a cafe in town. Because there wasn't much money around for tips, much less a meal, she did favors for the railroad men and truck drivers who came and went like tumbleweeds.

The Keeper survived childhood and was drafted into the military. The Korea of November 1950 was frigid. He and his buddies survived by filling spent 105 mm artillery casings with gasoline, setting them alight, and warming themselves like hobos around a burn barrel. He also survived by keeping his head down, but during the battle of Ch'ongch'on River, frost-bite took a foot, his left hand, a finger and a thumb on his right hand, and an ear.

Once back in the States, he checked the newspaper want ads. He looked for "Wanted: one-footed farm help" or "Wanted: three-fingered mechanic," but no one seemed to be looking for that. He decided instead to make use of the GI bill and go back to school. He figured his best bet was to make use of what he still had.

Once back in school, the Keeper settled on studying psychology. He told himself it was because he watched the war destroy the minds of his comrades, at least before a KPA or a PVA round destroyed their bodies. Besides, psychology was a lot like being an engine mechanic; the job was to figure out what went wrong under the hood. As time went by, he found he especially liked tinkering with what was wrong under the hoods of wayward teens.

Turning forty-five, the Keeper had enough of trying to fix what lay within Kansas's schools. He hopped on his Harley and headed out for what lay beyond the sunset. What he found was disappointing. What he found was the end of the road. What he found was Aberdeen.

Despondent yet resourceful, the Keeper applied for and received a grant "to help transition at-risk youth in Grays Harbor County." And what he found was that the wayward youth in these parts grew fast and thick. He found they were like what loggers called scrub. Around here these kids were considered little more than slash ready for a one-match burn.

So the Keeper of the Child Redemption Center put up his shingle on Aberdeen's Heron Avenue near the Wishkah River because the rent was cheap and the competition was sparse. He waited for potential clients, essentially late model versions of himself, to crawl off their slash pile and onto his.

CPS VERSUS THE ART OF ADOLESCENT MAINTENANCE

When Petr stepped into the Child Redemption Center, he looked like fresh meat for Child Protective Services.

The Keeper thought differently. He was pretty sure that working the proverbial CPS Creek wouldn't pan out because Petr didn't look like he'd take to foster care.

So the Keeper proceeded in this way. He gave Petr some time to size up not only the place but also him. The Keeper sat on his desk, one foot on the floor, relaxed yet aware, not wary, not distracted, but most assuredly owning his own space.

Petr reacted as a man should entering a stranger's camp. He made eye contact and then disengaged. He pawed the floor a bit with his right foot and then announced in a muffled voice his intention. "Saw your sign."

"Uh-huh."

"Not sure what it means."

"Well, I find out where you're at, and we try and make it better."

"Huh?"

"Safe to say things aren't going good?"

"Maybe."

"Safe to say you'd like things to get better?

"Maybe."

"Well, then maybe we can make things better. All depends on where you're at. All depends too on if you got the gumption."

"Gumption?"

"Yeah, gumption. A Scot's word. Means can you get up off your arse? That's an Old English word. Nobody shits out of a donkey. Know what I mean?"

Petr allowed his mouth to curl ever so slightly. Not his whole mouth, just the right side. And the Keeper knew he had him.

"If you want, you can sit anywhere you're comfortable. We'll talk some and see what we come up with."

"Okay."

This began a late afternoon and evening of shooting the shit. Of course, the Keeper had therapeutic goals in mind, and he had learned all about classical and operant conditioning as well as person-centered therapy, but experience had taught him that people were more like coyotes: they had a nose for traps. Fact was the Keeper's end goal behind shooting the shit with Petr was to have no end goal in mind other than coming to some agreement on how the sun might best come up tomorrow. Then, if all went well, come to some agreement on how the sun might best come up the next day, and maybe the next, and if they were lucky, the next, and so on. He liked to think of it as "tomorrow therapy," his very own special brand of psychology.

After a cookie, and then dinner, and then sleeping on the couch in the Child Redemption Center, and then breakfast, and then more shooting the shit, and then a shower and a trip a few blocks away to pick up some fresh clothes at the Salvation Army, and then lunch and even more shooting the shit, Petr and the Keeper settled on a nonenforceable agreement.

"So, you probably need to find a roof over your head and food for your belly?"

"Guess so."

"Well, I know of this shake mill that's walking distance. They'll hire you right off the street on a trial basis. If you work good, they'll keep you on. That'll put money in your pocket for that roof and food we're talking about."

"Okay."

"Now, I got an idea for a roof. There's this old hotel not far from here that's got room up in the attic. If you go down there, you can say I sent you. Ask for Jessie. She'll take a liking to you if you tell her you can pay fifty a month. Here's the fifty. Give it to her and you're in."

"Okay."

"So we come to this thing called school. Ever been?"

"No."

"Can you read and write?"

"Yeah."

"Can you add and subtract?"

"Yeah."

"Can you multiply and divide?"

"Multiply?"

"Say you got five boxes with fifty matches in each box. How many matches you got?"

"Two hundred and fifty."

"Yep, you can multiply. Can you divide?"

"Divide?"

"Say you got a hundred matches, and you need to put them in three boxes that hold twenty-five matches. Does that work?"

"I need another box 'cause I got twenty-five matches left over."

"Yep, you can divide. Like as I was saying, we come to this thing called school. I need to enroll you in school to keep my job. Since you never been in a regular school, and you're no kid, I can enroll you in the Steam Donkey Academy. They're what you call an alternative school. They won't get in the way of your work. If you got the gumption, you can even earn a high school diploma."

"Okay."

"You sure?"

"Maybe."

WHAT'S UP WITH JESSIE?

Sitting up here as I am on this empty osprey nest on top of this power pole, I thought you might be curious about the woman who took a liking to Petr. You might wonder about the sort of woman who consorts with the guy down at the Child Redemption Center, not to mention the sort of woman who rents out dusty attics for fifty bucks and smiles when payment in dog-eared tens is forthcoming.

Her story goes like this.

Jessie married a bootlegger who didn't quit running whiskey out of Victoria, Canada, just because prohibition was over. No, he had established a good supply chain, and if nothing else, illegal whiskey was tax free. Unfortunately, his enterprise came to an end during the "Gale of '34." The big blow capsized his whiskey running boat, and he, the love of Jessie's life, drowned.

Being it was the Depression, Jessie's husband didn't put his earnings in the bank. Instead, he stacked his ill-gotten gains neatly in a Pukka suitcase: British-made canvas with leather, the sort of thing made for traveling light, especially during a quick getaway.

Needless to say, Jessie was sad, what with the disappearance of her husband, gone for good, or at least until he surfaced decomposed with a Dungeness crab inside his body and a lugworm in his left eye. But she made do. She mourned for a time. She iced the money among her dance set underwear: bandeau brassieres, shaped vests, and step-ins. She only spent a few tens and a twenty along the way.

Then Jessie went all out. As it so happened, World War II was all the rage, and Japanese folks were being boxed and shipped to internment camps, their property sold or stolen. Jessie figured she had enough money in that Pukka suitcase to acquire her own ill-gotten hotel. She also figured she had enough money to spruce it up and open a brothel. She was proud to offer her employees a respectable amount of money from clients with respectable incomes. She named her brothel the Giggles Hotel in honor of her dearly departed husband's talent for importing giggle juice to Seattle.

For a time, Jessie ran a highly successful business. She provided services for the needs of monied men and employment for needy women, a scratch for an itch. But times changed, and the growing class of Seattle's mothers pressured Seattle's fathers to stop all this providing for the needs of monied men and employment for needy women.

Jessie could see that Seattle was being proverbially strung with a lot of barbed wire, and that was bad for business. What she needed was to strike out for some open rangeland. And when it came to open rangeland, Aberdeen fit the bill.

So she sold the Giggles Hotel and bought a building in Aberdeen. It was a derelict hotel on H Street near the confluence of the Chehalis and Wishkah Rivers. Of course, she also spruced the place up. She named her new brothel Grain Fed Fillies, a wink to her woodsy and seafaring clientele. If there was one thing Jessie knew, it was that when these boys came in from the woods or off the sea, they were lonely for girls and buxom ones at that.

This then was what I observed from this power pole just outside Grain Fed Fillies. From there I watched Jessie take a liking not only to the fifty dollars but also to Petr. And, hey, maybe Petr could have called this woman Grandma Jessie. He didn't, but he could have.

SACRAMENT

libraries safe and
warm, dented spam and bean cans,
trash day Eucharist

SCHOOL

We here on the Olympic Peninsula don't do school. It's not that we don't have schools, and it's not that we don't learn. We learn plenty around here. It's just that the whole notion of "doing school" always feels foreign, especially when we are inside a school. Leaving the woods and sitting at a desk is a bit like leaving the womb and sitting on a block of ice.

It should come then as no surprise that Petr didn't thrive at the Steam Donkey Academy, although his time at the shake mill went well. He had no problem splitting wood, and he did what he was told. At a shake mill that was good enough. But at the Steam Donkey Academy, Petr had trouble reading and writing words and numbers on packets of paper. And he didn't do what he was told.

The teachers there were very nice. They had many good conversations together about his experiences, but they told him that if he didn't do his work, they were going to have to get rid of him.

"So Petr, did you get a doughnut? It's hard to get your work done if you're hungry."

"I just had a jelly-filled and, boy, was it good. They're from Chow Dog's Doughnuts down on Alder and Ontario. You should get one. You'll be glad you did."

"Sure thing, Petr. Now how's your science packet coming? How many pages have you finished?"

"Don't know."

"Well, let's look and see. Not much so far. You were here for a few hours yesterday, and you didn't really get anything done?"

"I guess not."

"Why not?"

"Don't know."

"Well, if you can't get your work done and earn credits, you can't earn a diploma. You want a diploma, don't you?"

"Don't know."

"It seems like you are always looking out the window instead of doing your work. What do you see out there?"

"Right now I see a raven sitting on that pole. Sometimes I ask him questions like, 'I see your feathers are black. Why is that?' And he answers like, 'I was just a teenager when I first learned to fly. Of course, I wanted to fly as far and as high as I could. I looked up at the sun and decided I was going to fly up there.' And then I ask him another question like, 'So I'm thinking that didn't go so well. Did you make it?' and he says, 'Not quite, but as you can see, I got so close my feathers burned to charcoal!'"

Petr went on like this all through '82 and into '83. He worked at the cedar shake mill, lived at Grain Fed Fillies, and attended the Steam Donkey Academy, but finally his teachers decided that try as they might, Petr wasn't going to earn enough credits to get a diploma and punch his ticket out of the woods.

Fortunately, any alternative school worth its mark treats students like logs, which is to say, both loggers and teachers buck for grade. Fact was the school not only had a plan A for high grade students but also plans B through Q for those who weren't.

So after two years, an alternative school teacher filled out the entrance and financial aid paperwork to Olympia, WA's Black Hills Technical Institute. Turns out some colleges don't require high school diplomas. Turns out they are in the child redemption business, too.

Not wanting to leave Petr hanging, the Keeper put the bus fare to Olympia in Petr's hand, and Jessie, well, she put a kiss on Petr's cheek, pressing her ample breasts suggestively close, and was that her tongue that brushed his lips?

TRANSIT TO OLYMPIA

trans people sit here
in kaos' bus'ness office,
auto caution door

A CURIOUS EFFECT

It was Petr's first day at Black Hills Technical Institute, and he had a meeting with his academic adviser. While looking for her office, he stopped at an information kiosk and saw this flyer.

BHCR 87.9

Black Hills College Radio

ORGANIZATIONAL MEETING

April 6, 9:00 p.m.
212 Dissemination Workshop
Meet the Staff
Share Sustenance

NEEDS FOR SPRING TERM
DJs
Production Staff
Front Desk

Reading this flyer had a curious effect on Petr, which is to say it made him wonder. Bird chirps made him wonder. A crack of what might be a branch made him wonder. The wind. But never something he read.

Petr read "BHCR 87.9" and concluded those were radio station call letters. Then he read "NEEDS FOR SPRING TERM" and wondered if he might fill that need.

BUT I DIGRESS, THE LOVE SONG OF R. A. DIO

Go up in the sky like a satellite launched into the ionosphere of half-garbled messages, the reflected languages of lonely gigs in graveyard studios and blear-eyed beds bathed in radio, of transmissions that speak like demi-gods of eschatology leading to a proverbial cliff . . . not to worry about the height, so don your wings and take flight.

STEPH AND MORE

When Petr went to the BHCR organizational meeting, the first thing he noticed was a large bowl of tortilla chips and a tub of cheddar dip. Remembering the timber beast code, that food was third only to air and water, he picked up a paper plate and piled a large mound of chips in the middle and a smaller mound of dip nearer the side. So far, college was turning out to be squirrel heaven, a magic midden of pine nuts with acorn butter.

While Petr dipped and crunched, a woman he thought a bit older interrupted him midchew. She wore a gray flannel hoodie with the words COR-MORANT COVEN emblazoned in crimson across the front. She had added brick-red highlights to her naturally black hair. And she touched her oversized glasses before saying, "Pretty cool, huh?"

"Uh" —chew, chew, chew— "sure."

"They're not plastic. They are real goat horn. Not Galapagos tortoise, of course, but goat horn."

Chew. "Okay." Chew.

"My name's Steph. I'm the program director."

Chew. "Petr." Chew, chew.

"So you're interested in radio?"

"Yeah." Chew.

"Is there something you'd like to do here? If you saw our flyers, we really need help this spring. We need DJs, production staff, and front desk help."

"I'd like to broadcast. I do interviews." Chew, chew, chew, chew.

"That sounds interesting. What sort of interviews?"

Petr stopped chewing. "I talk with frogs and ravens and otters. Cormo-rants, too." He nodded at her hoodie.

"Oh, really?"

"Yeah, sometimes I talk with Bernard Huelsdonk. Folks called him John. Called him Iron Man of the Hoh, too. He homesteaded there. Did a lot of cougar hunting for the bounty."

"Oh, really."

"Yeah, and I really like talking with kushtakas."

"Kushtakas?"

"Yeah, they help people who get lost in the woods or out to sea. Instead of letting them freeze or drown, they make them into another kushtaka. That way they don't die."

"Wow, that's pretty strange."

"Yeah, most people don't believe in them, but my daddy Bear told me about them. He said the Indians knew all about them, and, uh, I've talked with them some."

"I can tell you we don't have anyone that does a show like that. I think the local ecology angle is interesting, what with the ravens and otters. I also like that you know about local history and folklore. It's a pretty psychedelic take on the interview format. Do you do all the voices and everything?"

"Yeah, you might say that. They speak through me."

"Weird, but it might work. I'll tell you what. Peter, right?"

"Petr."

"Oh, sorry. Well Petr, we have a volunteer orientation this Wednesday evening at seven p.m. right in this room. Then if you're still interested, we have a DJ training coming up next week. It's down the hall in Studio 2. What do you think?"

"Okay."

THE RADIO STUDIO

The main control panel, the one the DJ used, was an RCA broadcast console. Nine volume knobs, the ones DJs called pots (short for potentiometers), lay ready to mix radiant symphonies. The backlight of the control panel's single volume unit meter, the one DJs called a VU meter, shone like an Olympic lighthouse calling mariners into harmonic harbors and up to melodious moorings.

Two turntables were to the DJ's right.

A reel-to-reel tape recorder was behind.

Between the broadcast console and the turntables was a rack with two cart machines. DJs used these two-track tape players to play carts, short for cartridges, recorded with oft-used promos, advertisements, station identifications, and PSAs, better known as public service announcements.

And extended over the control panel were two arms. One arm, bent at the elbow, cast a yellow moonlight. The other, thrust assertively forward, held a microphone, the one Petr was to use to broadcast voices from the Olympics, the ones he brought from his childhood.

"Tonight I have Pacific Chorus Frog with us. Could you start us out with your signature call? I think it's what our listeners know best."

"Cre-ee-ee-ee-eeek."

"That was great. Welcome to the BHCR studio."

"Good to be here, Petr."

"What I'd like to talk about is this interesting ability you have. Most of our listeners have heard you singing at night but probably don't know you change color. Tell us about how this happens."

"It all started with Raven. He got into that black thing of his by hangin' up in the sun."

"So you're saying your changing color has something to do with Raven?"

"Yeah, I'm getting to that."

"Sorry, please continue."

"Well, Raven, you know, once he saw that he changed to black, he started seeing all the other colors differently. He thought things would be way more interesting if other things changed color, too. Like leaves, right? Or lakes. If you watch, a lake changes color all day long. So does snow.

"What happened was, one day Raven was out riding the thermals and heard me out singin' with my swampers. It was that time of year, you know, out cruisin' for some swampettes. We've all been there, right?

"So, Raven, he homes in on my solo and lands right next to me. He figured he'd dress me and my swampers up a little, make us more the mating type. He dressed us all up in green like the lady ferns we were next to. And he didn't stop there. Get us warm, and he yellows us up some. And when we go muddin' in our down time, he turns us out in a nice cinnamon."

"You might say Raven was the first artist," Petr interjected.

"Sure, you might say that."

THE END OF SPRING QUARTER

When did Petr leave school? The answer to that question is easy. At the end of spring quarter.

When did I, Raven, take off from this Doug-fir branch just outside the BHCR studio, lift into the thermals just below a fluffy cumulus cloud and right above the Black Hills Technical Institute campus, and follow what comes next? The answer to that question is just as easy. At the end of spring quarter.

BOOK TWO

BAIE'S BEGINNING

IN HER BEGINNING

In her beginning
She shed a tear.
She felt alone,
solitary,
only.
One.

And She walked out.
She walked across a plain.
She walked through a valley.
She walked alongside a mountain.

And She felt wistful,
a deep longing,
dreamy,
so much so,
that rising from
below came
a wellspring,
gushing.
The fountain mist
froze.
The fountain edges

melted
turning ice to
rain,
turning rain to
rivers,
turning rivers to
oceans.

And She birthed souls.
The wistful
dreaming inside
took root,
ripening,
bursting outside.
Sea otters.
Orcas.
Eulachon.
Humans.

And She birthed a forest.
The profound
blessing inside
took root,
ripening,
bursting outside.
Giant kelp.
Sugar kelp.
Bull kelp.
Rainbow-leaf kelp.

And She wandered
forlorn.
She yearned

fancy.
She bore Baie.
She bore Petr.

And She bore you,
dear reader.

And She bore me,
yours truly,
White Otter.

HOMECOMING

BAIE'S JOURNAL

Entry 1

I am home,
dear Mother,
your precious Baie,
pronounced bay,
French for berry,
the one you
faithfully planted,
the one who
deeply rooted,
the one you
lovingly nurtured in
your cranberry bog.

As I grew,
I heard your call.

Dinner was served,
the warm applesauce
spooned onto
spatter-blue tin plates.
My mouth curled like
a tart apple slice.
Your finger twig wagged
—Cranberry blossom,
take up your pen and
write your soul.

PRAYER

BAIE'S JOURNAL

Entry 2

Saint Thérèse de Lisieux,
Carmelite little flower,
who died a nun at
twenty-four,
who let fall
a shower of roses,
forgive me.
Unacceptable,
I have left you,
me a failed postulant,
not even a novitiate,
two years in
your French monastery
unsuitable,
unworthy.

Dear Father,
Dear Mother,
forgive me.
Abject,
I have returned,
me a prodigal heir
after your passing,
well past the mourning,
my inheritance
your cranberry bog,
blessed,
born-again.

Mother,
Father,
Saint Thérèse de Lisieux,
in the presence of
your angels,
I will prepare the soil.
I will tend the ground.
God willing,
the blossoms will fruit.

MORE HOMECOMING

BAIE'S JOURNAL

Entry 3

Tears.
Neglected bog.
Words.

MY BIRTH

BAIE'S JOURNAL

Entry 4

You said, dear Mother,
I was conceived under
a green aurora.
I flourished with
our bog's blooming.
I ripened in
the first October rain.

When I broke your water,
Dear Father was gone.
He returned with
a basket filled with
golden chanterelles.
He pulled you,
a splitting chrysalis, from
our worn turquoise couch.

We took off in
our '52 pickup,
Rust-o-leum orange.
We hunkered down,
you cramping,
me deep inside.
We barreled up
the Humptulips and onto
Olympic logging grades.

We headed for
a cedar shack,
one silvered by
the weight of
many years' rain.

When we arrived,
we found your midwife,
Madame Brighid:
all fair skin,
seafoam irises,
long, gray-flecked hair,
faithfully holding
the paschal
and moving inside
a congregation of
votive candles.

Of my birth
you said
—I was so afraid.
I couldn't cry.
I hurt too much.
You were ready to
come out, but
I wasn't ready to
let you go.
I was your father's
lucky bloom.
You were
my drupelet.
But then you came:
head,
shoulders, and

praise the Blessed Virgin,
the flood!

AFTER BIRTH

BAIE'S JOURNAL

Entry 5

Nineteen years later
what have you birthed,
dear Mother?
my afterbirth
fresh cut liver,
my body
a slippery salamander,
my shadow
Olympic *skookum*,
my spirit
a white-lined sphinx moth.

EXCUSE ME, WHITE OTTER HAS SOMETHING TO SAY

Orca, you raped me.
Slick and powerful,
harboring sea lice,
you came big out of
the rolling surf.
You mounted my back.
You smothered my squeals.

I couldn't breathe under
your blubber's breadth.
You hurt me deeply,
spirit powered by
the rich, ruby flesh of
numberless salmon.
I was devastated.
I could not understand
why I, White Otter,
was the target of
your seminal abuse.

In this world ephemeral,
I said a prayer with
my new moon eyes,
my fog-silver breath.
I said a prayer for
endless forests of
rich, green kelp.

You said nothing.
Your belly descended like
a suffocating night.
Your weight erased me.
Ghost Porpoise and Seal,
strong and aware,
possessed you.

I was crushed breathless on
these soft Pacific sands.
I was reduced to
rhythmic wave action.
I was rocked with

a spasmic quake.
I was filled to bursting.
I split open like
a ratfish egg case.

Once it was finished,
your voice, a seal club,
came crushingly down.
—White Otter, come
sound the depths among
the gray whales.
Come and chase through
the salmon schools.
If you follow,
I will fulfill your desire.

A mere razor clam squirt,
my voice responded
—Orca, I can't be yours.
Your depths are not mine.
I can't follow where
your chase leads.

Emptying its bilge,
your voice replied
—Though you refuse me,
I'll answer your desire.

And you returned to
the rolling surf.
The skies deepened.
Kelp fell thick on

the water's surface.
Roots stretched out
their fervid mouths.

Kyrie eleison.
Christe eleison.
Kyrie eleison.
Je ne suis plus un créature
de la terre
or the air.
I am a creature
de la mer.

LA VOLONTÉ DE DIEU

BAIE'S JOURNAL

Entry 6

You said, dear Father,
you were raised in
a French monastery.
—*J'étais orphelin!*
Qui, moi!
The nuns teach me
read and write French.
The nuns teach me
say English.
They teach me read
Saint Thérèse de Lisieux.
I repair tables and chairs.

Place shingles on
antique roof.
Fabricate crucifixes with
hammer and chisel.

—They teach me
l'oeuvre de Dieu est
un grand plaisir.
They offer me a name,
le petit ange.

—When I grow,
a man stop at
the monastery,
my home.
He has backpack.
We have same age.
He want meal.
He want bed.
He and I repair chapel.
We remove floor planks.
We nail new planks.

—We work, and we speak.
He say new college,
no university program.
He say Black Hills Technical Institute.
He say Olympia, Washington,
so green, it is black.
He say I be happy.
He say my soul grow natural.

And I say
—*Qui! Providence!*

Oui! C'est
la volonté de Dieu
that make me leave
my good Sisters.

—I send papers,
then I go, but
how do you say?
I am on probation.
They give me job.
I repair school.
They give me room.
They give me food.
I have class of English
and of botany.

—We go to
Tahola Shaker Chapel.
It is here
I see *ta mère*
very beautiful in
the red sunset!

—I find bench.
I sit down.
One old man ask
if I need help?
Il été incroyable, oui?

—I ask work
I sweep church.
I repair windows.
I repair roof.
I wash fish.

I shake.
I say French prayers, and
no people fall maladies.
C'est incroyable, oui?

—He say I idiot but
see I serious.
He see I sincere.
I sleep in church.
I eat in church.
I work what they say.
Oui! C'est
la volonté de Dieu.

—I see *ta mère* all time.
Ta mère see me all time.
People see me see *ta mère*.
People know.
People joyous.
I work sunup to
sunset.

—I work and work and
see sign "For Sale."
Oh, *ma chère* Baie!
Oui! C'est
la volonté de Dieu.
Home for my wife.
A place for
cranberries and
mon enfant,
you my Baie,
my berry.

—I obtain new work at
Hoquiam sawmill.
I obtain loan of
Timber Beast Credit Union.
I eliminate "For Sale."
Ta mère and I,
we plant bushes of
wild cranberries.
We make sign of
the cross Carmelite.
I say prayer of
Saint Thérèse de Lisieux.

Ce fruit quand de le touche
Me paraît un trésor.
Le portant à ma bouche,
Il m'est plus doux encore.

Il me donne en ce monde
Un océan de paix.
En cette paix profonde
Je repose à jamais . . .

And, dear Mother,
again in English.

When I touch this fruit,
it seems a treasure.
Putting it in my mouth,
it is sweet again.

It brings me an ocean
of peace in this world.
In this profound peace,
I rest forever.

HERE

BAIE'S JOURNAL

Entry 7

Today,
I cling to
the elements.
Lying out among
our cranberry bushes,
the Pacific clouds
float above,
luminous from
within.

Before me grow
our dwarf bog cranberries.
Scientists call these
Vaccinium oxycoccus.

The big farms,
the big companies
drown their plants.
Their berries are stem-bound.
Their berries are breath-starved.

Here
we have no flood.
Our berries are delivered
one and then another,
each stem lovingly broken,
each cord reverently cut.

WAITING FOR DORI

BAIE'S JOURNAL

Entry 8

I

Over Humptulips
and through the fog
to Baie's farm
Dori comes.
Her truck rattles along
an asynchronous song
like spent and spawning
chu-um.

II

Rattle, rattle
her truck's tattle
all in the Sitka
spruce.

Sister, sister,
second daughter,
will be put to
use.

Harvest, harvest
latent largess,
squeezed cranberry
juice.

III

I have a plan
that Dori and I
will get busy:
a cranberry bog
resurrection of
sorts,
a wayward
women's roadhouse,
a monastery for
wildsisters.
We will put
our gumption
where our mouth is:
as my dear Dori says,
wildsisters got t' do
what we got t' do.

IV

Kyrie eleison.
Christe eleison.
Kyrie eleison.
Tout
est perdre.
Tout
est retrouver.
Now and
here,
wildsisters.

HOOD CANAL

Remember me, your ol' pal Raven? I've just been hanging up here in the thermals. I've been biding my time while you went off to the Humptulips, sampled our local cranberries, and strolled through a shower of sea kelp. All this time I've been tailing Petr over the northeast corner of the Black Hills. I've been shadowing him all the way to the Olympic Peninsula's east coast, all the way to the Hood Canal.

Some might say Petr was running away from school. Others might say he was trying to find himself. I'd say let's not overthink this. I'd say let's not go down that mountain beaver hole. Let's not dream where no other dreamer has dreamed before.

If you look west from here, this Hood Canal region abruptly ends with the steep rise of the Olympic Mountains, the same mountains some have said are dirty clothes strewn about God's bedbug floor. Others have called this little patch of chaos God's green bedlam.

And if you dive straight into the Hood Canal, what you'll find isn't exactly oceanic. True, the waters of the Hood Canal are salty and subject to Pacific tides, but the waterway itself is only 65 miles in length and on average only 1.5 miles in width.

The water quality is irregular to say the least. Back in the ice age, the north end of the Hood Canal was fairly silted in by glaciers so that in places the depth is only 150 feet. Moving south the depth drops to 425 feet. Here the Hood Canal becomes a big bathtub. The salty Pacific comes in from the big spigot. Snow-fed rivers come in from smaller spigots.

The bathtub's water lies in three layers. The bottom layer is sea water brought in on the new tide. The middle layer is brackish and anerobic, old, a commonwealth of decomposition. And the top layer is a freshet fed by many rivers: Skokomish, Liliwaup, Jorsted, Hamma Hamma, Duckabush, Dosewallips, Quilcene.

This place, the Hood Canal, is about to become the starting point for Radio Free Olympia. Sure, Petr could have, maybe should have, left school and taken the familiar way home, that paved road which leads from Olympia to Aberdeen to Forks and beyond. That paved road could have been, probably should have been, only his naked thumb away.

But he didn't do that. Instead, Petr did the Jesus and Elijah thing. He did the Siddhārtha Gautama and Muhammad thing. The Čháŋ Óhaŋ, Crazy Horse thing.

Yes, you guessed it; Petr plunged right into the dirty clothes strewn about God's bedbug floor, right into God's green bedlam, into this patch of chaos just west of the Hood Canal.

BECAUSE YOU MIGHT BE CURIOUS

Bear taught child-Petr that only hippie and yuppie hiker types go into the Olympic Mountains. He said that National Park regulations made it impossible for anyone to be a mountain man. But Petr wasn't a hippie. He certainly wasn't a yuppie. And hiking to him was as foreign as swimming to a Townsend's mole or flying to a bull trout.

You might be curious WHAT exactly Petr packed for his plunge into the Olympics. You might think that a list of what Petr took with him would help you figure out what the hell Petr was up to. Here is that list. Good luck.

1. Military surplus canvas backpack (from Corvids: a supermarket, a wonderland, a big-box swap meet)
2. Military surplus wool blanket

3. Stack of military surplus C-Rations aka Charlie Rats (HAM & EGGS CHOPPED, BEANS W/FRANKFURTER CHUNKS, BEANS W/MEAT BALLS IN TOMATO SAUCE, SPAGHETTI W/BEEF CHUNKS IN SAUCE)

4. Homemade trail mix (peanuts, raisins, M&M's candy, Grape Nuts cereal)

5. Empty five-pound coffee can

6. Empty two-liter pop bottle with cap

7. Ferrocerium rod, six-inch hacksaw blade, cotton balls, petroleum jelly, and plastic sandwich bags (for starting fires, well worth the investment)

8. Military surplus mess kit, chow set, and can opener aka P-38

9. Blue poly tarp (the fabric of America)

10. Coils of double-braid nylon rope

11. Rusty-then, polished-now Bowie knife and well-worn leather sheath

12. Do-it-yourself FM radio transmitter with eggbeater charger (more on this later)

Bear also taught child-Petr a number of other things about the Olympic Peninsula. For example, one night long before Petr rolled Bear off the log caddy and into a shallow grave, Bear said to Petr, "Y'seen any Indians around? Y'know, way back folks new to these parts did all manner of stuff to them like give them the flu and smallpox. Killed a whole bunch of them. Then folks did stuff that made the salmon real scarce."

"Why'd they do that?"

"Well, it wasn't because they wanted the salmon to go away, but let me tell you, some folks are greedy. They built logging and electric dams that kept the salmon from spawning. They fished out the rivers, too. They even made boats with big nets that started fishing out the ocean."

"Sounds dumb."

"Yes siree, that it was. Course, y'know the Indians all got stuck on reservations. I wouldn't want to be stuck on no reservation."

"Me neither."

"Even so, the Indians back then didn't go up in the mountains. They stuck pretty much to the coast and traveled around by canoe."

"Bear?"

"What li'l Petr?"

"Bear, I was talking to Raven last night."

"Yep, sometimes I caw back at all the racket those birds make."

"No, I mean I was talking to RAVEN."

"Oh, y' talking to the radio again?"

"Well, yeah, sort of."

"And what did this Raven have to say?"

"He told me that there was a time the Old Growth Folk had summer lodges up in the Olympics. He said, 'Petr my boy, the mountains and the trees and rivers all have a spirit. All the logging is stripping that spirit away.'

"I told him I didn't exactly get what he meant.

"He said, 'Sure, that's a lot for a little boy like yourself, for a very serious, spiritual boy like yourself.'

"So I told him thanks.

"Then he said, 'Think nothing of it. The thing is, we Old Growth Folks used to have winter lodges down here near the ocean and summer lodges up in the mountains. But when the loggers cut down all the trees, especially the cedars—you know, that's a really powerful tree—well, it was time for us Old Growthers to move to the mountains full-time. Like I said, we Old Growth Folks once had summer lodges up in the Olympics, but now those lodges are more or less year 'round.'

"I asked him why he was down here talking to me.

"He said, 'Birds got to fly, Petr. You know, birds got to fly. Besides, I've had my eye on you ever since you washed up on Shi Shi Beach. And I expect some day you'll come visit all of us Old Growthers'."

So now, dear reader, as you can see, my expectation is about to be met, you know, the one where Petr comes to visit me in the Olympics, the one I expressed to child-Petr some time before Bear said, "I wouldn't want to be stuck on no reservation."

LEAVING HOME

sucking very hard and long
at Mother America's teat

all seemed foolhardy
all seemed foolhardy

shotgun blast to the mouth of
the American Dream

real estate suitcase
toss me a cigarette

bathing in intoxicating
Olympic Squirrel Scold

infant of the squall
infant of the squall

bleeding bloom to the heart of
the Universal Dream

real estate suitcase
toss me a cigarette

KATE

Petr stood for a while, military surplus canvas pack heavy against his shoulders, Hood Canal at his back, eastern face of the Olympics starting, black-etched tree line against the gray-naked stone higher, rock face then snow, selfsame clouds. He imagined the ridge behind the first and the ridge behind that until his mind's eye came to Mount Anderson, its ice a ghostly white, a sepulchral blue.

He imagined assembling his transmitter and broadcasting across the tangle of green-to-black valleys. His first step was to follow the steep ascent of the Dosewallips River, and while on this trail, he planned to test out his equipment. Then when he reached Mount Anderson's south flank, just short of its snow fields, buffeted by the same updraft which pushed ravens sunward, he planned to initiate his first broadcast from Radio Free Olympia.

To this end, Petr started his plunge just off the black asphalt of Highway 101 and along the chipseal of Dosewallips Road. At this intersection stood a building. A sign read Bayshore Motel. Down the road and on the left stood a few houses and another significant building. A sign read Brinnon School. Further on the right stood a building with a cupola topped by a cross.

This sight reminded Petr of the Quileute Indian Shaker Church of his childhood, so he decided to investigate. He walked off the road and through a thin line of Doug-fir. On his right a sign read Brinnon Community Church. On his left a sign read Brinnon Cemetery.

Petr's eye was drawn to a stone pillar. He walked beyond the cemetery sign and discovered that the pillar was encompassed by a stone circle, the sort of fairy ring that once had been built to enclose well-to-do family plots, the sort of stone circle that Celts built.

Coming upon the circle's southern edge, Petr stepped over the boundary and inside. Here he stopped. At his feet lay a gray granite marker. The marker read

Carrie Snyder
1876–1961

He had no idea who Carrie Snyder was. She was certainly born way before he was, and she died a few years before Bear had collected infant-Petr off Shi Shi Beach. He thought she had lived a long life. He thought that someone had dug a hole here and dumped in what was left. He thought that standing here felt weird. He felt queerly cold.

Petr's eye was then drawn away from the marker to the stone pillar. He walked a few steps and then confronted the pillar, an outlandish monument on the circle's western slope, an obelisk cut with four upward tapering sides, a phallic thing. Words were chiseled on three of the four sides. The stone faces read

Alfred D Fisher
1814

Ewell P Brinnon
May 20, 1830 — December 29, 1895

Kate Brinnon
wife of
Ewell P Brinnon
1840–1898

Again, he had no idea who Alfred D Fisher or Ewell P Brinnon were, but when he read Kate Brinnon's name, he felt different. He thought Kate felt familiar. He felt graciously warmed, intimate.

O'WOTA

Let's get a few things straight. First, Petr had no way of knowing that Kate Brinnon's S'Klallam name was O'wota. He also didn't know that O'wota was the daughter of the tribal leader Lach-ka-nam (also known to Europeans as Lord Nelson) and his wife Qua-tum-a-low. And he didn't know O'wota had many brothers who were famous on the northern and western Olympic Peninsula: S-hai-ak (also known to Europeans as King George), Cheech-ma-ham (also known as the Duke of York and Chetzemoka), Sna-talc (also known as General Scott), and Yaht-le-min (also known as General Taylor).

Oh, and there's more. For example, Petr didn't know that Lach-ka-nam's oldest son, S-hai-ak, who was slated to become the next S'Klallam chief, had either died or had an argument (depends on who you ask) with his younger brother and shipped himself out to San Francisco. Later this younger brother, Cheech-ma-ham, the new next in line to become chief, visited San Francisco and got a good soak in the European flood, all of which led to the S'Klallam signing onto newbie governor Isaac Steven's treaty, the one which traded the locals $60,000 and "three thousand eight hundred and forty acres, situated at the head of Hood's Canal" for all of the eastern and much of the northern Olympic Peninsula. Not surprisingly, many of the locals in attendance had their doubts. L'Hau-at-scha-uk, a Toanhooch leader, figured this was not so much a real estate deal as it was a death sentence. But all in attendance signed on anyway because Steven's death-sentence-wrapped-in-a-treaty wasn't something they could refuse.

Needless to say, not all the locals packed up and moved to what is now the Skokomish Reservation on the Hood Canal's Great Bend. Some S'Klallam took up William Talbot and Andrew Pope's offer to work at the new Port Gamble lumber mill. Then in 1936 these Port Gamble S'Klallam were granted a 1,231-acre reservation at Point Julia. Others bought the land which now is the Jamestown S'Klallam Reservation at the southern end of Sequim Bay. And some simply stayed put for a while, eventually either moving away or dying.

But don't forget Kate, the name on the stone pillar who was born O'wota, the name associated with someone Petr didn't know but with whom he felt familiar. It turns out that O'wota was one of the locals who didn't move to any reservation. Instead, she married the European newbie Ewell Brinnon, a man who maybe came from Virginia and who reportedly told someone he was from Ireland. After the wedding, O'wota told Ewell that she feared his homestead along the Duckabush River was going to flood over and over and over and over and over again. To his credit, Ewell respected her local knowledge, sold his Duckabush homestead, and bought land in what some back then called Quagaboor and others called Ducaboos. And it just so happened that some of the newbies thought these words were too hard to spell, so Jessi Macomber, the wife of Julius, the first postmaster in the area, changed the name to Brinnon. I mean, who really gives a damn about thousands of years of cultural and linguistic history?

And while we're on the subject of naming, who gives a damn that Kate was named O'wota by her mother and father, and all of her childhood family and friends knew her as O'wota, and no matter how many newbies, including her husband, called her Kate, her deepest, probably quite secret gull cry, emotional bonegame self would always respond to O'wota, not Kate, always O'wota, even if the newbies thought Kate was nice, a great housekeeper, and a good cook? Even if Mrs. McCutchen, another newbie, of course, said that Kate, not O'wota, saw Jesus looking in the window when Kate was dying? Even if Kate, not O'wota, was buried in the Brinnon Cemetery, the land donated by her husband?

Which brings us back to the one thing Petr did know, Kate's adopted name, the one chiseled on the cold stone phallus, the one he stepped close to, the one he traced with his finger. And out of this tracing he imagined red cedar plank houses with structural outer poles and angled shed roofs. He smelled the punk of wood smoke infused with salmon, seal, shellfish, birds, berries, and roots. He heard the pulse of child-chatter, raven-gurgle, frog-chirrup, breeze-swell, and drizzle-drip, drip, drip. He tasted burnt bone, a pith of salt, red ochre in deer tallow, spruce, and clam shell.

Petr felt home. He closed his eyes and imagined O'wota's finger pointing straight to the sacred heart of the Olympic Peninsula.

OFF ROAD

Petr walked out of the Brinnon Cemetery and back onto the Dosewallips Road. To his left and to his right he came upon a few homesteads and hunting camps, some stick-built, others manufactured. One had a red Peterbilt 351 log truck parked out front with an empty logging trailer, a Peerless two-axle stinger pulled up on the bed.

Further along Petr passed through a few private clear-cuts slashed across steep embankments. As a boy, he always thought of clear-cuts as burial grounds where people had been planted upside down, their legs chopped at the waist. He never understood who would do such a thing, so he picked up his pace. He didn't want to be the next head shrouded in the soil. He didn't want a red huckleberry bush to sprout from the scar on his bloody stump.

Leaving the clear-cuts behind, Petr encountered a formidable monument constructed of mortar and rounded river rock. From this monument hung a milled timber sign of painted brown boards with yellow-painted lettering. The message read Olympic National Forest.

Beyond the sign, the chipseal road turned to gravel access and dropped into the woods along the Dosewallips River. As he walked, Petr was greeted on either side by crowds of sword fern. He smiled to remember his childhood, a time when the occasional blue, but more likely gray patches above became the heavens, the tree canopy the sky, and the sword ferns the trees.

This sort of forest floor was where child-Petr explored his first game trails. This was where he disappeared into dens unseen: sanctuaries for the unschooled and studios for his imagination. This was the time child-Petr grabbed a hatchet and thought himself a bygone logger out to do what Bear called "an honest day's work." He used his hatchet to fell, buck, and yard a choice sword fern, carefully arranging the fronds the way Bear's storied timber beasts placed logs on the landing.

Continuing along the gravel access, Petr walked over this rise and around that declivity, and then he decided to stroll offroad. He walked into a stand of Doug-fir intermixed with red cedar, and here he stopped among a congregation of redwood sorrel lit in converging shafts of cathedral light. He recalled Bear showing him that redwood sorrel behavior was counterintuitive. Instead of reaching for the light, the leaves of these plants bent earthward like a hymnal dangling from a child's hand. Petr knew that if he cast his green shadow across these sunlit sorrels, he could watch these leafy hymnals open ever so slowly. This he did.

Before returning to the gravel access, Petr walked up a short, steady rise and stopped once more, this time in a stand of bleeding heart. These pink heart-shaped flowers had lured a multitude of small worker bumblebees, the majority colored black and yellow, a few colored black and orange. Petr was fascinated by these hairy thimbles, the way each hung from the two white inner petals, the way each extended her tongue to drink from pools of sugary nectar.

Closing his eyes, Petr dropped to his knees, lay back along the game trail, and thought his heart a construction of bleeding heart petals. He imagined bumblebees moving toward him from all directions. He felt the bees land on his chest and crawl inside his shirt, their tongues probing and testing, searching for an entry. No break was found.

Petr then imagined a thundercloud brooding overhead. He felt the pregnant mass release a tsunami of steely air, a microburst which plunged with such force that it snapped a Doug-fir limb. He heard the crack and felt the branch split his rib cage, pierce his petal-formed heart, and spike him to the earth.

Gathering about the wooden stake, the bumblebees fed from his heart-bloomed nectar. Satiated, the congregants took flight and whizzed for home.

AFTER THE PICTURE SHOW

ravished and alone:
haven a hermit crab shell,
mother a cuckoo

BUT I DIGRESS, SAPLING MOLESTER VERSUS VAINGLORIOUS BIRDBRAIN

Now that we've got Petr stowed away on a bed of bleeding heart, I thought you'd like to hear another of my personal stories. I got a million of 'em.

But before I quork one your way, I should tell you, full disclosure and all, that my buddy Boomer (outsiders call him Mountain Beaver and scientists call him *Aplodontia rufa*) would tell this story differently. The way Boomer would tell it, he is the sand of the earth, and although that is true, that is also quite dull. Fact is my buddy Boomer doesn't season his stew, and as for me, when it comes to storytelling, I use a bit more spice, if you know what I mean.

Now my version starts back in my younger days, back to that time when I caught an Olympic Mountain updraft and headed straight for the sun. If you remember, I was intent on snatching a bit of sunlight, but instead of hitting my target, I skipped off the upper atmosphere, reversed direction, and tumbled down, down, down until I thwacked into the hard-as-marble surface of the Hood Canal.

No matter. If I've learned anything, I've learned to keep my ear open for opportunity, and with that in mind, I put up my antenna and tuned into OZZ. It was the top of the hour and time for the afternoon news.

"OZZ news time is two p.m. Now for the headlines on the hour, every hour. Today in the news the space shuttle has for the first time retrieved a satellite, everybody's buying compact discs instead of records, and it's Anti-Fascist Struggle Day in Croatia. On the harbor, local mountain beaver Boomer has put a bit of sunshine in a box. And now here's Chip Wood with the weather. Hey, Chip, I'll bet it's foggy trails again. Am I right, or am I right?"

Naturally, I thought to myself, "Well, well, seems like ol' Boomer's got a bit of sunshine on a cloudy day," and no sooner had I thought this, than I pushed off from my trusty branch, swept down into the Queets Valley, pulled up on a conky snag, and gazed down at Boomer finishing off a western hemlock seedling.

"Hey, Boomer, ol' pal, long time no see! How's my favorite mountain beaver? Cache any boletus buttons lately?"

"Don't eat fungus." Nip. Chew, chew.

"So I hear you've been inviting people for lunch, and I thought I'd save you the trouble of looking me up. You know how I'm not home much. I like to let the lichens grow good and strong on my perches. Besides, I found something I know you'll like, so I caught the first thermal that came along. Long story short, I brought you a present."

Chew. "Present? Really?" Chew.

"Where are your manners, Boomer? How about we do this back at your place? I haven't seen your lovely home in ages."

"Hm" —gulp— "where's my manners? Follow me," and I stayed hot on his itty-bitty butt, that is, until it disappeared down a large boomer hole. I thought nothing ventured, nothing gained, right? So I trimmed my wings, inhaled, and dropped like an anchor.

Once at the bottom, I found Boomer's burrow continued along a sloping passage, and let me tell you, his mineshaft was dark. Dark like the flipside of the moon. Dark like six feet down in a peat bog, like the obsidian cavern of Boomer's monster-berry heart. Not to worry, I knew that while Boomer busied himself over serving lunch, he also was worrying over the seed I had planted in his brain.

Tick, tock, tick, and Boomer served up an assortment of huckleberries and licorice fern generously coated in banana slug slime. Yum! Fortunately for me, Boomer couldn't contain himself, and after a single bite, he blurted out, "So about that pres—"

"Boomer! You cagey connoisseur, you patron of pipsissewa pâté, you really know how to stuff a bird. I can't remember—"

"My present!"

"Oh my yes, Boomer, you're feeding me so well all the blood's drained from my brain. Now, come closer. Look under my wing."

As quickly as his spadefeet would carry him, Boomer ambled over to me and stopped in the gloom. He then peered deeply where he fancied his present to be, but try as he might, frustrated by the darkness, he could make out only shadow.

"Can't see anything! Where's my present?"

"Why, Boomer, look right here. Just reach out and take it."

Again Boomer came up empty, extending his long-clawed fore paw and swiping the air. "Nothing!"

"Really, Boomer, get some light. You don't want to miss out on what I've brought."

"Light?" Boomer thought out loud. "Yeah, must get some light," and he shuffled off to retrieve the box, the one that I learned about from the radio newscast.

Once again, tick, tock, tick, and Boomer returned along one of his artisanal corridors, sensed my presence, stopped, sat up on his haunches, and snapped open his little light-filled box, filling the chamber with a glorious glow and, in turn, illuminating the bit of oyster shell nestled in my underwing.

"Pearls, pearls!" Boomer gasped, and as he let go of the box, he plucked the shell from my wing, and as the box fell, I swept it from the air and snapped it shut, plunging the burrow into darkness. Fortunately, I had a mind map of the escape route, and soon enough, I was up, up, and away into the sky!

But before you get all judgy, let me take a moment to say that I'm not heartless. I fully acknowledge that the rumor mongering we call "word on the game trail" has been cruel to Boomer, tagging him with names like Sapling Molester. I am also aware that he's been Cougar and Bear's plaything. They love to roll my buddy into streams and bat him into thickets. I do feel bad about all that.

Furthermore, let me take another moment to say that all words on the game trail are equal opportunity imps, tagging me with names like Vainglorious Birdbrain. And sure, I have an egotistical side, so you won't be surprised that I'd really prefer to be known as Ravenus Rex. And, yes, Light Giver.

GO FIGURE

Sign said, "No Rebar
Spiking the Trail," flashing his
dream like a child's face

GOSSIP

Hauling himself up from his bed of bleeding heart, Petr returned to the gravel access road, and with the sun now behind the ridgeline, he entered the long summer twilight, the time it took the sun to descend from the ridgetop to below the Pacific's horizon. And in this time Petr wanted to cover some territory, so he picked up the pace, one step leading to another, the rhythm lulling him into a fanciful conversation.

He remembered being a child and playing a game where he turned every sound of the forest into a conversation with the animals, the plants, and even the stones. Any sound could become animated. He especially liked returning to his memories of playing beside a creek, recollections of the *chee-chee-chee* of tiny kinglets in the hemlock and the rattle of belted kingfishers on overhanging branches.

He thought the kinglets terrible gossips, complaining about every little nuisance: the lack of insects to eat, their cousins one tree over who couldn't control their chicks, the heat of the afternoon sun, and the embarrassing sister who spent very little time keeping her feathers presentable.

In response, the belted kingfishers chattered endless somethings about those on the other side of the stream, whinging about weasel coming home empty-handed or queen bumblebee having yet another brood under her wings. When was she ever going to learn that more children just meant more larvae to feed, the little maggots! And what about those kinglets? Yak, yak, yak, weren't they enough to drive you to distraction?

Absorbed in his memory, Petr lost track of time. Walking became a mediation of muscles, a physical trance. The weight of his pack dissolved, at least until he reached a final clear-cut where the trees disappeared, and the canopy opened to the sky.

Here he stopped, the trance broken, the weight of his pack a mockery.

THE DOOHICKEY VERSUS THE THINGAMAJIG

Looking from the gravel access into the clear-cut's succession of fireweed, oxeye daisy, and foxglove, Petr decided he'd stop for the night. In the morning he'd start up again out where a brown metal rectangle read Elkhorn Campground. He'd head in that direction, the way the arrow pointed.

But right now, the sun already below the ridgetop, Petr hauled himself off the gravel access and into the clear-cut. He stopped at an old red cedar stump, cut long ago, six feet in diameter if it were an inch, not a part of the what-came-next, not a part of the recently departed second growth, but now a headstone in a vast Olympic Peninsula graveyard, a monument sculpted by axe and whipsaw.

While looking over the stump's flanks, Petr recalled one of Bear's stories. He imagined two men in a gloomy December drizzle wearing hickory shirts, high-water pants, and suspenders. The men used their sharpened axes to cut notches into the red cedar buttress above the root swell. Into these notches the men inserted springboards, sawmill cut planks with steel plates attached to one end, each steel plate possessing a sharp cleat which bit upward into the tree. Once inserted into the notch, the plate and its protruding plank extended horizontally some five feet off the ground.

Petr imagined one man applying kerosene-based saw oil to their misery whip, a two-man crosscut saw with a handle at each end. The man kept the saw oil in an old cork-stoppered bottle. The cork had a notch in it to allow the saw oil to dribble out onto the saw blade. The men relied on their saw oil because as they worked, the oil dissolved the tree's sticky resin. Without the saw oil the misery whip would have become hopelessly gummed up in the fresh cut. "Hey, toss me that saw oil. I hate when my tool gets stuck." "Oh, shit, that's funny." "Ain't it though, my doohickey all glued inside a what-chamacallit, you know, that thingamajig, like my finger caught in a damn bitch's mouth."

The men then pulled themselves onto their springboards, and from this perch one grabbed the handle of the misery whip, the saw he had propped vertically against the tree. Next, the one with the handle sliced the air with the freshly sharpened blade, and the other caught the free handle. Both men spit a tightly packed wad of wet-worked snus into the salal-choked under-story. Breath . . . breath . . . breath . . . and the men, now sawyers, pulled the blade through the trunk, releasing the aromatic pungence of red cedar. Over time the pair developed a rhythm, muscle against saw against wood grain, until snap . . . creak, creak . . . snap, snap, snap . . . c-r-r-r-ea-ea-ea-ea-k-k-k-k, the giant fell and then the giant crashed. Directly above, a murky fog replaced the red cedar canopy.

DANCE OF THE RADIO PARTS

We on the Olympic Peninsula don't consider sleep to be some sort of inconvenience to our waking productivity. We've not heard John Calvin's sermons on the virtues of labor, and we're pretty disinterested in Max Weber's *The Protestant Ethic and the Spirit of Capitalism*. Of course, it's not because we don't work. Oh no, if getting stuff done sets you free, then every night our dreams are highly productive.

Case in point: when Petr got tired from all his walking and imagining, he sat down, propped his back up against that red cedar stump, the one he had taken such a fancy to, and promptly fell asleep. All about him lay fallen white and purple foxglove blossoms atop old skidder tracks.

Then a most curious thing happened, well, not so much curious as generative, fertile, productive. What happened was that while he slept, Petr's mind opened wide its needful fish mouth, and what Petr imagined were not blooms set loose upon the breeze, but blooms tightly gloved on the hands of fairies passionately paired in an aerial *pas de duex, totalement en l'air*.

And as he dreamed, Petr also became aware of a hush of fairy voices. At first he enjoyed their song washing over, waves renewing like an August tide pool. As time passed, he began to make out words, then phrases, and finally sentences. "No . . . more . . . no . . . more . . . long . . . long gone . . . no more . . . no more . . . long long gone . . . no more, no more . . . long long song . . . gather all . . . the fairy folk . . . rocky outcrop, cloaked in moss . . . mousy sleeps, can't be woke . . . people don't believe in us . . . no more, no more, long long gone . . . no more, no more, long long gone . . . no more, no more, long long song . . . gather all the fairy folk . . . alder catkin windy tossed . . . rough skin newt, tail is broke . . . people don't believe in us . . . no more, no more, long long gone . . . no more, no more, long long gone . . . no more, no more, long long song."

"Muss his hair!"

"Monster-berry juice his eyes!"

"Braid his lashes!"

"Dump his bag! Whee-ee-ee-ee-ee-ee-ee."

"Look at this. What's all this?"

"What is this?"

"What is that?"

"It can speak!"

"Grab its tongue!"

What was once a paired ballet, now became a quadrille of fairies, one pair coupled with blossoms, the other pair coupled with radio parts. And hovering above these dancers, three other fairies, ones with different technical abilities, provided music. They played a bone whistle, a *bodhrán*, and a *timpán*. While the musicians played, the dancing fairies sang.

> Oscillator, oscillator, phase-locked loop,
> Oscillator, oscillator, phase-locked loop,
> Gain stage, gain stage, one-half watt.

> Power supply, power supply, twenty-four amps,
> Power supply, power supply, just five watts,
> Nickel, cadmium battery.

> Coaxial, coaxial, fifty ohm,
> Coaxial, coaxial, impedance,
> J-Pole, J-Pole antenna.

Fast and faster the quadrilles reeled, violet blurring into pink blurring into white, the tart of red huckleberry, the sweet of ozone.

Faster and fastest the quadrilles reeled, the voices becoming feverish, an aria sampled directly from a night mirage.

And then the voices became not at all. Nothing. Nothing but crackle and fizz.

SNEAKER WAVE

"Newt's got your tongue,"
log truck coming 'round the bend.
"Newt's got your tongue."

"Newt's got your tongue,"
tumbled down a waterfall.
"Newt's got your tongue."

"Newt's got your tongue."
"Yes, Mum, I am headed home.
Newt's got my tongue."

BOOK FOUR

WILDSISTERS

BLESSED ART THOU AMONG WOMEN

BAIE'S JOURNAL

Entry 9

I sit,
dear Mother,
the elements all about:
breeze-blown fog,
earth-bound dew,
vapor-filtered sun.

I count,
dear Mother,
the things I feel:
our bog spotted with
cranberry blossoms,
our roof covered in
red cedar shakes,
my rosary strung with
broken cockle shells.
I count

Dori's approaching
engine shifts.

I remember
her Subaru Brat's birth,
a gift from
a broken stepdad.
I remember
her Brat's girlhood,
our memory baby,
its body composed of
patch and primer.
I remember
her Brat's adolescence,
riding along
our Humptulips.

Then just short of
the cranberry bog,
Dori's half car,
Dori's half truck,
abruptly halted.
Her engine quieted.

A wind blew through.
Her door opened.
Then Dori rolled out:
my Dori of
the crucible,
my Dori of
the anvil,
my Dori of

the hammer,
my Dori of
the punch:
tempering,
swaging,
stamping.

She shouted against
a fresh Pacific gust
—Good gawd Baie,
get over here an'
give me a big ol' hug.
Jeez-us, it's been a while.
Sure as shit
wasn't my idea for
you t' run off
two years ago.

Our greetings twined like
orange honeysuckle vines.
Our embrace fruited like
black elderberry blossoms.
Our tears flowed,
carried away on
the salt breeze.

Hail Dori,
full of grace,
the Lord is with thee.
Blessed art thou among
women.

BLESSED IS THE FRUIT OF THY WOMB

BAIE'S JOURNAL

Entry 10

—Baie, come meet Aces!
He's still all strapped in.
Damn, he got buried in
all my stuff! An' look,
he's sleepin' all cozy!

Dori dug down,
unsnapped her love child, and
lifted Aces free and clear.
She then planted him on
Humptulips' soil.
Stippled sunshine
fairy danced about
his seal-eyed face.
I thought him many things:
a ripening cranberry,
a Sitka spruce seed,
an oyster-nestled pearl.

Full to bursting,
I blurted out
—Let's take him to
the Humptulips!
All God's otters
need a baptism!

—Good gawd, Baie,
there's crazy shit in

that head o'yours.
Sure as shit, why not.
And so we went to
the Humptulips.
The air was a barm:
sea-salted,
peat-spiced,
shot through with
glaucous gull cries.
We stopped at
our river's edge.
We stood on
green grass fed by
Olympic silts.
We watched its waters
steadfastly stream by.
We felt its waters
potently drawn toward
the slack coastal tide.
We knelt down.

Turning reverential
I prayed for
Dori. I prayed for
Aces. I prayed for
community.
—Dear Mother,
dear Father,
we gather on
our Humptulips to
baptize dear Aces in
God's graceful love and
God's loving grace.
Like haircap moss,

dear Aces will thrive.
Dear Aces,
child of dear Dori,
I baptize you in
Jesus' name, who
suffers the children, who
washes women's feet, who
plants the mustard seed.

—Now, Baie,
none o' that
immersion shit.
Don't make him cry.

I dipped my hand into
the murk and swirl of
our Humptulips,
this congregation of
Sockeye and Dog Salmon,
Fisher and Otter,
Crow and Cormorant.
A water droplet
trickled from
my hand and
kissed his cheek.
He did not cry.

—Jeez-us, Baie,
that was, damn . . .
hmm, well, guess it's okay.
Let's get on back.
I'm not used t' all
this churchy stuff.

OPEN

BAIE'S JOURNAL

Entry 11

an otter beheld
Dori; then it beheld me,
windblown open door

THE WAY BACK

BAIE'S JOURNAL

Entry 12

On the way back,
we stopped.
We picked first fruits,
the soft-fleshed salmonberry.
These yellow druplets,
tinged with red,
fell free into
our needful hands.
Their subtle sweetness
fed our eager tongues.

first fruits are very
nice, priming our taste for the
stronger fruits to come

BACK TO OUR FARMHOUSE

BAIE'S JOURNAL

Entry 13

I remember,
dear Mother,
your quilting stash.
It sat between
the maple rocker and
the iron wood stove.
Your gracious ragbag
contained a redemption of
work-worn pants,
sleep-worn sheets, and
wash-worn towels.

I remember your needles:
sharps and betweens,
embroidery and tapestry,
bodkins and chenille,
quilting and beading,
sailmakers and glovers,
darning and curved.

I remember your thimbles:
stainless steel cones,
one leather sheath with
a mercury dime tip,
fused wire ropes,
your wedding ring
a finger shield.

I remember
your mornings,
cutting free strips of
poplin and gingham.
I remember
your evenings,
cobbling together
crazy shapes from
dear Father's hickory shirt,
your calico house dress,
our jute burlap gunny sacks:
Tasty Tater Idaho spuds,
Pari Brand basmati rice,
Full-O-Pep chick starter.
I heard you call
your pieced patchwork
family album quilts.
I heard you call them
charm block crazy quilts.

OUT, OUT

BAIE'S JOURNAL

Entry 14

quilts warm the body;
memories warm the spirit:
out, out damnéd chill

WHAT'S UP WITH DORI?

BAIE'S JOURNAL

Entry 15

I badgered up,
dear Mother,
your beggar's block quilt.
I gifted it to
Dori who tightly wound
her Aces against
the Pacific cold.
She then swept up
her child-in-a-blanket and
freely reeled about
the farmhouse kitchen.
The two weaved between
the table and chairs and
then plunked down,
exhausted, onto
the Doug-fir floor.

—Jeez-us, Baie!
I'm glad you're home.
When you took off,
I got a pack o' boyfriends.
We went muddin' in
our ol' pickups.
We went drinkin' all over
this gawd-damn harbor.
I was havin' a grand time.
I s'pose they was, too.
Sure as shit better have.

—I was dumb as
a green-ass choker.
Before I knew it,
I was sure as shit late.
Then I got all sick.
I was pullin' over an'
barfin' big time on
the side o' the road.
I was buyin' up
boxes o' saltines an'
eatin' them like
sea salt taffy.

—Got t'admit,
I got real scared.
Me, mornin' glory Dori,
was gettin' filled up.
Sometimes I felt like
a hand sledge
was poundin' inside.
Cramps ain't nothin' like
forgin' some hot stock.

—So I turned out
this high-grade boy.
It wasn't easy, but
I press forged him good.
Then me an' Aces,
we took the hell off.
We kept goin' 'til
we got t' Elkhorn,
the Montana one, an'
we crashed there hard;
I mean real hard, like

we dropped a turdzilla.
I couldn't be nobody's mother.
You know, ain't nobody
been a mother t' me.

—Now don't get me started.
I s'pose ol' Alicia
did her best; that's if
promisin' every guy
the keys t' my . . . shit,
you and I know,
it got so bad
I looked forward
t' the big hairy bust up.
We'd start all over,
just me an' Alicia.
We always got by on
box mac'n'cheese an'
surplus peanut butter.

—Jeez-us, Baie,
remember how
she'd always come home?
She'd be dumb drunk
wearin' some rat's asshole.
They'd be talkin' 'bout how
great it's goin' t' be,
him evil eyein' me like
hot crispy bacon.
That's 'bout when
I'd jump my Brat,
go t' findin' you,
crash a few days 'til
the dirty asswipe took off,

then jump my Brat back.
The next days were for
gettin' Alicia out o'
her gawd-damn bed.

—And remember the day
ol' Barry showed up, an'
what do you know?
she sank her claws in.
He's so weasel-ass dumb
he married her, an'
what did she do?
turned the dumb fuck into
her personal slave.
She'd cougar scream
—Hey, idiot,
son-of-a-whore,
where'd y' stash
the Robo?
And then she'd baby talk
—Hey, scrotum bag,
mix me up some
o' that purple drank.
But even shit-for-brains
couldn't stand it.
One day, poof, no Barry.

—The worst was Alex.
You remember,
yep, that sick one
she fish-snagged off
a hot dog roller.
Jeez-us, he was the worst.
I'm tellin' you,

he was a smack whore.
He was so bad,
we bunny hopped into
my ol' junker with
some o' your mom's
huckleberry pie an'
smoked salmon,
Good-gawd, I loved
that woman, and
we went tearin' up
the Humptulips past
Copalis Crossing onto
the one-O-one.
Then we buzzed
FS two-two-hundred an'
FS two-two-O-four.
We went straight on through
the Colonel Bob an'
near ran out o' road at
Campbell Tree Grove.
Had it all t' ourselves.

—I sure as shit remember!
A fat moon came over
that high east ridge.
We ate your mom's salmon.
We ate your mom's pie.
Our fingers got greasy, an'
our mouths turned all blue.
We should o' died right there.

—You know, Baie,
I can do without men.
Hate 'em, truth be told.

Aces and me, well,
we plan t' steer clear.
But you know, Baie,
those men're long gone.
Good gawd-damn riddance.
'Nough rememberin', an'
time t' get t' doin'.
Ain't that right, Aces?

EXCUSE ME, WHITE OTTER HAS MORE

Gray Whale,
Orca killed your husband.
Fattening on
seabed crustaceans and
spy-hopping for
your family,
your husband forgot to
read the silence.

On that fateful day,
he was majestic.
He was seminal.
He was damn near epic.
His breech sparkled,
the diatoms flashing across
his skin like
sticky diamonds.
He was the pearl in
your oyster.

On that same day,
Orca was degenerate.

Transient and hungry,
he sounded into
an offshore trench.
After a single deep breath,
he dropped like
a ballast stone.
He located your husband,
his mind's ear triangulating
the pounding surf against
your beloved's splash.

Then came the end.
A lightning bolt of
negative adrenaline,
Orca hit your husband's belly,
teeth tearing away pounds of
Pacific-kissed flesh.
The gash leaked like
a ruptured aneurysm.
He didn't stand a chance.
Jaw torn free,
tail severed,
blowhole sucking,
he sank.
He surfaced in
pieces.

Gray Whale,
distant from
the calving lagoon,
you and your child
are now refugees.
Close your eyes to

your terrific memory.
Rub away
the sea lice.
Come out of
the incessant surf.
Feast on
upswelling krill.
Stay offshore in
my Olympic waters.
You are weary.
I am alone.
Together
we may find peace.

Kyrie eleison.
Christe eleison.
Kyrie eleison.
Je ne suis plus un créature
de la terre
or the air.
I am a creature
de la mer.

AFTER REELING WITH ACES

BAIE'S JOURNAL

Entry 16

We leave
the living room.
We pass through

the door.
We step onto
the porch.

The boards squeak:
loose against
their nails,
nothing
to be done,
the boards
never quite
lined up right.

The boards converse:
one grain
to another,
weathered,
each squeak
a ghost of
footsteps.

DREAMING WILDSISTERS

BAIE'S JOURNAL

Entry 17

Aces was playing a game,
testing his legs in
the cranberry bog,
his toddler body
towering above
the verdant bushes.

Dori and I
watched and encouraged,
laughed and marveled:
pure angelic joy.

Then I started talking
—I think you're right,
dear Dori;
it's time to start doing.
You and dear Aces
will live right here.
This will be your home.

—Let's make this place our own.
Let's make a safe harbor.
Women need a safe port.
Their kids need a safe berth.

—We'll rebuild the barn.
We'll add a kitchen.
We'll frame loft rooms.
We'll open a roadhouse.

—We'll have good strong coffee.
We'll have cranberries and
wild nootka roses, too.
We'll call it Wildsisters.

Then Dori answered back
—Je-e-e-zus T. Christ, Baie,
give me a second, will you?
You sure think mighty big.
Aces, what d'you think?
He looks pretty settled.

Sure as shit, you'll
need some muscle, an'
sure as shit, I don't
need no more trouble.
Last time I looked 'round,
prayin's worthless without
a whole lot o' doin'.

—Where should we start,
dear Dori?

—Like you said,
the barn's a good place.
How old is it, anyway?
If the structure's good,
we add some insulation.
We build up a few walls.
We wire the electrical.
We plumb some pipes', an'
then we throw open
this Wildsisters like
a crack-ho's backdoor!

BLESSING WILDSISTERS

BAIE'S JOURNAL

Entry 18

Saint Thérèse de Lisieux:
Aux premiers instants de ma vie,
Vous m'avez prise entre vos bras;
Depuis ce jour, Mère chérie,

Vous me protegez ici-bas.
Pour conserver mon innocence,
Vous m'avez mise en un doux nid,
Vous avez gardé mon enfance
A l'ombre d'un cloître béni.

In the first moments of my life,
you have taken me in your arms.
Since that day, dear Mother,
you have protected me here below.
To preserve my innocence,
you have put me in a sweet nest.
You have guarded my childhood
in the shade of this blessed cloister.

SISTER OBBLIGATO

BAIE'S JOURNAL

Entry 19

I think about
the word sister:
the sister who
never came,
the sisters whom
I left behind, and
the sister who
brought her child.

After thinking
I imagine:
a raven

take flight and
disappear across
the harbor,
an otter
slip beneath without
a surface swirl,
a hawk moth
settle onto
dear Ace's cheek, and
somewhere beyond
the horizon,
candlefish,
eulochon in Chinook,
tiny oily torches,
mass for
the journey home.

Then I wonder:
what's to be sewn,
dear Mother;
how shall we gather?
What's to be built,
dear Father;
how shall we inhabit?
What's to be conceived,
dear Sisters;
how shall we desire?

Thinking,
imagining,
wondering, and
now,
Dori and I,
doing.

Kyrie eleison.
Christe eleison.
Kyrie eleison.
Tout
est perdre.
Tout
est retrouver.
Now and
here,
wildsisters.

BOOK FIVE

PASTURE POODLE AND THE LOST CHILDREN

FREE WILL IN AMERICA

We here on the Olympic Peninsula are unlike most Americans; we don't waste our time wondering about free will. Oh sure, we make decisions, but we don't wonder why we went this way instead of that way. Fact is our trees are three blue whales tall, and our devil's club suffers from gigantism. Our storms and currents roll past like old-timey smallpox and influenza. And our banana slugs, well, these slimy buggers put men's penises to shame.

Truth is, we view our decisions much like Tsutomu Yamaguchi must have viewed his. Maybe you've heard of Tsutomu Yamaguchi, the only documented survivor of both the Hiroshima and Nagasaki nuclear attacks. The story goes that Yamaguchi-san, who lived in Nagasaki and was away from home on business, was walking to Hiroshima's Mitsubishi shipyard on August 6, 1945. Above him Yamaguchi-san saw an American B-29 bomber. He also saw a parachute with something attached. FLASH! BANG! And he spun up into the air and landed in a potato patch. He woke up. His face and arms were burned. Both eardrums were broken. He stumbled toward the shipyard, found two friends, Iwanaga-san and Sato-san, and spent the night in an air raid shelter. He got up, swam through a river filled with dead bodies, and boarded a train home to his wife and infant son.

But there's more. August 9, 1945, Yamaguchi, deaf and burned, went to work at Nagasaki's Mitsubishi office. He told his supervisor his survival story. The supervisor did not believe him. After all, a single bomb could not destroy an entire city. FLASH. And Yamaguchi dropped to the floor. SHOCK WAVE. FLYING GLASS. SWIRLING DEBRIS.

Then what? Yamaguchi-san found his home destroyed. He feared the worst but found his wife and son unharmed. She had gone to find ointment for his burns. She and their child escaped the bomb in a tunnel.

So while you've been off witnessing local Humptulips' customs like impromptu baptisms, an Orca murder most foul, and ghost footsteps, I've been, like Yamaguchi-san, all without cause, all without reason, perched up in this red cedar.

And now that you're back, take a seat next to me on this branch. Relax, look down, and see, as the sun filters through, that Petr's arms are wrapped around his backpack like it's the ark of covenant, like it's Mary Magdalene's left breast, like it's a bottle filled with messages addressed to no one. No need to wonder who they're for. Relax, look down, and let's explore.

A DOSEWALLIPS SUMMER MORNING COMING DOWN

Petr awoke. The mist had settled in the valley, but it wasn't a blinded-world mist. Instead, the mist was suffused with light, no cloud cover above, only a cloud on the ground, a veiled-world mist.

Petr opened his eyes. He felt his radio transmitter safely spooned against him. He remembered sitting with his back against a massive red cedar stump but did not remember slipping down and clamshelling around his backpack. He also remembered weird images of dancing foxglove blooms and songs in fairy tongues and radio static. But he didn't remember assembling his radio transmitter, the one not in his backpack, the one lying out where it didn't belong.

Puzzled, Petr sat up and looked toward the east. He remembered an earlier time when a patchouli-scented hippie chick had flipped her hair and sat next to him on the Grays Harbor and Olympia bus. Back then he thought she smelled like walking through the front door of 123 Future Street.

Shaking away this pleasant memory, Petr prepared to break camp. He stowed his transmitter in his backpack, slung his possessions up across his shoulder, stood, and began to stumble back to the trail. He found the first bit easy, the track a civilized ten feet wide, the path gently rising along the

Dosewallips River. As he strolled, he imagined well-heeled urban hikers shod in Malaysian rubber, Chinese polytetrafluoroethylene, and English suede.

By mid-morning Petr found himself more than a hundred feet above the Dosewallips River. Below the trail white-capped, dark water rushed over glacial boulders and deadfall. Red cedar lined the riverbank. Doug-fir and western hemlock held the cliff face. Above the trail more Doug-fir continued with Pacific silver fir starting.

With the sun at its zenith, Petr came upon a series of switchbacks that returned him to the Dosewallips. Here the air chilled, and from above a seasonal rill, now a seep, trickled down and muddied the path. Sheltered from the afternoon sun by a fold in the ridge, the foliage changed dramatically. Occasional red huckleberry and vine maple gave way to vanilla leaf, redwood sorrel, and bleeding heart.

Continuing on, Petr clambered over a rotting log. Years before, the shallow-rooted tree had lost its balance, its heavy branches sending it ass-over-tits. "Holy Mary Mother McCree, how the fuckin' 'ell did I end up here?" "Johnny, I said y' was shit-faced an hour ago. Can I give y' a hand?" "No, jus' leave me be. I'll jus' rot here awhile."

Petr imagined the rotting log as it had once been, a majestic red cedar. Then one day it fell, CRASH, and in its falling tore a hole in the forest canopy. The resulting rush of sunlight had opened the way for a salmonberry stand, the one growing all about this now rotting log.

Petr stopped to pick the raspberry-like fruits from their canes. Some were red, others yellow. Early on, child-Petr had learned that the yellow ones were often tastier than the red, and although none of them were sweet by store-bought standards, each berry had a hint of sugar. He spent a good while, fat bumblebees busying about, pulling off the ripe fruit.

After foraging for a time, Petr noticed the sun tracking toward the western horizon. He decided to continue on, his progress steepening into the Olympics. UP UP UP, gravity began to weigh. His calves burned. His breath deepened. And as the trail narrowed, his steps fell into a rhythm. His wide-eyed gaze fixed on some indeterminate point.

UP UP UP, the trail began to level, and as it became less taxing, Petr came back to himself. His body was like a vessel, a cistern filling with a snowmelt of exhaustion tinged with pain. Finally he stopped. He found himself encircled by leggy bushes. He instinctively pulled fingernail-sized blueberries from their stems. He crushed them against his teeth. The resulting squirt of juice was a bit fresh, a bit tart. He then pulled thumbnail-sized black huckleberries from their stems. He split them on an eyetooth. The resulting earthy syrup spread sweetly throughout his mouth.

As he picked, Petr remembered walking many miles with Bear out to a place where a Makah sold black huckleberries in containers cut from the bottoms of gallon milk jugs. Fact was Bear didn't like messing with money, so his transactions were mostly executed by swapping one milk jug bottom filled with fresh-picked chanterelles for a similar one filled with fresh-picked black huckleberries.

Once upon a time, child-Petr had lived for a fresh berry snack. At the current moment, grown-Petr lived the same.

HUCKLEBERRY MILK JUG BOTTOM

huckleberry feast,
juice running from a child's lips,
an open-door breeze

BUT I DIGRESS, DUNG TRADER
TO DUNG TRADER

Now that you've read the chapter title, you know it's time for another digression, another one of my stories. And you also know that I've got a million of 'em, so here goes.

In this one you and I get to hook up with our ol' pal Coyote: aka Trickster, and my personal favorite, Pasture Poodle. I say ol' pal because I'm fairly confident you two have crossed paths, and if not, his name has, at the very least, graced your ears.

This story begins with me holding Boomer's light-filled box, an ace up my sleeve, you might say. And sure I could have gone all in, maybe got a nosebleed, done something monumental with that box, but where's the fun in that? Sometimes I like to play the long run, you know, so I decided to take a flier up Coyote's way, and after I pulled up on a particularly nice red cedar branch, I called down, "Hey, ol' buddy, sniffed any new butts lately?"

"Nah, things've been pretty slow."

"Ah, come on now, you've got to have something."

"Well, now that you mention it, maybe I can interest you in a little side deal."

"What you got in mind?"

"So I've been thinking. Seems to me, Raven, you've lost a bit of flush from your take off. Am I right? Seems to me that some mornings you just can't get off your perch. Now hear me out. In a recent study, four out of five cocks testified that a dolly bird got them up and flying high. Why waste another day grounded like some old coot? It all boils down to this: what would you give me if I could provide you with a heart-stopping hen?"

"Oh, I don't know. I might just fold."

"Come on, I've been around long enough to know a poker face when I see one. Dung trader to dung trader, I'll introduce you to some erotic action in exchange for you scouting me out some food."

Seemed fair to me, but then again, who's to say what's fair? At least it seemed interesting, so I responded, "Call, call, call," grasped the light-filled box tightly in my talons, and abruptly took off.

And once I was flying high, Coyote trotted off in search of the raven ravisher he'd bet but didn't have. Of course, he didn't want to go too far afield, too much work, but limiting his options meant he was down to his wife, Mole. Surprised? Don't be, because ol' Trickster had one house rule: lazy always beats love, a rule which might lead someone to conclude that he didn't love his wife, but that would be wrong. In point of fact, he loved her for a number of very good reasons: one, she was barepaw; two, she was present; three, she always had something in her pot; and four, even though she didn't rub up against him very often, she didn't go out scent marking either. Truth was he loved her because she was always subservient, always simpering, in a word, sexy.

"Hey baby, do I got a plan for us. I know I never get enough to fill that pot of yours, but I've fixed all that. You see, I got Raven out scouting up some grub. Now, here's the deal: I promised him a paramour in return. Do you think you could spruce this place up a bit? And yeah, how about sprucing yourself up, too. That should get his attention."

Mole did as she was told. She always did. A little musk and whisker trimming here, some barbecued salmon fat there, and finally she dug in and transformed their treefall into Salon d'Olympia.

While Coyote trotted off to take a nap, I hooked up with a hotblooded updraft, the perfect place to weigh my next move. Hey, I was in no hurry, don't mess with a good thing, right? But that all changed when the sun dipped toward the Pacific and the mountains began to cool. Seems the love affair between me and the atmosphere was over, so I decided to make a clean break of it. I decided to leave that waning updraft behind, barrel roll DOWN DOWN DOWN into the deep, damp Satsop River drainage, and pull up on a red cedar bough set above a black eddy beside the bleached skeletons.

Just below my perch, one particular skeleton stood out. It looked like it was still alive, like it might swish. It looked so spirited, in fact, that I dropped to the river's edge and stashed my light-filled box under a red cedar root tangle. Then I flew back to my perch, and with a sturdy tool, my hard, handsome beak, I wrenched free a choice piece of greenery only to drop back to the water's edge and place the foliage atop the skull, ribs, and tail bones. And let me tell you, that's when the magic started. I say magic because the flora and bones writhed in unison, and finally they fused into Dog Salmon Brother, my ol' chum, the one who I revisit every year, the one who asks me along when he returns to his undersea home.

"Raven, isn't it?"

"Yeah, you betcha."

"Ready to take the plunge?"

"Do you know the way to O-lym-pE-A?"

THE TIME-LAPSE COMPOST BIN

Once his dietary and psychic berry needs were satisfied, Petr pushed his legs further up the trail. Soon he came upon a warmer, drier subalpine habitat. The vista was breathtaking, the air spiced by fragrant mountain hemlock and silver fir oils.

Again Petr forgot about the pack against his back, the weight becoming one with his body's rhythm, and as he walked into the early evening, he brought to mind the faded map of the Olympics that Bear had tacked on their logger bunkhouse wall. Orienting himself inside the image, Petr judged that he was not only leaving behind Crystal Mountain to the west but also heading straight for the triple peaks of Mount Anderson. He figured he was following a crest just east of Diamond Mountain.

Then Petr unwittingly left the crest trail and wandered down into a valley. He found himself back among red huckleberry bushes and downed logs, the latter festooned with thick mats of moss and western hemlock seedlings. He stopped for a moment to view a fairly substantial western hemlock that stood solidly on tip-toed stilts of roots.

This unique situation, a tree trunk standing on the pillars of its exposed roots, comes about through an extraordinary process. It all begins when a sizable tree falls, rots, and becomes a seedbed. This fallen tree is called a nurse log, a situation where a mother-tree rots and nurses her child-seedlings. Over time, one successful seedling becomes a sapling, and the sapling's roots grow around the nurse log, eventually finding their way into the soil below. As mother-tree continues to rot, becoming a compost bin of a log, and then becoming nothing at all, her child-sapling's roots strengthen, becoming substantial posts, like so many concrete piers supporting their high-rise above, the same western hemlock roots and trunk that stopped Petr.

FREEBOOTING RADIO

eyelid dance
down and back
moist electric
hard magnetic
freebooting
radio

freebooting
amnion
freebooting

cambium
freebooting
radio

Pacific
Olympia
Pacific
Olympia
freebooting
radio

freebooting
western lands
freebooting
nether lands
freebooting
radio

eyelid dance
down and back
moist attraction
hard convection
freebooting
radio

AND THE EXTRAORDINARY CONTINUES

Standing in front of the stilted hemlock, Petr's experience took on completely new reference points:

left flipped right,
back split front,
past dissolved present.

One moment he was grown-Petr walking west through the Olympics; the next he was child-Petr caged, caught, helpless to leave.

One moment he was standing, gazing up at the height of the western hemlock's trunk; the next he was kneeling under the ramrod vigor of a sinuous spar.

One moment he was outside running his finger the length of a western hemlock root; the next he was inside running his finger over the moonlight luster of a precipitous pale.

OTHERS

Curious. Petr saw a number of others, each under a tree, each looking through western hemlock roots. Petr tried to take it all in. The Valley of the Nurse Logs. Children in the Dosewallips Stockade.

The first moved sharply about, nervous. Balled within itself, it had been trapped by loss, pent up by a world stolen and murdered. Once a fabulous life force, its world had been shrunk to what was contained between the stilts.

Behind the first, another lay piteously open. Soiled, it had been sliced by a rusty blade and bruised by an ill-made club. Existence just ghostly, exhaustion had blown it starved and battered into this safe eddy.

Further in the shadows, a third suggested itself as ripples on a black pool. A muffled echo, its world had been dampened, born upon a gone-to-pieces ear. Once a sonic symphony, it now played upon the bass drum of its experience for no one.

Petr felt them all to be mercurial, lonely, and deep, powerfully drawing his attention, so strong that he did not hear the rustle moving farther out among the trees.

SOMETHING'S HAPPENING HERE, WHAT IT IS AIN'T EXACTLY CLEAR

Maybe Petr didn't hear the source of the sound, but he did notice its motion, a shifting in space upon which to fix his eyes. Rectangular, he thought a skirt, but so wide that the knees it concealed were two feet across. He followed the line of the body upward. The totality was huge, a colossus shuffling about a central point, a bit red, mostly brown with charcoal accents.

Then Petr remembered a book from the Steam Donkey Academy called *Clamshell Boy, A Makah Legend* by Terri Cohlene. He remembered a central character named Basket Woman, a giantess, a collector of children.

Petr then had odd sensations. He felt on his tongue a sense of awe. He felt on his tongue a sense of Bear's eulochon candles, the ones Bear made from dried Pacific smelt strung through with a wick. And he felt on his tongue a sense, this one related to the other two, of earthquake.

BASKET WOMAN

Basket Woman got her name from her red cedar basket. When Basket Woman met willful children who stayed in the forest too late, she enticed them into her basket and took them home to her cook fire, no doubt putting them on the evening menu. In the end, these self-reliant children knocked Basket Woman into her own campfire.

SXWAYO'KLU

Petr thought about two things at once: about the character named Basket Woman, the one from the storybook; and about the enormous figure, the one he was experiencing in the shadows. His thoughts connected the two, and then his thoughts disconnected them.

Petr watched the unnerving figure come closer, so close he was overpowered by the smell of wood smoke and charred salmon on her red cedar clothes and body. The figure knelt close to his tree enclosure, bent an eye to an opening in the roots, and let fall tangles of cedar-shred hair. He thought he should be afraid. He was not.

Petr heard the figure mumbling, maybe singing, but the sound was more like raven chatter from the other side of a ridge. The voice seemed to pull at his entrails. He wanted to vomit, but the pull did not have a hold of his stomach's contents; instead, it had a hold of the organ itself. Then, when he felt the pull was about to tear his entrails from his body, his eyeballs slid, swoosh, back through his throat, and he found himself back outside the root enclosure. He turned and saw the opaque emptiness of the figure's unblinking eye at his left shoulder and felt the mumbling to be a migraine in his ears.

Seemingly unconcerned, the figure rose, turned, walked toward a smoldering fire, a burn he had not noticed until now. She bent and blew a steady breeze through the coals. Once the flames began to dance among the coals, the figure turned and began to sing again, this time to the others in their root enclosures, this time in a way Petr found intelligible.

> —Huckleberry children, children.
> Dosewallips children, children.
> Sxwayo'klu's lovely children, children.
> Huckleberry children, children.

Petr felt tears running down his cheeks. He felt invited. He felt as if he were one of Sxwayo'klu's children.

Then Sxwayo'klu stopped singing and turned toward him. He tried to think. He imagined the red cedar mask carving which held the frozen expression of a face. He heard the raven chatter that was a voice, "Bird got your tongue."

Petr turned and watched a whisky jack, aka gray jay, camp robber, or in Salish, *wisakedjak*, race in flight through the trees. In its beak the bird had a hold of Petr's tongue. The bird carried his tongue in the direction he thought he was headed.

BOOK SIX

STRANGERS

FEEDING THE BOG

BAIE'S JOURNAL

Entry 20

Dear Mother,
you said
—Shit.

Dear Father,
you said
—Merde.

Dear Dori,
you say
—Toxic dump.

Today
I spread
rabbit manure from
four orphaned

bunnies:
each bought
along with
a cage and
water bottle
at the 4-H fair;
each filled with
the tiniest light;
each devouring
weedy upstarts;
each leaving behind
bog food.

Later
I will spread
manure from
mounds of
mushroomy
angel wings
leavings
bought on
the cheap in
burlap sacks from
the Humptulips
Fungus Farm.

big Pacific rains
sweep across the luscious soil
brewing a dark tea

WHAT DORI DID

BAIE'S JOURNAL

Entry 21

Dori took up
dear Father's tools,
the ones
acquired from
Olympic old-timers,
the ones
aglow with
a patina of
sweat.

Dori sharpened
the plane blade,
chisel bevels,
the saw teeth.
She oiled up
a spade helve,
hammer handles.
She cleaned
a file's teeth,
drill-bit grooves.

Dori eyed
the barn's footings,
enchanted glacial erratics

laid by
dear Father.
Gloire soit au Père.

Dori touched
the wood skeleton,
spirit living Doug-fir,
carpentered by
dear Father.
Et au Fils.

Dori stitched
the building's skin,
salvaged, vagrant shiplap,
nailed out by
her.
Et au Saint-Esprit.

Dori laid
the structure's skull,
redeemed red cedar blocks
axe-split by
her.
Monde sans fin.
Amen.

strong morning coffee,
two cups; weird wildsisters' work,
dovetailed Doug-fir lengths

AH SHIT AND SORRY TO BOTHER

BAIE'S JOURNAL

Entry 22

A rufous hummingbird
came up out of
the blossoming snowberry.
Hovering motionless,
it froze above
Dori's left shoulder.

Instinctively Dori slipped
dear Father's hammer into
her leather-belted jeans and
slid clairvoyant across
the roof's drip edge.
She quickly descended.
The footworn ladder creaked.
A few red cedar shakes
lay askew.

I looked to Dori,
her willful feet
firmly planted on
Humptulips' sandy silt.
She looked to me,
my hand anxiously grasping
the loaded manure bucket.
We waited motionless for
what would come next.

A woman appeared off
the Humptulips trail,
slowly walking out of
a Sitka spruce stand.
Her gait was side to side,
her bearing tentative.
She felt a silvery thing.
She felt exhausted,
a dog salmon
nosing upriver.

Dori stood her ground,
narrowed her eyes, and
barked out a warning
—Now, watch yourself there.
Don't know you from
the devil himself.

The woman took off.
She darted past us.
After entering our barn,
she was gone.

Two men then walked wild off
the same Humptulips trail,
the same Sitka spruce stand.
They felt shadowy.
They felt two starved coyotes
stalking downwind.

Dori faced them, and
they stopped, standing in
a triangular configuration,
one flanking Dori,

the other trailing.
Dori's glare challenged.
The men, feculent,
felt like two omegas
pointedly sniffing for
cat truffles.

The one leading
hastily baited a line and
tentatively threw it out.
—So-o-o-o-o sorry to disturb.
Doin' all this yourselves?
Husbands must be out
bringin' home supplies.
Am I right?

Dori did not reply.
I did not reply.
Silence.
Ocean breeze pressed
our raw cheeks, ruffled
our loose hair.

—Yass, we been tryin' to
find our precious sister.
Her name's Shasta Lynn.
She's been worryin' us
considerable much.
Real jumpy, eh.
Just a bundle of nerves.
Speed freak, eh.
You didn't see the b—,
our precious sister?

The second grinned at
the ground, maybe at
a skipjack beetle.

Then Dori growled,
exploding the triangle with
her mother-wolf voice.
—No, I don't know.
My husband'll be back soon.
He expects chores t' be done.
Know what I mean?
Now, you all clear off.
Best be back t' work.
Best not disappoint.
He don't ask questions first.

Dori's stare cut each one,
ripping an emotional wound,
leaving a psychic scar.
She then set her heal,
powerfully spun around,
entered the barn, and
suddenly reappeared.
Her left hand gripped a rifle.
Her right hand worked the bolt.

—Ah shit,
you have a good day.
Sorry to bother, eh.

The two headed out.

Cold and quivering,
manure bucket in hand,

I looked to Dori.
I didn't know about
her difference maker.

—Found it cleanin' up.
Springfield nineteen-O-three,
a thirty-aught-six.
It's a deer an' bear gun.
Ain't loaded an' don't
think it'd fire anyway.
They don't know that.

EXCUSE ME, WHITE OTTER HAS A DIRTY BIRD'S TALE

Cormorant,
Dog Salmon told me
you rose with
the morning star and
headed off to
the Three Devils along
Rattlesnake Creek.
Here you found two strangers.
They were tending to
a pine and rabbit brush fire.
They passed a pipe between.
Contentment bubbled up like
a wellspring.

The first stranger's name was Gull.
He blew a snare-shaped ring and
cried the only note he knew.

—Cor mor . . . ant,
please . . . join us.

Gull passed the pipe to
the second stranger.
His name was Orca, and
he too casually blew
a snare-shaped ring.
The wisp cinched tight about
the icy sun dog in
the high azure sky.
—Sit a while.

Reading your hunger,
Gull took his spit from
the crackling fire and
thrust it your way.
You in turn
gladly accepted.
The morsel,
not quite pink,
nor orange exactly,
melted rich on
your eager tongue.
Your belly demanded more.
—Brothers,
you are powerful hunters.
This is extraordinary!
What is this called?
How do I find my own?

Gull thinly smiled,
his bill open like

an empty purse.
Orca damply spoke,
his answer an unctuous
evangelist's pitch.
—We have no art,
brother Cormorant,
except that brothers share.
If we work together,
we all can live well.
Wouldn't you agree?
This tasty bit is salmon.
When the shadows are long,
walk into the sunset.
There you will find more.

So you waited, and
soon the shadows of
the basalt ridge came down.
You walked toward
the waning twilight.
You followed the coulee to
the Columbia's tumbling edge.
You picked up
salmon's rich decadent scent.
You found salmon's
sun-bleached bone crumbs.
You went down through
Crescent Bar, down past
the Snake River, down past
the Umatilla River, down through
Cielo Falls, and down to
the Columbia's mad mouth.
Here stood the Pacific.

Silently following,
Orca stopped on
your unsuspecting right.
He pointed his fin into
the rolling surf under
the naked thirsty sun.
He then cast his hook.
—Salmon's home is there.

And a moment later,
Gull stopped on
your unsuspecting left.
He then set the hook.
—Cor mor . . . ant, you . . .
will be . . . fa mous . . .
You will . . . be known . . .
Sal mon . . . find er . . .
be stow . . . er of . . .
un told . . . rich es.

Your anticipation was
passionate and profound,
a spoil melting in
your needful mouth.
You dove in.
You swam out.
You plunged straight to
an Old Growth Village,
Salmon's beating heart.
You didn't notice
the hook snagged deep in
your ravenous gut.

This then brings us to
your tragic climax,
the fatal place where
Gull and Orca commenced
a feeding frenzy.
After the bloody rape,
after the gory killing,
you became a dirty bird,
a filthy fowl destined to
spend the rest of
your black familiar days
incessantly bobbing in
foul Pacific flotsam.

Cormorant,
you peck away
our eyes' flesh.
Grant us mercy.
Cormorant,
you peck away
our eyes' flesh.
Grant us mercy.
Cormorant,
you peck away
our eyes' flesh.
Take us home.

Kyrie eleison.
Christe eleison.
Kyrie eleison.
Je ne suis plus un créature
de la terre

or the air.
I am a creature
de la mer.

SHASTA LYNN

BAIE'S JOURNAL

Entry 23

After the two men left,
I set my bucket by
la cathédrale de lapin.
Here my parishioners
chewed their rosary.

Then Dori and I
reentered the barn.
We jointly stepped around
an ongoing repair and
abruptly stopped at
a sizable hole between
two old-growth joists.
Here dear Dori hooked
a woman-sized lunker, and
after some struggle,
she landed her prize:
a coarse creature
humbly draped in
a coral polka dot
grandma's house dress.

Wary, the creature blinked up.
Uncertain, we blinked down.

And when the creature spoke,
her voice came well-deep.
—Them boys out there,
they went huntin' me, but
I rabbit-holed good.
Them boys came close, eh.
Ever since I read the leaves,
them leaves said D E A T H.
Yass, them leaves,
they don't lie.

And Dori snarled back
—So, you got a name?

—Me? Shasta Lynn.

—Where'd those boys go?

—Them two? Not far.
Wanted a piece, eh.
Yass, yass, them boys did.

Dori reached out and
touched Shasta Lynn's mop.
Shasta Lynn looked up and
grasped Dori's hand.
Shasta Lynn's smile was
a crooked cartoon line, and
Dori's growl softened,
less white vinegar,
more lavender honey.
—I got that, but where
you think they're headed?
Think they'll double back?

—The earth's shakin', and
I splits open; fish eggs,
they all tumblin' out.
Babies all got an eye.
They watchin' me and you.
I splits open, and
babies got an eye.

—Jesus L M N O P Christ,
Baie, I'm callin' it quits.
This one's all yours.
She ain't my department.

MORE SHASTA LYNN

BAIE'S JOURNAL

Entry 24

So I smiled and said
—Now, dear Shasta Lynn,
you just follow me.
We'll check the fridge.

And off we went:
three ragamuffins,
three guttersnipes, waifs,
three offscoured strays
trooping gallantly past
the cranberry bog.

When we arrived in
the farmhouse kitchen,
Shasta Lynn directly spied
a bright yellow label,

ripped straight through
the cellophane bag,
grabbed a salty handful, and
stuffed her mouth full.
All the while she mumbled
—Yummy cuttlefish!
Love cuttlefish!
O-o-o-o-o-h. A-a-a-a-h!
Cuttlefish!

As I watched her
nearly choke on
the rehydrating mess,
I thought Shasta Lynn
a proper wildsister.
—Dear Dori, how about
some garden greens with
our dried cranberries?
Some just-baked bread?

—Sounds all right, Baie.
I'll make the salads.
You can put out
the bread and butter.

First Dori washed
our garden-picked greens.
Then she tossed our salad.
I broke the bread and
mixed cranberry butter.
Shasta Lynn doggedly licked
the empty cuttlefish bag.

Once all was prepared,
we eagerly circled

our bigleaf maple table.
As we shared our greens and
passed our hand-sliced bread,
Dori spoke her mind.
—Now, Shasta Lynn,
we need to know 'bout
those boys chasin' you.
I've seen them before.
They didn't know me, but
I sure as shit know them.
What I don't know is where
they're holin' up.
Are they always movin', or
they got their own place?

—Them boys're my brothers.
Nothin's safe when
Daddy's gone loggin'.
The 'Tulips is dark.
The earth shakes, and
the air stinks rotten eggs.
The chickens split and
eggs come tumblin' out.
Bleak, black nights.
Dirty fingers.
So I took off, eh.
The shakin' and stinkin'.
I just got out, eh.

Setting her eyes as
high climbing osprey do,
Dori saw the end.
—Been there, an' . . .
Je-e-e-e-e-zus Shasta,

we got work to do.
Must be holed up at
your family shack.
Daddy still there?

Shasta Lynn shut tight as
a low tide horse clam.

—So, here's the plan.
You got to stay here now.
You can't go back.
She can't go back,
right, Baie?

—Oh my yes, dear Dori.
Dear Shasta Lynn,
we're putting rooms in
our cranberry barn, and
you will sleep there.
We're starting a cafe, and
you can work there.
You belong here now.
You're a wildsister.

DEAR FATHER'S RADIO

BAIE'S JOURNAL

Entry 25

Once Dori lay
her tools to rest,
once Aces shut

his eyes to dream,
once Shasta Lynn set
her alder leaves to brew,
I expectantly switched on
dear Father's radio.
I tuned its big disc dial.
I sought an engaging voice.

—OLYP radio time is later than you think. In local news, it seems the
Humptulips boys are up to their old tricks. In world news, astrology nuts
report that everyone born today has got the negative polarity. What's that, you
ask? Well, it means you're an introvert, and a pretty feminine one at that. And
now here's that OLYP original tune you've all been waiting for, "Haunt My
Flesh" by Fisher and the Weasel Folk.

—Haunt my flesh incarnate soul,
the one I hear and smell,
and when I boil your angel blood,
you'll saturate and fill,
me,
you'll saturate and fill,
me,
you'll saturate and fill,
me.

—Haunt my flesh incarnate soul,
the one I taste and feel,
and when you break my martyred bud,
the rapture will fulfill,
me,
the rapture will fulfill,
me,
the rapture will fulfill,
me.

Such an inflaming tongue,
dear Mother.
It seduced my soul and
rippled the tea leaves
freshly spent in
Shasta Lynn's cup.
It queerly blended with
Shasta Lynn singing
—I'm a little berry
ripe and round.
I been all broken.
I can't be found.

All this led me to
say a fervent prayer,
one dutifully said to
Saint Thérèse de Lisieux,
one profoundly said for
a healing shower of
Pacific kelp.

Kyrie eleison.
Christe eleison.
Kyrie eleison.
Tout
est perdre.
Tout
est retrouver.
Now and
here,
wildsisters.

BOOK SEVEN

DOG SALMON BROTHER AND THE WHISKY JACKS

ALL TOGETHER NOW

So now you've got it, right? Radio Free Olympia. It's all connected: carrier waves, audio signals, frequency modulation, microwaves, and so on. It's all sonically and harmonically connected: sines, cosines, position, speed, phase shift, and so forth. It's all connected: eye and ear, tongue and nose, skin. It's all connected.

Whether it is I, Raven, in the air or White Otter in the water or Petr in the pulse or Baie in the spirit, it's all together now.

THE FREQUENCY OF GRAYWACKE

Petr's eye opened to see another eye. His ear heard a whir. He thought the buzz a morning alarm clock. A hummingbird lingered and subjected him to a lengthy examination, making a few deft feints toward Petr's face. Then the bird buzzed off, circled once around his radio equipment, the transmitter lying out on the ground, and whizzed away into the green and brown and black background.

Petr wondered why he didn't recall assembling his transmitter. His brick-sized electronics box, antenna up, eggbeater charger motionless, lay in the vanilla leaf and bleeding heart. This wasn't the first time. The first time was when he woke up against a red cedar stump among some foxglove blossoms. This time he was sitting against the stilt roots of a western hemlock.

He thought forward about his plans to transmit from the east slope of Mount Anderson. Given the height boost, he imagined his signal making it all the way to Seattle. He smiled. He then imagined his ultra-low-wattage transmitter ruffling the ear feathers of a few spotted owls a mile or two down-range.

Petr hoped to get up close and personal with Mount Anderson's glacier. He knew he was in for a serious climb, one that would start after he passed the place where Elk Lick Creek joined up with the Dosewallips River. From there he planned to climb over one thousand feet. He judged this should take a full day. His thoughts made his muscles ache.

In preparation, Petr squirreled around in his backpack. There he found an unopened C-Ration can, BEANS W/FRANKFURTER CHUNKS. He found his can opener and worked it around the edge of the can, and then he found his chow set spoon and went to eating. No, it wasn't hot. It wasn't even warm. But it was food, and because it was not only edible but also filling, life was good. After he had finished half the can, he pushed the lid down on what remained and stowed it, his spoon, and his radio equipment securely in his backpack. He would finish the can later, but right now he wanted to get to his feet and start on his way.

Soon he came upon an old National Park Service footbridge. Someone a long time ago had cut, limbed, and bucked two trees. Then they chopped one side of each flat and placed the logs across an unnamed, snow-fed run. Petr liked the bridge's simplicity, no muss, no fuss, and he crossed the bridge and walked another mile, raising his elevation over three hundred feet.

Then Petr came to another National Park Service footbridge, this one crossing the Dosewallips River. Someone a long time ago had placed this second bridge, and then that someone must have taken one look at the ensuing steep grade and just stopped. "Hey, Jerry, you think we ought to blast in some switchbacks?" "Nah, Gus, anybody gets this far is peerless enough t' goat their way on up." "I hear y' there. Let's turn around. Last one down is buyin'!"

Once across the second bridge, Petr paused and breathed deeply. He then put his head down and took his first step. His instep met the path at a painful angle. His knee took the weight of his body. He used his thigh, back, and stomach muscles as a fulcrum against his bones. Now it was a matter of STEP, BREATHE, STEP, BREATHE, STEP, BREATHE.

But the trail was so steep that Petr couldn't maintain a rhythm. He found it necessary to stop every hundred feet or so to catch his breath. During one of these stops, a white parnassian butterfly, two red eyespots on each hind wing, crossed his path.

Petr was unnerved by the silence. He felt there were two kinds of silence. There was the human silence he remembered surrounding his childhood, a silence that wasn't silent at all, a silence filled with a symphony of bird trill, creature scuttle, and wind breath. Then there was another silence, pure and void, the frequency of graywacke sandstone. His intestines twisted. He felt wrong. He felt watched.

HONEYMOON MEADOWS

Petr craned his head to find the trail's horizon. Nothing moved on top, so he brought his eyes down on the zigzag, examining trees, rock outcroppings, and undergrowth. The hair on his arms and legs stood on end. He imagined a stalking cougar, and then smiled, picking up the chatter of an alarmed, territorial Douglas squirrel. He thought he wouldn't be the first predator's meal nor the last object of a squirrel's derision. He decided to keep pushing.

STEP, BREATHE, STEP, BREATHE, STEP, BREATHE—Petr moved along until the trail leveled out onto an alpine bottom, a meadow. Here he stopped to watch a mariposa copper flit about a stand of bistort and fleeceflower. Petr was captivated by the white of the bistorts' flowers, the red of the fleeceflowers' leaves, and the metallic iridescence of the butterfly's wings. The bright alpine sunshine, so different from the muted marine light to which he was accustomed, illuminated this enticing picture, an egg fertilized in Caravaggio's eye.

GETTING SOME PERSPECTIVE

look, a wildflower;
in the still periphery
a shadow crouches

BERNARD HUELSDONK

"Bet I startled you," it said, keeping its eyes purposefully distant. "Don't mind if I take a breather with you? Not too many folks go off trail. Too steep. Wrong way to th' Enchanted Valley. You headed through th' side door? Me, too. That's a fact."

Too tired to refuse, Petr accepted the offer of companionship even though it appeared out of the twilight. No matter.

"Yep, been out cougar huntin'. Gov'ment gives four-fifty for each pair of ears I bring in. Call 'im Big Mouser. He holes up 'long a game trail and cat-naps most th' day 'til somethin' catches his 'ttention, mostly elk. Took me some time t' think like 'im, learnin' where elk go and findin' my own perches downwind. Soon 'nough they pass through, movin' from one grub spot t'nother. That's what I'm doin' now, elk all just 'bout moved up out of th' valleys lookin' for meadows where th' snow's just melted. Big Mouser followin' 'em, and I'm followin' Big Mouser. Bernard's the name. What's yours?"

Petr tried to speak but couldn't. He recalled a dream he had, the one with the whisky jack flying away with his tongue.

"Yep, been sleepin' out under th' sky. Wife and kids are back cozy and warm on th' homestead. Done some loggin' and carried pack for some folks prospectin', explorin', or just gettin' lost. Got t' rustle up some money some way or 'nother. Been walkin' these trails as long as I can remember. Ain't a bend in a cr'ck I ain't been through one time or 'nother."

With unblinking eyes, Bernard caught, locked, and held Petr's gaze. "This here's far as I like t' go. Open places make me nervous. Always like bein' down in th' trees keepin' an eye out, so nothin' sneaks up on me. Like t' watch my back, you might say. Now, you go on out and set up camp. I know you got it in your head that's where you want t' be. I'll just rest here before I get back at it. Now, go 'head. Much obliged for th' company."

After Bernard settled on his stomach, front legs tucked under his chest, back legs stretched out from his tummy, Petr walked away from the stunted subalpine fir and whitebark pine. He headed up into the paintbrush and avalanche lily, the blooms which lay below the scree and snow fields of the Anderson Glacier. In the descending Olympic sun, the ice glowed out of proportion, orange, and when he turned back, what once were individual trees were now a color block of blue edged with fiery red.

Petr looked for Bernard but couldn't find him. Then he heard, "Up here folks been known t' dream . . .," ending in a cat scream.

HIS TONGUE

Petr busied himself. First he set up camp and finished his can of BEANS W/FRANKFURTER CHUNKS. Then he hooked up his transmitter and stretched his dipole antenna.

A family of whisky jacks swooped low out of the firs and joined him. Mom and Dad walked about looking for leavings. Their young one perched on Petr's backpack.

It was time to broadcast Radio Free Olympia. Petr started by generating electricity. He had a small brushed twenty-four-volt DC motor that he turned with a kitchen eggbeater. He used the power he generated to charge four D-cell batteries, which in turn powered his five-watt FM transmitter.

Petr turned, and the energy he produced mixed with that of the slowly grinding glacier, the retreating Bernard, the whisky jacks, the half sun on the ridgeline. He remembered Bear telling him about the Haida shaman who went into the forest with an assistant. There the shaman fasted and received power from the otters. He became transparent as cave fish. His eyes turned to angel wing mushrooms. He danced and entered a trance, and when he awoke, he searched out an otter and cut out its tongue, the organ a potent talisman.

With batteries charged, Petr flipped the transmitter's power switch and danced about the transmitter. He felt an Olympic frequency. He stepped to the blooms. He stepped to the ice. He stepped to the rock. He stepped to the stars. He felt part of a harmonic chorus.

Then Petr became exhausted and stopped. He found the whisky jacks' fledgling dead, its tiny talons grasping the dipole. Tiny blood feathers lay about its cheek and breast. Its fish-egg eyes had turned to moonjelly.

Mourning, Petr thought about whisky jacks. When the breezes chilled and ice crystals formed, other birds followed the warm retreating air. Elk headed down from the subalpine meadows to take shelter in the valleys. Only the whisky jacks remained. They survived on their wits, and they survived using their superglue saliva, sticking bits of cached food on fir twigs and in rough bark. They wintered through Olympic nights huddled in woodpecker-squirrel hollows or under snow-covered boughs.

Mourning still, Petr pulled his jackknife from his pocket, opened it, and used it to pry apart the fledgling's tiny bill. He recalled Sxwayo'klu's question, "Bird got your tongue?" It had.

Now high in the Olympics, just below the Anderson Glacier, Petr began to speak in whisky jack tongue. He spoke to the avalanche lily. He spoke to the paintbrush. He spoke to the skyrocket. *"Wa ah ee er uh araa ta . . . wa-ah-ee-er-uh-araa ta . . . wa ah ee er uh araa ta ta.*

"A cha ee cha . . . e cha . . . a cha eh eh eh eh . . . wa wa ah ah uh . . . ee wh wh wh wh . . . wh wh wh wh wh . . . whee wee wee wee . . . whee wee wee wee.

"Wa ah ee-er uh araa ta . . . wa ah ee er uh araa ta . . . wa ah ee er uh araa ta ta.

Skin transparent as cave fish, eyes turned to angel wings, Petr spoke throughout the night, and when the horizon showed almost dawn, Petr plunged deeply into a pool of dream.

BUT I DIGRESS, THE GARDEN
OF OCEANIC DELIGHTS

Now that Petr's safely asleep, I propose that we get back to my story, you know, the one where I wrapped my black wing about my ol' chum Dog Salmon Brother, the one where we dove into the Satsop's current and swam

DOWN, DOWN, DOWN to his sea bottom home. And it should come as no surprise that along the way we engaged in some playful conversation, some talk about a mutual friend of ours. "So what about that Coyote? He really doesn't seem to know his ass from a hole in the ground."

"Half-assed, you mean," Dog Salmon Brother quipped.

"Yeah, word around the campfire is Raccoon weaseled Coyote out of a salmon dinner."

"You heard that right, brother."

"Did Raccoon really broil up Coyote's butt while he was sleeping? Did he really pull the old switcheroo, you know, a piece of salmon for a piece of arse?"

"Yep, and even though he figured Raccoon was up to no good, he ate most of his greasy old anus anyway. He always puts one and one together and gets a fraction."

"Explains why he's always cinched up in his own snare."

"All's ill that ends ill, you mean," Dog Salmon Brother gibed.

"Exactly!"

As we continued swimming, Dog Salmon Brother and I passed a downed oil tanker. Crude oil bubbled from cracks in its corroded hull. The dissolving hydrocarbons short-circuited our powerful *skookum* and diverted our rapidly flowing *chuck*. Accumulated mercury lay heavy upon our livers.

"But you got to like the guy," Dog Salmon Brother reflected, "Don't you think you got to root for the omega dog?"

"Yeah, if nothing else he's tenacious. He must've been dealt at least one more life than Bobcat. And that wife of his, Mole, she keeps the home fires burning, don't you think?"

"I don't know; does she dote on him, or what? I mean, she'd do him a little more good if she had a little backbone. And speaking of bones, she even quit returning salmon ribs to the riverbank. You know the arrangement, the fewer bones returned, the fewer of us come back to spawn. That Coyote may be a kick in the fins, but our relationship is just about spawned out, if you know what I mean."

DOWN, DOWN, DOWN some more, and then Dog Salmon Brother's village appeared out of the depth, a condition that those of us who swim these parts know as Pacific murk and swirl. First Dog Salmon Brother and I made out the defining angles of plank houses and then the supporting posts, individual planks, and some doorways. Next we saw figures moving about, and finally we found ourselves among Dog Salmon Brother's siblings, parents and grandparents, his cousins, uncles and aunts—all living their lives: the Chum, the Coho, the Humpy, the Sockeye, and the Tyee. Some were off shrimping; others mended their nets and lines. Some were repairing a plank house at the village end; others fashioned a canoe, pounding out the charcoal, the scoria left from burning a red cedar log. Children lazily played hide and seek among the dwellings. Smoke curled up into the pull of the Pacific current.

As it turned out, Dog Salmon Brother's return home was not a cause for celebration. He explained to me over a dinner of krill pâté that a gray carrion sickness had been visited upon the Old Growth Salmon, the illness rotting the victims both inside and out. He confessed to having recurring day and night visions of the end time, a plague of shipworms chewing the plank houses into sawdust and excrement, a whirlpool of current scattering life and memory across a barren ocean bottom.

Although I traveled to Dog Salmon Brother's home to honor our long-standing friendship, he had more immediate concerns, a hope that I might rid him of these disturbing visions. He went on to tell me that his own people had taken to ostracizing him for becoming a raving madman. He had called them lazy because fewer and fewer were leaving to return to the rivers of their birth. He had said their future was to live an endless ironic thirst, their flesh gone gelatinous, purulent, their remains urchin and starfish-eaten. In return his people had charged him with betrayal, accusing him of throwing their ancestral bones to the gulls.

Then we were quiet, and no sooner had our conversation ceased, than Silver Salmon Sister entered the room, passed through, and left. Although Dog Salmon Brother had told me about his sister, I hadn't met her, and because her time in the room was so brief, we remained strangers. Even so, she made a diaphanous impression. I thought her a Picasso sketch cast in pewter, a Monet shadow painted blue, a Bruegel grisaille carved in stone.

And as if on cue, Dog Salmon Brother stood and motioned for me to follow. We walked through a long windowless corridor lit only by passing bobtail squid, and we entered into Silver Salmon Sister's garden of oceanic delights. Crystal jellies languidly moved about in an atmosphere of sea sparkle. Lush mats of sea grape lay across a basalt outcropping. Hell's fire anemones and fire coral rhythmically released milky clouds of spawn. Shamefaced incognito gobies and drowsy spider crabs lay secure in thick stands of snake-locks anemone.

A blue-ringed octopus passed by.

BOOK EIGHT

TRESPASS

PRAISE BE THE GOD-GIVEN TIME

BAIE'S JOURNAL

Entry 26

What is a year, dear Mother:
someone's measure,
a segment, a radius,
God's little orbit?

Praise be
the God-given time for
this past year,
enough time to ready
the barn's sleeping rooms,
the barn's nurturing kitchen,
the barn's sheltered hall.

Praise be to
dear Dori for
sawing the framing,
laying the plumbing,
stringing the electrics,
nailing the dry wall.

Praise be to
dear Shasta Lynn for
scavenging the furniture,
organizing the kitchen,
planning the menu,
divining our future.

GUEST REGISTER

BAIE'S JOURNAL

Entry 27

In the name of
Vincent de Paul's
immaculate heart,
I made
a guest register for
opening Wildsisters:
a moorage,
a sanctuary,
our women's roadhouse.

I gathered
materials.

I cut
the pages from
an old account book.

I sewed
the lot together.

I used
dental floss.

Covetous of its "W,"
I tore free
the cover from
an odd encyclopedia.

I glued
the sewn pages and
the cover to
grocery bag endpapers.

REGISTRATION

BAIE'S JOURNAL

Entry 28

Wildsisters
Guest Register

Name: Sesily Phink
Coming from: pregnancy
Going to: delivery

Name: Misty Meran
Coming from: an uncertain slough
Going to: a certain oxbow

Name: Ruth Ann Delaney
Coming from: a dark road
Going to: the straight and narrow

SESILY PHINK

BAIE'S JOURNAL

Entry 29

She crossed from
door to table.
She ordered no drink:
not juice,
not cola,
not water.

I fancied her.
I felt her thirty years old.
I thought her ten years younger.
She purred about to
Dori and me,
wildsisters all.

I saw:
her hair
severely short,
her hips
powerfully gentle,
her mouth
lipstick-glossed,
her belly
full-to-bursting.

She wore:
a scarlet-dyed mushroom
encased in

blown glass crystal
lying against
her freckled chest.

I thought:
a rabbit in
search of
a secret thicket.

I felt:
a spirit kit
stir within.

From the kitchen,
Shasta Lynn called
—What breathes
first through
its gills,
next through
its lungs, and
finally through
its skin, eh.

THE ONGOING WORK

BAIE'S JOURNAL

Entry 30

nailing thinly split
red cedar against Doug-fir,
tight against the rain

joining table legs
to dismembered maple tops,
coffee cup mornings

feeding cranberries
to press, bittersweet droplets
fall east of sunrise

MISTY MERAN

BAIE'S JOURNAL

Entry 31

Her feet clicked across
the floor.
She ordered a drink:
lemon spritzer,
sugared cranberries,
self-spiked vodka.

I distrusted her.
I felt her fifteen years old.
I thought her six years older.
Her breath
filled the room,
a caustic breeze
rustling
snakeskin.

I saw:
her eyes
done in
cougar black,
her fingers
coiled in
silver,
studded with
turquoise.

She wore:
a ruby polka dot
sheer blouse under
a fringe leather vest
attracting
want-crazed coyotes.

I thought:
a welp,
motherless,
starved.
I felt:
an image in
a wolverine's
eye.

From behind the counter,
Shasta Lynn said
—If you know good and evil,
aren't you God, eh?

SOMETHING'S IN THE WIND

BAIE'S JOURNAL

Entry 32

Wildsisters fell to gaming.
Little Aces played with
Monopoly pieces.
The wildsisters toyed with
new acquaintances.

As for me?
I clicked and tuned
dear Father's radio.
— ... every breath you take, every ...
— ... it's the Lord Je-e-e-e-zus that ...
— ... just an invitation would've been ...
— ... an arcade game about an Italian ...
— ... sweet dreams are made of ...

And then a man's voice,
provocative, exotic,
enticing.

—BHCR time kind of depends, and how about last night's guest, Pacific Chorus Frog? Don't he put the slip back in slippery for all you she-frogs out there. And tonight, in honor of sexy sensuality everywhere, I've invited Rough-Skinned Newt to the studio. Many of you may remember that Rough-Skinned Newt was named the Amphibian-American Poet Laureate for 1983. So please welcome to the BHCR studio for the very first time, Mr. Newt.

—Good to be with you, Petr.

—For those listeners who are unfamiliar with your work, it seems, at least to me, pretty old-fashioned. Is that safe to say?

—That's safe to say, Petr.

—And why do you think that is?

—I suppose it has something to do with hanging around bogs and dead-fall. All that rot, it just becomes part of one's soul. Does that make sense?

—I think so. I also think that most of your poems are super sexy, and now that I think about it, I wish last night's guest, Pacific Chorus Frog, were with us here right now. I'll bet your poems would turn him on.

—Yes, I'm fairly well acquainted with Pacific Chorus Frog. We're not exactly cousins, but we do share a certain pheromonal signature. Let's just say that I get the song he's singing.

—Very good. And speaking of songs, I'm hoping you'll share one of your sexy poems. Would you do that for us? I know our listeners would love to hear one. Maybe lull them into a sweet dream of their own.

—Sure thing, this one is a bit of a meditation. It's written as a villanelle, an old French form, where I pose a few questions about the relationship between a frog and the object of his desire.

> You looking for the fairy frog,
> her marshy breath and mossy touch?
> She's lost because she's never been.

> When mists rise up,
> when moth tongues roll uncinched,
> you looking for the fairy frog?

> The draining of our summer swamp
> has really been too much
> She's lost because she's never been.

> When praying to squirrel middens,
> when brewing moon drops punch,
> you looking for the fairy frog?

Cut, yarded, trucked, forgotten,
the slash bones white as slush.
She's lost because she's never been.

When will the sad and empty end,
no point to chirp—Stop! Enough.
You looking for the fairy frog?
She's lost because she's never been.

Oh, I was intrigued.
I was warmed.
I was fluttered even.
Who was this man,
this voice, this angel
who enflamed me so?
No way to know, so
I clicked off
the radio and
turned to Shasta Lynn
who sat spreading
her tarot cards across
our floorboards,
the ones toiled upon,
the ones worn smooth.

She smiled up,
Queen of Cups.
She puzzled down,
Page of Cups.
She clouded over,
Judgment,
reversed,
a cruel Pacific squall
blowing.

RUTH ANN DELANEY

BAIE'S JOURNAL

Entry 33

After Shasta Lynn served
the last round,
Dori held the door for
the last one out.
Or so I thought.
An ocean gust pushed off
the Pacific and
tossed about
Shasta Lynn's
tarot cards like
fallen
vine maple leaves.

Before the door closed,
I witnessed her.
I thought her thirty-five years old.
I felt her much older.
Once a logged red cedar
tumbling over
a flooded flume,
she now was
a sinker log
come to rest.

I saw:
her hair
a tangled
salal thicket,

her body
an east-facing
tight-ringed
silver fir.

I heard:
she hunted
black bear for
big timber dollars;
she drove
rain forest roads,
dark,
finding roadkill.

I thought:
her lightning bolts
quickened
her bear spirit;
her bear breath
revived
her alcohol-soaked
bags of God.

I felt:
a slew of
our fathers'
sins.
Retrieving her Chance card,
Shasta Lynn exclaimed
—Yass, yass,
lust, envy, greed.
Take
a ride on
the Deadly Sin Railroad.

Pay
the white otter
twice
the token.

Then, softer
—Yass,
lust, envy, greed . . .

EXCUSE ME, WORD ON THE TIDE

Ghost Shrimp, swim through
the gaping hole burned in
my immaculate heart.
Singed is our fixed belief.
Charred is our abiding faith.

Word on the tide is
you know the ghost dance.
You dance for the one who
was spy hopping, who
heard hard candy songs, who
was shamelessly smeared with
spilled heavy crude, who
was forcibly entered.
Word on the tide is
you dance for the one who
was deceived and defiled.

Ghost shrimp,
this is a tricky place;
this is a babbling time.
The tide brings only bones.

Pray night will become day.
Pray hole will become home.
Pray sky will shower
green Pacific kelp.

Kyrie eleison.
Christe eleison.
Kyrie eleison.
Je ne suis plus un créature
de la terre
or the air.
I am a creature
de la mer.

RIPTIDE

BAIE'S JOURNAL

Entry 34

a premonition:
one of you will betray us,
rip current setdown

WAKING UP

BAIE'S JOURNAL

Entry 35

Sacré Dieu!
dear Mother,

this early morning
I found Sesily
fearfully curled on
Wildsisters' Doug-fir floor.
I judged she was in
labor's incarnate magic.
I knelt beside her.
I began to pray.
—As seals exhale in
our morning fog,
as birds molt in
our increasing light,
as frogs chorus in
our spring showers,
may Sesily,
dear God,
be delivered.
Amen.

After I quieted,
Ruth Ann came down from
our now-occupied loft.
She looked us over and
thought out loud
—Hey now, missy, I see
y're havin' a baby.

After Ruth Ann's pronouncement,
Shasta Lynn came down and
stopped as if before
a secret fairy well.
She narrowed her eyes.
She opened her mouth wide.
She emanated no sound.

Inside this silence
Ruth Ann crossed her arms and
stiffened her jaw.
I felt her impatience.
I heard her take charge.
—Havin' a kid's hard, and
I see y'r scared, Ses, but
y' need some relaxin', and
as f'r ev'rybody else,
let's get first things first.
Somebody rustle up
some clean towels.
Find somethin' so clean
y'can eat off it,
not somethin' y'washed
my dirty rig with.

That's when Shasta Lynn flushed.
She took wing, dear Mother.
She flew right through
Wildsisters' door and
melted into
the morning push of
thick Pacific fog.

BIRTH

BAIE'S JOURNAL

Entry 36

And that's when
Ruth Ann went about

the necessary job of
delivering Sesily's baby.
She headed straight for
the wood stove, fed in
some firewood, put on
a soup pot, and went to
boiling water.

All the while
Sesily went about
having her baby.
Her fists balled.
Her jaw clenched.
Her eyelids squeezed.
And her uterus contracted.

I puzzled over where
my dear Dori could be.
Then a little head crowned.

When Ruth Ann returned,
she gently brushed away
Sesily's bangs.
She reached down and
grasped the quick from
crown to chin.
She lovingly cradled
God's tiny basket.

For a second time
I puzzled over where
my dear Dori could be.
Then the contractions stilled.

Until Ruth Ann shouted
—PUSH, Sesily!
PUSH like
y'r own life depended!
PUSH like
y'r baby's life depended!
PUSH like
y're Saint Helens
ready t' blow!

Once more her fists balled.
Her jaw clenched.
Her eyelids squeezed.
And her uterus contacted,
this one powerful,
this one so big that
the slippery shoulders
came fully free and
a glorious girl
washed perfectly out.

For a third time
I puzzled over where
my dear Dori could be.
Her absence was strange, but
as I mused, she appeared in
the doorway, ready for
the necessary job of
cutting the umbilical.
Her steady hand possessed
our steel wool-scrubbed,
wood fire-sterilized
cranberry pruners.

She cut the cord,
a blood jet coming.

—PUSH, Sesily!
Y'ain't done!
Just one more!
PUSH like
y're goin' t' be done!
PUSH like
y're bull sticked and
fully loaded on
y'r daddy's stump ranch!

One last time her fists balled.
Her jaw clenched.
Her eyelids squeezed.
And her uterus contracted,
the rich, thick placenta
washing out.

FREYA PHISH

BAIE'S JOURNAL

Entry 37

Who is she?
dear Mother.
Monica of Hippo?
Rita of Cascia?
Agnes of Rome?
Margaret the Barefooted?

Ruth Ann lay
the child in
Sesily's arms.

Feeling
her child
close,
Sesily,
safe and delivered,
brightened.

Feeling
her mother
close,
the child,
safe and embraced,
stirred.

Sesily
looked to
her wildsisters.
—She's Freya,
Freya Phish.

INKY CAP

BAIE'S JOURNAL

Entry 38

After the delivery
Misty came down
the loft stairs and

stopped just outside
our wildsister's circle,
chewing the tips of
her old man's beard hair.
A dark spirit,
her presence troubled me.

In response
I broke our circle.
I poured a glass of
tart cranberry juice.
I retrieved a slice of
heavy rye bread.
I dipped the slice in
a Saint Vinny's glass.
I offered Misty
the juice-soaked bread.

Misty accepted, ate, and
then entered our circle.
She softly chanted
Shasta Lynn's catechism.
—If you know good and evil,
aren't you God, eh?

And then it happened,
that thing beyond
our imaginings,
our wildsister Misty,
a liquefying inky cap,
lingered no longer.
She broke the circle,
ripped Freya from
Sesily's arms, and

disappeared, just like
Shasta Lynn, through
Wildsisters' door.

Dori reacted first
—Damn it to hell,
she surprised me.
I should've cut her off!

Ruth Ann reacted second
—I'll track 'er down.
Got a nose f'r such things.
Me an 'er go way back.
Things ain't right f'r
any o'er kind, you know.
She come from
thievin' stock,
easier t' steal than
do f'r y'rself.
Takes good care
o' what's 'ers, though.
Got t' give 'er that.
I'll track 'er down.
Make this right, you know.
No harm'll come t' Freya.
Won't let it.
Y' can be sure o' that.

Then Ruth Ann started off to
catch Misty, and
Dori started for
Wildsisters' phone, but
before disappearing,
Ruth Ann stopped, frozen in

the open doorway, and
hard as nails said
—No, no need.
Police'll jus' stir th' pot.
Be all runnin' 'round in
squad cars, dogs barkin'.
Treein' Misty ain't how
Freya comes home, you know.
Don' need no bad endin'.

Dori put the phone down.

Ruth Ann then offered a smile,
gap-toothed, sincere.
—'Sides, this might be
th' best place
we never had.

Kyrie eleison.
Christe eleison.
Kyrie eleison.
Tout
est perdre.
Tout
est retrouver.
Now and
here,
wildsisters.

BOOK NINE

KUSHTAKAS AND SALMON WINGS

STEPPING OUT

As it just so happens, we, you and I, have come down from Petr's campsite, that place where he stepped to the blooms, the ice, the rocks, and the stars, that place where he broadcast from Radio Free Olympia in whisky jack tongue. And now we are perched together up in this subalpine fir, a roost above Anderson Pass, a particularly good spot to take a moment to wonder about Mount Anderson, the Anderson Glacier, and Anderson Pass—or more simply put, what's up with all the Andersons? Fact is we here on the Olympic Peninsula don't take much stock in names that some soldier pulled out of his arse and dropped on a map. After all, a mountain is merely its immense interior, its water and windswept exterior, a bedazzled sight one moment, a muted maw the next—not at all a mountain. A glacier is merely its fickle interior, its faceted exterior, a blind-struck sight one moment, a haunted shroud the next—not at all a glacier. A pass is merely its singular infinity—not at all a pass.

But there they remain, all these Andersons on maps, all coming about because U.S. Army Second Lieutenant Joseph P. O'Neil "was attracted by the grand noble front of the Jupiter hills [our northeast Olympic Moun- tains], rising with their boldness and abruptness, presenting a seemingly impenetrable barrier to the farther advance of man and civilization."[*]

---

* Joseph P. O'Neil, handwritten manuscript, 1885, in Robert B. Hitchman Collection, Washington State Historical Society, Tacoma.

Now that's something, wouldn't you say? I guess Joseph P. O'Neil thought the Olympics were some sort of girl, a missy with some sass, one decked out in jeans and a top with pointed front and back yokes, a spread collar, snap flap pockets, and a three-snap bust. I guess O'Neil thought nobody had penetrated her, but apparently he thought he was up to the challenge. He was the one to take the sass out of her.

I think it's important to note that Joseph P. O'Neil did not reach the summit. Oh, he came mighty close. He most likely stepped out on one of her unspoiled flanks. But he did not scale her. He most certainly failed to couple onto this turn-too-big-to-handle. At least that's what loggers around here used to say.

O'Neil's story continues when, back in the bunkhouse, Joseph P. O'Neil saved face by slapping names on his failed conquests. He chose the name Anderson because Thomas M. Anderson was his commanding officer. Anderson was a captain the first time and a colonel the second time that O'Neil stepped out with the Olympics.

Fittingly, Thomas M. Anderson was a man of many experiences and conquests. He stepped out with the Civil War's Spotsylvania and Wilderness campaigns. He stepped out with the Alaska Gold Rush. Then after O'Neil memorialized Anderson with a mountain, a glacier, and a pass, and the military promoted Anderson to general, he stepped out with the Philippines in both the Spanish and Philippine-American Wars. Clearly, Anderson stepped out a lot.

AND ONE MORE THING

Before we take a flier off this perch above the crest of Anderson Pass and follow Petr into the Enchanted Valley, let's wonder some more. Let's wonder about this tidbit Joseph P. O'Neil left behind concerning his first attempt at penetration.

The camp was aroused several times after this by the panther's cry resounding through the woods. If there is anything that will make a man's blood creep it is to be suddenly awakened in the night by that terrible salutation from our king of the mountains.

There is a curious legend among some Indians that a God, a bird of some kind, an eagle or raven, makes its home in these mountains, and it will inflict a terrible punishment on those who by entering them desecrates its home. Among what Indians or tribes this exist I know not, but when our copper-colored friend saw where we were and found out where we were going, neither big pay or the fear of being shot, both were promised him, could detrain [sic] him. He reluctantly camped with us but during the night folded his tent and quietly stole away.¨

"Stole away," huh? I don't know about you, but we here on the Olympic Peninsula know where and when we don't belong. Money don't get you an invite. Violence don't get you an invite. And don't say Big Mouser didn't warn us.

DESCENT

Petr Bauer, the strong *skookum* of the littlest whisky jack's tongue still in his mouth, set his back to the east, the Dosewallips River falling behind, and set his course to the west, the Quinault River falling forward.

Petr's descent felt steeper than his ascent. His knees took a pounding, the trail dropping a hundred feet down for every hundred feet ahead. When the trail turned left, he dropped another three hundred feet, the trail finally leveling off. Here he stopped, and here his mind backtracked. He imagined meltwater from the Anderson Glacier above journeying downslope, becoming a nameless creek, and emptying into the larger flow at his feet, the Quinault River. His mind then advanced. He imagined a blue line from Bear's long-gone map, the blue line of the Quinault River entering and leaving the Enchanted Valley, entering and leaving Lake Quinault, and merging into the solid blue of the Pacific.

He thought about the whisky jack family, the mom and dad alighting nearby and gleaning from his leavings.

¨ O'Neill, handwritten manuscript.

He thought about the little one perched on his antenna, dead, and about how he had pried loose its little tongue, now leathery, now silent, from its delicate beak.

Then Petr thought about Bernard, about where he might be. True, he and Bernard had only shared a short bit of trail, but he imagined where Bernard might be holed up and in what shadowy thicket along what cascading river or on what basalt ledge overlooking what trail, a place from where Bernard's terrible voice might say, "I enjoy a walk as much as the next guy, especially one through Honeymoon Meadows, but, dear me . . ."

ROCK LEDGE INTERLUDE

Back on the trail, Petr found this stretch along the Quinault River less rigorous, and as the sun reached its zenith, he looked to a rock ledge overhead. Once more he thought about Bernard and about this ledge being the sort of place Bernard would choose, a perfect place to hide, blue-shadowed and delicious, the perfect place to observe.

So Petr went off trail. He plunged into a stand of young, sturdy silver firs, grabbing one trunk after another, pulling himself up the hundred-foot rise. Once on top, he found himself sheltered from the sun by larger trees above and the north-facing ridge further out. Here a patch of snow remained in the trees. Setting his pack on a moss-matted rock, he settled in, secure.

Petr then broke out his trail mix. The peanuts, raisins, M&M'S, and Grape-Nuts gave him a rush. He wasn't eating much, passively foraging the Olympics, actively burning youthful reserves, but soon he was newly energized, and he focused on the wildflowers beginning to emerge, the snow recently receding.

Poking about like a bear cub on a termite log, Petr uprooted a number of plants. He broke free the bulbs from the green stems and star-shaped, pink-tinged petals. He shook off the dirt and then popped the soft, smooth bulbs into his mouth. They tasted of snowy peat, then nuts.

Not satisfied, Petr crawled along the bench, farther away from the snow and into a duff of wood rot and emergent ferns. He came upon a lump which reminded him of bread dough, the sort Bear set out to proof on rare sunny mornings. Pinching two fingers and a thumb into the mass, Petr fetched a piece to his nose. He smelled fungus, imagined an earth brain, and heard Bear's gravel voice exhort him to avoid mushrooms that turned blue or red when broken. This did neither, so Petr judged it safe. He popped the fungal fruit into his mouth and chewed slowly, indulgent, saliva coming. With Olympic bulbs and mushrooms coursing through his veins, he felt like the famous Kalaloch red cedar, all 175 feet, meghalayan, all one thousand years of age.

And he felt as if Bear had never died.

RIP RAP

Petr unclipped his backpack's main flap and pulled free his radio outfit. He connected the battery source to the transmitter, linked the eggbeater-generator to the battery, pushed two sticks into the ground, spread his antenna from one stick to the other, and attached the antenna to the transmitter. Now ready to broadcast, he sat, a Jesus bug on an eddy. He relaxed, a marmot sunbathing on a rock. He turned his eggbeater and opened his mouth darkly, an expectant Dolly Varden below a riffle. He imagined speaking into his low-impedance mic, a nighthawk rising.

"You're tuned to HOO HOO FM radio, voice of the whisky jack for all you coastal tailed frogs who would rather reproduce in our cold, swift currents than speak your mind."

And then he stopped.

Petr's eyes settled on the drip, drip, drip, drip, drip from the snowmelt and then followed the drips as they formed a trickle which joined a rivulet which ended in a puddle. And there, just beyond the puddle, wet, atop a collection of sticks, he saw a lipless mouth, two nostrils, and two ink-drop eyes—a tiny face. And then, extending from the tiny face, muddy, atop decaying leaves, he saw a rusty back stripe, embryonic limbs, and fetus fingers—yes, a western red-backed salamander, the sort child-Petr had found when he overturned logs.

Petr again turned the eggbeater. He hummed a bagpipe drone. The hum brought on a trance, which brought on a dream.

"Down in the deep pools, down in the deep pools, dream the dawn souls, down in the deep pools.

"Bara of breathing, flashes into living, flooding the brae-side, bonded in dirt-self. Fiddle the rye quitch, weaving the fen-knit. Fiddle the quack grass, braiding the bog-knot. Brawl in the brooding, fires into lightning. Brimming the bosky, born in sin-shade.

"Down in the deep pools, down in the deep pools, dream the dawn souls, down in the deep pools.

"Carry the cauldron, coal-glows for heating. Bragging the bole, carrel the keep. Cleave the feie-cwen, skiving sloe-sinew. Cleave the kelpie, gnawing on gore-grist. Call on the chub-clutch, in linne-lair for lying. Mingling with minnows, slither with sild.

"Down in the deep pools, down in the deep pools, Dream the dawn souls, down in the deep pools.

"Seek the moor-milk, morels for the morning. Mouthing on mold-must, dawn the moon-day. Know the seed-fiend, seeping the gray-gift. Know the slimp-milt, seething the bond-kin. Lisp in the low-light, lithe an-ewte lip-skinning. Slurring the dulse-skin, sund the holy.

"Down in the deep pools, down in the deep pools, dream the dawn souls, down in the deep pools."

Again Petr stopped.

His eyes settled on the scree field coming down from a northern ridge. He remembered Bear once saying "rip rap" to child-Petr and explaining that rip rap was an accumulation of rock which had formed over time when individual stones had broken free from a cliff face. Upon hearing this, child-Petr fell in love with saying "rip rap" over and over and over. Bear often told child-Petr to take "rip rap, rip rap, rip rap, rip rap, rip rap, rip rap, rip rap" outside.

Petr imagined speaking, "Rip rap, rip rap, rip rap, rip rap, rip rap, rip rap, rip rap," and he continued until he felt fulfilled, disassembled his transmitter, packed the parts away, hopped to his feet, put his palms together, and bowed to sibling salamander. Soon after, he headed down to the trail, the silver firs anchoring his descent.

As Petr became smaller and then not all, the salamander remained, unblinking.

BUT I DIGRESS, *DEUS EX SALMONINA*

Yep, you're right, Petr's crossed over Anderson Pass, and, yep, you're right again, it's all downhill from here, so let's take this moment to check in on Mole. You remember Mole, Coyote's dutiful, long-suffering, earthy wife, the one who uncharacteristically was beginning to engage in a little compare and contrast: Coyote or Yours Truly, Yours Truly or Coyote?

The thing was, ever since Coyote told her to spruce herself up, Mole was becoming increasingly convinced that her sad situation was probably, most assuredly, all Coyote's fault. After all, he was the one who got her thinking, the one who said to her, "Do you think you could put a little musk behind your ears?" And he was the one who got her looking back to the time when she was first ripe, more ready than she knew, and remembering when he blew into camp from somewhere out there.

Back then Mole and her folk hadn't seen or heard anything like him. Back then he had gathered them around the campfire and enthralled them with stories of his exploits beyond the horizon. He said he had hunted and dined with all the Old Growthers. He had traveled with Eagle, who gave him the feather he wove into his tail. He had shot the shit with Dog Salmon Brother, who gave him the eye teeth called canines. He had haggled with Raven!

Coyote also mesmerized them with dancing in the campfire's dying embers, and what a dancer he was! Back then he seemed like lightning, sparks shooting from his guard hairs. He seemed to turn to the rhythm of some inner drum. She was sure that this dervish, the fakir who had danced into her dreams, was beyond compare. She was completely open to him. When he was near, life seemed a romance instead of a routine. She was convinced that he would provide an endless supply of magic!

But that was a long time ago. Today when she went down to pan in her stream of consciousness, she wanted to separate what was from what is. She thought that for all the friends Coyote claimed to have, insisted he had, told stories about, anecdotes too wondrous and too fantastic to be false, he was a loner. None of his fellow heroes ever joined him; his talk was a monologue, his dance a solo, his dream a psychosis. She also thought that for all the boundless energy he claimed to possess, he slept in most mornings and napped away most afternoons. He was just as likely to be snoozing in a sunny, quiet meadow or positioned like a fetus in a salmonberry thicket as to be off building the blueprint drawn from his yipscapes.

And as Mole continued to think, her idea of Coyote became a dream fish, a female salmon, her tail tip and dorsal fin cutting a riffle. Then this dream fish became a dream eye, and the eye grew so large that it framed a village, a place where the inhabitants moved ever so slowly, sad, and before long the eye became a tear drop, and the inhabitants' eyes were not just eyes, but also tiny tear drops inside this larger tear drop.

Soon she saw herself reflected in all the tear drops inside this tear drop. Then this tear drop became Raven's dream eye. She felt there was something very sexy about his eye, and a bit later, his eye became a candlefish flame, a fervor which burned for Raven: Raven High Flier, Raven Seer, Raven All That My Husband Is Not.

Putting her dreams at arm's length, Mole thought about how her dreams were always small. She also thought about how her small dreams only led to small actions, not like her husband's dreams. His big dreams only led to big words, never to any actions at all.

So Mole became determined to do something she had never done. In fact, she was determined to do something that Coyote had never done. She was determined to turn a big dream into some big action, and to this end she returned to their den, dug in her forepaws, and went to work. She began by gathering up all the salmon bones that her husband had pitched into a dark corner. As she collected, she seethed at her husband's sloppiness, the way that she always was entangled in the wreckage of his schemes. She, Mole, knew better, and clearly the time had come to scour away the shit Coyote had wedded to her.

To realize her big dream, Mole carefully used her foreclaws to rummage through the salmon bones: classifying, sorting, and distributing them into distinct piles. Then she used these piles to reconstruct a backbone upon which she attached a single line of rib bones. After completing this framework, she repeated the process, so that when she was finished, two headless half-salmon lay before her, inventions that someone like Mole, or even you or I, might dream to be wings. All that remained was for Mole to coat her creations with spruce sap and affix a flurry of salmon scales.

In the firelight Mole dreamed her new wings to be the double rainbow which sometimes formed across the western Olympic sunset. She dreamed of shedding her mangy Coyote skin and dressing herself in newly hatched Raven feathers. And she dreamed of flying off with Raven on salmon wings, a red band of rainbow coming into sight above, a pile of Coyote scat passing out of sight below.

CLOUDS

Sitka spruce, blood spattered
beard lichens, only a bit
lower than the angels

CLOSE TO THE BONE

The rain came. Sharp and drenching. Sweeping clouds of fog. A cold gust. Deadfall. Opening in the canopy. Deluge. Rain weight. Bending limbs of giants. Heavier shower. Cold.

Petr began to shiver involuntarily, and he remembered Bear teaching him the sanctity of warm and the righteousness of dry. Sure, Bear and child-Petr had lived close to the bone and far away from any store, but they bucked timber to raise their core temperature. Sure, they had lived without electricity and minus society, but they split rounds to burn away the rot.

So Petr found this present situation to be like no other. Because the rainwater ran over his eyelids and into his eyes, he struggled to scan for shelter. He thought the Enchanted Valley to be a shadow cast upon a shadow cast upon a third. He felt it a place on the tip of his tongue, irretrievable. He feared washing away into the Quinault.

And then dumb luck wrapped her warm-hearth arms about him. Wiping his eyes with his rain-drenched sleeve, Petr found that water no longer ran from his hair on to his cheeks and down his neck. He also found himself surrounded in a half-circle formed by the twisted buttresses of an ancient red cedar and sheltered beneath the dense canopy of a young western hemlock.

No longer drenched, Petr quickened into action, unclipping his soaked pack, rooting past his wrapped-in-plastic radio parts, and finding the waterproof pouch where he kept his fire-starting equipment. He imagined Bear's old wood stove and remembered his child-self being chored with rekindling the fire every morning. Unfortunately, all the available tinder was cold and wet, and the embers of the past were dead like Bear.

Defeated, Petr sat down in his dry niche of peaty duff, pulled his knees close to his chest, and closed his eyes. If he didn't wake, he might split and leak hemlock sap. He might heal over with frog skin.

MASS

Deep ocean clouds snuffed the sun.
Maidenhair and licorice ferns arched their fronds and released an ecstasy of
spores.
Ghost plants rose, slippery and erect.
King boletus mushrooms swelled out of proportion, their caps splitting,
their spongy womb tumescent, ripe.
Banana slugs slid atop crystalline mucous trails. Some were three-inch
saffron-glistening fingers. Some were eight-inch blackberry-spoiling
members.

called to sacred mass,
new skin encapsulated
in unctuous desire

THE KUSHTAKAS

Slick, heavy, it stopped short. It stood over Petr. Curious. Several others followed. They arranged themselves in a semicircle. The first picked up Petr's backpack, turning the slug mass and its transmitter contents this way and that. It turned to the others, presented the backpack so that they could see it, turned it upside down, held it by one strap, dangled its weight, and finally set it down.

Then all became a flurry of activity. Brush was cleared away. Erratics were rolled in, forming an igloo-like den. A smaller one began to construct a fireplace, expertly stacking round stones to absorb heat. The smaller one then sparked a red cedar fire: split tinder and kindling, cut hot-fire rounds, and quartered all-nighter logs.

In the firelight, features slowly began to emerge. Bodies were long and lean. Short arms extended from chests. Sharp claws were attached to tiny close-packed fingers. Wide-set eyes. Harelip on dark, downy faces.

They worked quickly, furtively, appearing and disappearing over and through thickets and deadfall. Everything was transformed, the completion a signal for all to assemble around the fire.

The smaller one silently turned to Petr, and just beyond the fire, the first one assertively spoke, "We're so glad we found you when we did. I can see you're warming up. We'll have something to eat soon."

The whisky jack tongue in Petr's mouth answered, *"Wa ah ee er uh araa ta."*

"We were worried. You look pale. Your cheeks are blue. Traveling in rain like this isn't good for you."

Another one across from Petr looked back through the growing flames, "Ah, let him alone. He needs to warm up and rest. A good dinner will do him good."

A fourth then turned and slipped between the stones.

"He'll be back soon," the first one explained. "He's off looking for dinner. We don't eat anything he doesn't want. It's best to keep him happy."

"E cha . . . a cha eh eh eh eh."

Then the one who had left returned. Grunting, it dragged a freshly killed elk by the horns, the body lodging between two erratics. It addressed the others, soliciting help. "Hey, grab a hold here. I'll lift up the hind quarters from the other side. It'll fit through that way. Pull on its horns, and I'll push from there."

"We can't eat all that," the one tending the fire said.

The first replied, "I'm glad we have it," and then turned to Petr. "This is a homecoming. You've changed so much since we last saw you. You've grown up."

"Whee wee wee wee."

With that, the one tending the fire grabbed the antlers and pulled, dragging the haunches through the gap. The dead weight stopped just short of the fire, its body a wrong angle. The back hooves almost head kicked the one across from Petr.

In the firelight the elk's eyes were still dewy, its lashes poised to blink. The only signs of violence were two neck wounds punctured at the carotid. Out of the shadows came two others. They slinked about, eyeing the others, the elk, and then the others again. The first said to them, "Let's all sit and relax."

Then the one who had brought the elk said, "We eat in remembrance of our ocean neighbor Salmon. We eat in the hope that our ocean neighbor will return to our rivers and restore life in our mountains. We eat that they will swim us into dreaming. We eat not to forget," and with that it went to work on the belly of the elk. Using incisors like scissors, it neatly unzipped the soft, lean hide, exposing the warm insides.

Steam rose as each waited its turn, and when the opportunity presented itself, one and then another used its short forelimbs in a swimming motion to clear away fat and fluid. The organs went first, chunks of slippery liver, lengths of uncoiled intestine.

After tearing loose a chunk of heart, the first spoke to Petr, "You really should eat. Come on, have a bite. You'll feel a lot better."

"Wa wa ah ah uh."

"Ah, come on." It came so near that Petr felt its moist, ferrous breath on his cheek. "While they're busy, I need to share something." Petr thought he heard his mother's voice. "I'm glad you're here. Maybe it's because I'm lonely. I've always been lonely. I hope you stay."

Then it raised its voice, calling to the others. "Dig in. There's more than enough for everybody."

Again it came closer and lowered its voice, conspiratorial, "You got an eye for one of those two? Can't say I blame you. It's healthy. They got eyes for the weasel boys. Those two leave carcasses rotting in creek beds, but they're good providers. Trust me, I can put in a good word. They all listen to me. They'd really like a good match. You're a good boy."

The pull was irresistible, nauseating, entering Petr's ear, coursing throughout his arteries. Mother. He began to convulse.

"Listen, go get yourself something to eat. There's time for that now and other things later."

A spasm brought Petr to his knees. Convulsed, he emptied his stomach.

NOTHIN' TO UNDERSTAND, REALLY

A stick cracked. The sound resounded among the trees. The sound brought up their heads, ears erect, and just as dark as they came, they slid away, absences.

Petr was on his knees, waiting for another spasm. What he got instead was a different voice, this one also familiar. "Kushtakas." This one was Bernard's.

Looking up, Petr saw Bernard's back. He also saw the glint of Bernard's polished hunting knife. The knife's antler bone handle seemed to grow out of a joint on Bernard's right hand. The knife's blade cut the elk's hide away from the muscle.

Petr looked down. The whisky jack tongue was stuck on a banana slug's back. Both lay in a pool of Petr's vomit.

"Kushtakas, Old Growth Otters, I thought they might've got you. You were almost a goner."

Petr blinked.

"Don't know 'bout 'em? Course not. They're always out when somebody gets in trouble. Looked like your family? Mom, Dad, brothers, sisters, I expect. They want you t' stay; give up on your life and go with 'em. I'll bet you almost did. Yep, bet you almost did."

Petr blinked some more.

"Don't trouble yourself. Nothin' t'understand, really. Kushtakas're Kushtakas; elk're elk; Bernard's Bernard. Important thing's you didn't go with 'em. Suppose it mightn't be so bad, maybe, bein' a Kushtaka. Saved many a man drownin', many a man lost. Suppose they do more good than harm. They're a clannish bunch, takin' care of their own. All th' same, don't want t' be no Kushtaka. Don't want no short, hairy arms growin' out of my chest. Don't suppose you do either.

"So you're wonderin' where they went? Oh, they're about, don't you worry. They play on your mind if you let 'em. They won't bother you while you're with me. We're well acquainted, them and me. We may be neighbors, but we don't got much in common. Don't need t' get adopted by no Kushtakas."

Petr looked on as Bernard continued to work over the elk. It was clear that Bernard was practiced in the art of dressing a kill. The Kushtakas had gone a long way to eviscerating the elk. All that was left to Bernard was to hide and butcher.

Petr felt soothed by the sound of Bernard's knife separating the elk's haunch from its back. The rhythm made Petr sleepy. Then he was asleep.

When Petr awoke, broken clouds rolled directly overhead. The heavy weather had passed, and the sun now shone at such an angle, that while he lay in the murky valley, a billow of cloud became lined with a radiant border.

Beneath this glory-filled sky, Petr's radio antenna stretched from one red cedar bough to another. A banana slug, the whisky jack tongue now held fast to its mantle, crawled up the antenna's feeder. The transmitter, free from its plastic wrapping, lay in his open backpack.

Where Petr remembered the elk carcass to have been, stiff white-to-brown hairs were strewn.

BOOK TEN

BURNING FOR YOU BURNING FOR ME

SUBMISSION

BAIE'S JOURNAL

Entry 39

Out on
the bushes,
the hard, green
tumescences
form and
grow and then
split.

Petals,
like delicate
moth wings,
appear.

These blossoms
broadcast
their scent,
seducing.
Their flavor
stirs

honeybees,
submitting.

Smell their fragrance!
Their perfume swings from
heaven's censer.

See their conception!
Each berry swells to
spirited fruition.

Taste the ripening flesh!
The sweet arises out of
subterranean bitter.

Feel the blessing,
that one and this one,
each a eucharist!

BUSY

BAIE'S JOURNAL

Entry 40

Dori
busies herself
finishing the barn:
imagining,
measuring,
cutting,
joining.

Shasta Lynn
busies herself
tending the kitchen:
planning,
ordering,
preparing,
serving.

Aces
busies himself
becoming himself:
wondering,
exploring,
trying,
growing.

I
busy myself
cutting the deadwood:
surveying,
choosing,
snipping,
discarding.

Ruth Ann
busies herself
hunting salvation:
searching,
acting,
searching again,
acting again.

Sesily
busies herself
hoping to be restored:
grieving,
expecting,
praying,
believing.

I TOOK A MUG

BAIE'S JOURNAL

Entry 41

Shasta Lynn missed
Sesily's birth.
She also missed
Freya's kidnapping.
Needless to say
I was surprised when
I saw her come down
our barn loft stairs and
begin the work of
making morning coffee.

Once the coffee was on,
Sesily found me.
She grabbed my elbow and
tearfully pulled me to
the mournful place where
her Freya was born.

Her tears were a squall,
cold.
Her mouth was a well,
dark.
—O-o-o-o-o-o-h.

I left Sesily and
found a chipped
bone china mug,
one redeemed from
The Whistle Punk Tavern's
"Soon To Be Gone Sale."
I filled full the cup.
Rings spread across
the coffee's surface.
Steam curled into
our Wildsisters' air.
I gave thanks and
rejoined Sesily.
I gave her coffee, but
she was not tempted.

I could not find her child.
I could not fix her hurt.
Maybe I could create
a distraction.
Maybe I could bring
temporary relief.
—Dear Ruth Ann
will bring good news.
I really think so,
dear Sesily.

We should listen to
dear Father's radio.

And although I hoped to
amuse Sesily,
I too desired to take into
my eager ears
a man now familiar,
now foretasted,
now arousing,
yes,
a nice way to
begin the day.

KNOCK, KNOCK

BAIE'S JOURNAL

Entry 42

I sparked and tuned the radio.
— . . . now I'm dancing for my life . . .
— . . . a high of eighty . . .
— . . . she's a maneater . . .
— . . . U.S. Says Army Shielded Barbie . . .
— . . . oh Mickey, what a pity . . .

— . . . quork, quork.

—Hey Raven, hop right on over here, will you? As commissioner the past forty thousand years or so, give or take a millennium, we'd really like to get your thoughts about this summer's Oly Fest.

—We know that participation's been down. It's been tough since the Wolf Folk quite probably, most certainly, were exterminated. Don't expect to see them again anytime soon. The Cougar Folk haven't stepped up like we hoped. From where I sit, this seems like the chance the Elk Folk have been waiting for.

—A while back on this same program, Father-Elk told me that it was time for the Elk Folk to show their stuff. So why do you think they haven't stepped up? You'd think they'd be all about showing us what real Oly spirit is all about! Why do you think we haven't heard their bellows up and down the valleys?

—Quork, quork, quork.
Knock, knock. Click.
Quork, quork.
—Quork.
flutter of feathers
Knock.
beak rub, hollow
—Quork, quork.
flutter
Click.
—Quork.

—That really is so true, isn't it? From where you're perched so much has happened just recently.

—I'm sure you'd agree that leadership isn't about who speaks the loudest or who puts on the biggest show. What I hear you saying is we really miss that working class spirit. We miss the way the Old Growth Salmon kept punching the clock, year in and year out.

—In your book, *Fighting the Downdraft*, you talk about the poverty which seems to have visited us all. I was particularly struck by what you wrote about the Mushroom Folk, about the contribution of the great Kingdom of Decomposition.

—Knock, knock.

—You're so right. Sometimes I get all, well, what would you call it? The whole . . . well, you know what I mean.

—Click.

—You're really too generous. Now, let's get back to the Mushroom Folk. You write about the ethical dilemma we face concerning our fungal brethren.

—Quork, quork.
flutter of feathers
Click.
Coo-oo-oo.
—Quork.
beak tap
Knock.
—Quork, quork, quork.
Click.
Coo-oo-oo-oo.

I turned off the radio.

—Baie, what was that?

—I'm not sure, dear Sesily.
Some nights I don't sleep.
One night I fiddled and
found this station.
Some nights I get it.
Some nights I don't, but
I can tell you one thing,
I love his voice.
I mean, that voice is like
cran-strawberry jam.
Put that voice on

a spoon, and I want to
lick it spotless.

LIGHT

BAIE'S JOURNAL

Entry 43

You told me,
dear Mother,
that I was born among
the paschal
and
a congregation of
votive candles.

In remembrance
I went under
Wildsisters' counter.
I found a box
filled with
your candles:
pure beeswax,
soulful wick,
divine light.

Moving about
Wildsisters,
I set a candle in
this place,
filling Freya's
awful absence with
light.

I set a candle in
that place,
forgiving Misty's
benumbed betrayal with
light.

I set a candle in
another place,
sanctifying Ruth Ann's
justifying journey with
light.

EXCUSE ME, WHITE OTTER WOULD LIKE TO SHED MORE LIGHT

Candlefish,
light of our world,
you mass and commune.
Rich is your existence,
each brother and sister,
each mother and father,
each aunt, uncle, and cousin,
a holy ampulla.
Your young are laid in
our fresh, chilly rivers:
Cowlitz, Quileute, Sooke.
Your young are delivered,
spirits freshly baptized.
Your young are carried in
pristine river run.
Your young return home,
the salt of
the sea.

As for you, Gray Whale,
night has forcibly fallen.
Your calf swims offshore,
now an after-hours snack.

As for you, Ghost Shrimp,
your home is a dead zone,
no longer secure,
now a septic sewer.

And as for you, Cormorant,
your conclusion has come,
your legacy written by
a miner's canary.

Candlefish,
light of our world,
you are our last hope.
I covet your body.
Dried and sparked alight,
you burn for me
dispelling the night.
Pressed like new grapes,
you sanctify all.
I take and eat,
dispelling the emptiness.
I give thanks and
pray you will return,
again and again,
world without end.

Kyrie eleison.
Christe eleison.
Kyrie eleison.

Je ne suis plus un créature
de la terre
or the air.
I am a creature
de la mer.

OVER HUMPTULIPS AND THROUGH THE WOODS TO THE OXBOW YOU MUST FLY

BAIE'S JOURNAL

Entry 44

Ruth Ann came through
the Sitka spruce.
She flung the door open.
She set her rifle down.

Dori came from
the cranberry bog.
She held Aces' hand.
She staked her territory.

Shasta Lynn came down
the barn loft stairs.
She gathered dirty cups.
She started the coffee.

Then Ruth Ann broke the silence.
—Don't think Misty's seekin'
no new territory.
She's no yearlin' tom.

Shasta told me 'bout
them boys Dori run off.

Immediately
we looked Shasta Lynn's way.
She tore a paper napkin.
She piled the remains.

Ruth Ann spoke again
—I did some diggin'.
Turns out Shasta and
Misty're stepsisters.
Turns out, too, that
they got two half-brothers.
Deal is they all
got a shack on
th' Humptulips' Oxbow.
I'll just bet y'that
Misty an' Freya're
tunneled in there like
two flathead wood borers.
Now all I got t' do is
'chop 'em out with
my Hudson Bay axe,
leastwise before
them boys go crazy on
all that girl scent.

Then Shasta Lynn declared
—Yass, yass, so sad.
Leaves fallin' on
a deep, dark pool, eh.
My daddy died on

the Mexican mud.
Years come drippin' from
that cold-blooded needle.
My momma stared down
that rusty barrel like
it was a wishin' gun.
Sometimes she would say
—Shasta Lynn,
we born of sadness, eh.
Oh, we howls a bit;
we whimpers a bit;
then we just quits.
We just up and quits.

Dori exploded
—Good gawd-damn, Shasta,
y'r fuller o' shit than
a twenty-year privy.
Ruthie's got an idea where
Misty's got Freya, an'
all y' can do is yap
a whole lot o' nonsense.
Now, forget 'bout
y'r junky family!

Aces, startled by
his mother's fury,
scampered directly out
Wildsisters' door.

Dori, her child gone,
grabbed Shasta Lynn's hair and
dragged her outside.
Ruth Ann, Sesily, and I

followed closely behind.
We all stopped next to
the cranberry bog.
Here Shasta Lynn knelt.
Here Dori loomed over.
—No more jabb'rin', y' hear!
See Sesily right there?
Say what y' know, or
so help me, Shasta!

Ruth Ann set her jaw.
—Better say somethin'.

Dori then tightened
Shasta Lynn's hair-noose.
That's when Shasta Lynn
sang this little song.
—Over Humptulips and
through the woods to
the oxbow you must fly.
The moth knows the course
to get to the source
through the black and
foggy ni . . . ight.
Over Humptulips and
through the woods to
the oxbow you must fly.
The frogs chirp high and
ravens spy as over
Humptulips we fly.

Her song now over,
Shasta Lynn showed us
her life-lived hand.

There rested a hawk moth,
etched and heavy.
The insect then rose,
alighting on
Ruth Ann's shoulder. Its wings,
God's natural psalter,
slowly opened, closed,
and opened again.

But Shasta Lynn had more.
She pointed and said
—Follow the roadkill.
Follow the crushed.
Follow the left-to-rot.
Stay away from
the wildman, eh.
I saw him before, and
he's out there again.
He's out there in
the pitchy woods.

She narrowed her eyes.
She spoke one last time
—Yass, yass, John Tornow,
you leave them be, eh.
I know you're real angry.
All those sins are heavy.
This isn't any of that, eh.
You know it, and I know it.
This here is not yours.
Just leave them be, eh.

And the hawk moth, as if
a hummingbird, as if
the white otter, as if

Mary Most Pure,
took flight from
Ruth Ann's shoulder into
our Humptulips' future.

Kyrie eleison.
Christe eleison.
Kyrie eleison.
Tout
est perdre.
Tout
est retrouver.
Now and
here,
wildsisters.

BOOK ELEVEN

SHE ONCE AND
SHE ONCE MORE

NO

I bet you're feeling right now like we, you and I, are in pretty deep. Ankle deep. Knee deep. Waist deep. Neck deep. I bet you're a bit uneasy with parodies of Thanksgiving songs being sung as treasure maps for digging up kidnapped babies. I bet you're having some trouble right now with Bernard and Kushtakas, or as the Tlingit say, *Kooshdakhaas*. And, hell, I bet you're having a good bit more trouble with me, a philosophical raven, if I do say so myself.

And you also may be annoyed with me always opening with "we here on the Olympic Peninsula," but bear with me because I'm going to say it again, we here on the Olympic Peninsula don't fuss much with being true to ourselves. We don't chase some true identity. And we don't go on journeys to find ourselves. It's not like we don't go on journeys. Hell, Petr's taking a stroll through the Olympic Mountains, but our journeys are always something we do, not something we are. Oh, don't get me wrong, it's not like we aren't a character in our own story, it's just that we aren't interested in verisimilitude. We aren't interested in being our own stock character for our own target audience. When it comes to the business of defining our brand, we say fuck that shit.

All this is to say that Petr, after being saved first by the Kushtakas and then by Bernard, was dealing with the effects of doing. He felt so much. He felt the seductive sound of the Kushtakas on his cheek and in his head, and he desperately desired to contact something to heighten his arousal. He touched the enticing whorls of haircap moss, the provocative tresses of maidenhair ferns, and although he reached out, he was not satisfied. He imagined himself folded in cedar boughs and sinking into a black pool. He imagined himself an alder leaf falling into the Quinault, diminishing downstream, and vanishing from sight.

Petr thought about the offer the Kushtakas made. They beckoned him to join their family. They offered the Enchanted Valley as his home.

No.

Petr's decision hurt, and although the pain was deep, after all he hadn't had a home since Bear died, he judged the pain of leaving to be less than the pain of staying.

And you may wonder how this decision fits his character. You may wonder about his motivation. You might think it should be neither his fate nor his destiny. Maybe it just doesn't fit the theme, some philosophical axioms and postulates that the godlike author put in place to govern the historical bedrock, the *weltanshauung*.

So let me, your good old buddy and pal Raven, give you a piece of advice, especially since you and I have come this far. Sure, Petr's a randy young weasel with a bit of the old biological, naturalistic imperative thing going for him, but don't get all tangled up in your Hegelian determinism. You might just face-plant in your own free will.

Since Petr has decided to distract himself with what's down the trail, I suggest you follow his lead. And me? well, to be sure I'll be riding that thermal just overhead.

HERE

No. Again.

No to Shi Shi Beach where Bear found the infant Petr.

No to the grave he dug.

No to the body he rolled off the log caddy and into the shallow grave.

No to whipsaw, axe, splitting maul, and chip-edged wedges.

No to hair greasy wet, the mother-of-pearl eyes staring up at him.

No to the final shovelful of earth.

Here, where the Enchanted Valley opened out into the wider lowland Olympic Rain Forest, Petr walked in vanilla leaf and wild ginger, devil's club and sword fern, Doug-fir and red cedar. He descended six hundred feet, but before he crossed the footbridge, he turned left.

Here, he felt seduced. Her eyes, dark, were open to his.

Here, he felt aroused. Her exposure, truffle musk and silky pelt, enveloped him like bigleaf maple syrup.

Here, he headed slam bang into the southern Olympics.

UP GRAVES CREEK

Petr followed the Graves Creek Trail. He ascended six hundred feet on a series of switchbacks and then followed the primitive trail above the tumbling creek. As he climbed, he dug in his toes, determined not to slip. His calves, thighs, and buttocks burned. He felt good. He preferred the sharp pain of working to the dull ache of getting by.

Then the trail evened out, so Petr did that for a while, at least until the trail met the rise of Graves Creek. Here the trail ended and began again on the creek's farther bank. The water was swift but down from its spring high-water mark. He thought about the logs the spring current had woven into the stream's bank. No question about it, he wouldn't have crossed Graves Creek in the spring.

Petr thought about lifting his pack above his head. He didn't want to soak his radio equipment, but this strategy would compromise his balance. He needed stability against the current. He didn't want to be a blown-down tree, so instead he placed his elbows akimbo and started across.

Chilled. Graves Creek wasn't glacier-fed, its source instead melting down from snowfields, the ones above at 3,600 feet.

Pulled. Graves Creek was a burn, a run, a race, and its waters wedded to gravity swelled to take him with it.

Exhilarated. Petr left the stream and continued hiking into the late afternoon. The next bit was a steep five-hundred-foot climb. He pushed forward, imagining his muscles smoldering to a fine ash. Then the grade became much easier but the footing at times precarious. He imagined mountain goats maintaining this trail. The goats had cut horn holes in their bright yellow hardhats. They became tiger lilies on a subalpine palette. He found fresh elk scat. A snowberry checkerspot butterfly was perched atop one dropping.

Eventually Graves Creek rose again to meet Petr, and he crossed once and then twice over the swift, now shallower stream. And then he stopped. The trail before him took on a daunting incline and appeared to switchback a few hundred feet above. He imagined what lay ahead, and his body gave way, broke down. He had skipped breakfast, then he skipped lunch, and now he was on the verge of skipping dinner, but with his energy reserves tapped out, stepping into this new climb was not an option. He thought about his remaining trail mix, a mass of Grape Nuts glued by the rain forest's humidity. He thought about venison steak. He thought about rich razor clams fried in saltines and butter. His throat burned, dehydrated. He even thought about earthworms, first wriggling in his hand and then wriggling in his stomach. His stomach grumbled.

And yet he still felt seduced.

He still felt aroused.

He reached into his backpack and then into the trail mix bag, balled his hand around the last of his provision, and pushed the mass into his mouth. Soon he felt somewhat revived, his renewed vigor shallow, twitchy.

Petr rocked his body into a trudging motion. He led with his shoulders. The ascent was a pisspot.

COYOTE AND THE BEER CAP

One trudge, two trudge, three trudge, four, Petr fell into woolgathering. He remembered his long-passed Bear. He thought maybe Bear was gone to hunt and capture. Or maybe he was gone to drink and black out.

To pass the time Petr began to gossip with the breeze like the two were on the radio. He then talked with a rosy-finch. "So what's on the menu?"

"*Choo, choo, choo, choo, choo.*"

"So you're recommending the sweat bees followed by a course of mariposa coppers. And some thistle and lupine seeds on the side. What's for dessert?"

"*Chirp, buzz, cho.*"

"Indian thistle seeds. Good choice."

Then came a commercial break, "Cold, clear, pristine Head Waters, quench that Olympic-sized thirst!" followed by Petr chatting up a lone raven, "So I hear you got us a story, the one about Coyote and the beer cap."

"Sure do, so here goes. One time my buddy Coyote caught sight of a beer cap. It was lying there in the moonshine, and it looked like a moon's egg.

"Well, Coyote looked into that moon's egg and saw me fly out high into the sky over the Olympics. And he had what you might call an epiphany. He thought I had the moon power. He thought I saw all at once from a bunch of different perspectives.

"Boy, was Coyote jealous. He thought, 'Now that's why Raven talks down to me from that high perch of his.'

"So Coyote decided right then and there to even the score. He picked up that old beer cap, wiped it in some fresh Sitka spruce sap, and stuck it on his forehead. He put that beer cap right between his eyes. Then he closed his eyes and started walking around. He thought he'd see the world the way I do. He thought he'd see the world from here, there, and everywhere.

"I must say Coyote was pretty pleased with himself. He grinned that slobbery, yellow-toothed grin of his. He thought, 'Raven, now I'm as good as you. I've figured out your secret. When word gets out that I've got new powers, everyone will respect me. They'll bring me expensive presents. They'll ask me to be their guest of honor. I'll eat until I'm fat, and everyone will invite me to visit their daughters!'

"Now, Coyote . . . and don't forget his eyes were closed."

"No, I won't."

"So Coyote stepped off a cliff. He tumbled ass-over-tits. When he cracked his head on one stone and then another, the beer cap was torn loose, and he was left with a bald spot between his eyes. Finally he went splat in the Satsop River. The slack water pool was just deep enough to break his fall but not deep enough to drown him."

"But what happened to the beer cap?"

"Good question. You see, the next morning, I was out stretching my wings, and there was that beer cap just lying there in the sunshine. It looked like a bottle blonde, and you know how I love cheap bling!"

"And did Coyote's fur grow back?"

"My, my, four-and-twenty questions, I like that. Well, it sure did, but it grew in white. You know that white spot on his forehead?"

"Yeah, sure."

"That's called a literary symbol, you know, like Coyote is both animal and human at the same time."

"Uh huh."

"And the point is, don't lose your way when looking at those pictures in your head. Of course, Coyote just thinks his white spot's a beauty mark. He's quite proud of it. Now that really cracks me up."

"Me, too."

SEX

Wynoochee Pass is a low point on the ridge between the Quinault and Wynoochee Rivers: beautiful, silvery-sighted, free, and cold-blooded. Its two black opal tarns, one here and the other there, are set in stygian-gray basalt, and its meadow is ghost-imaged and lies like a Guys *grisette* below a Millet Milky Way.

Here Petr collapsed and fell asleep, and while he slept, a family of whisky jacks, a dad, mom, and two fledglings, settled in a close-by silver fir. Looking down, they couldn't find anything to steal. They thought it worth their while to wait. Patience had been known to pay off.

Then a brown stain moved through the meadow and paused below the whisky jacks' perch. A second stain followed the first. The first shot upward. The later shot behind and latched onto the first. They spun, an arboreal dance, purple shadow on shadow in the moonshine.

oaky sweet urine adhering

nutty wet dog probing

savory sage onion penetrating
ruby-citron dream

juicy rotten straw seducing
earthy fermented cabbage biting
black olive wood succumbing
cherry-smear dream

When the coupling was done and the second moved on, she draped herself across a silver fir limb and rested against the trunk. Her eyes, jet-black beads, watched Petr.

But she wasn't satiated. She slowly came down the trunk and circled Petr. Her silhouette sliced the moon's crescent. She closed the circle, cinching him close, taut, wearing him like a war trophy.

Petr spoke in his sleep, his voice felt like his mother's.

My beautiful one,
I knocked on john's window.
I needed his money,
and he used my need.
Angel dust all about,
he held me by the wrists,
he fucked me 'til he burst,
and then he punched me out.

I woke to money
balled like my heart and
thrown between my feet.
I found the man
with his fancy bags
and fancy ended the pain.
I grabbed a hold,
I cooked,
I shot,
the dry ice in my veins.

Now I must let you go.
Dying's all it seems.
The lamp cord's tight;
my artery beats,
sweet Pacific dreams.

Quiet. And she whisked Petr from Wynoochee Pass up into the Olympic star-lit wash. Above was open and naked, delicious. Scintillant-white glitter beckoned from beyond. Halo and corona were thrown about, their germs sprightly dancing into space. The hearts and heads of beatific fetuses raptured inside the universal womb. Petr felt transcendent.

Below was exposed and stripped, sickening. Shit-brown clay bled from mechanical cat scratches. Douglas-fir and western hemlock were cut away, their limbs carelessly left behind in piles, the arms and legs of war-torn amputees heaped outside a hastily assembled field hospital.

And then she whisked Petr from the Olympic sky onto Humpnoochee Pass, a low point in the ridge between the Wynoochee and Humptulips Rivers.

She bit Petr's ear, hard, the flesh tearing and the blood collecting. She lapped at the ruby pool, his blood an aphrodisiac. She rouged one cheek and then another.

She spoke from her heat, her voice felt like Petr's mother's.

Needles and spoons,
needles and spoons,
your fingers in my brain.
Needles and spoons,
needles and spoons,
aren't you glad you came?

Where are you, my boy?
You've blown so far out to sea.
Been cast upon the waters
like loose leaves in my tea.

Where are you, my boy?
You're a bleeding in my head.
Tied up in plastic tubing;
fucked and left for dead.

Needles and spoons,
needles and spoons,
your fingers in my brain.
Needles and spoons
needles and spoons,
aren't you glad you came?

Where are you, my boy?
I pushed you far away.
My fingers broke and frozen
like tongues on judgment day.

Where are you, my boy?
My uterus a scar
from where you entered to this world
wished upon a star.

Needles and spoons,
needles and spoons,
your fingers in my brain.
Needles and spoons
needles and spoons,
aren't you glad you came?

Quiet again. And then she bounded away and took to the crook of a different silver fir. Again she reclined, this time licking from her what remained of Petr, the one who lay asleep, his pants twisted about one ankle, his shirt wrapped about his backpack strap, the feeder to his transmitter's antenna coiled about his sex.

BUT I DIGRESS, WHAT'S LANGSTON HUGHES GOT TO DO, GOT TO DO WITH IT?

Bestiality, you say? Mama darling fetish? My goodness, dream sex is one thing, but radio sex is quite another!

It won't surprise you that I, Raven, have got some part in all this, even if it's tangential. And you may remember that I admitted to having an egotistical side. I may possess a bird's-eye view, but as wide-angled as my vision can be, it's still firmly my point of view. All that being said, allow me to continue with my story. You'll catch on soon enough as to where my tangent line meets Petr's curve.

You see, I've never thought myself to be the messianic sort, but at the same time, I don't mind being thought of as a hero. Who wouldn't? But a funny thing happened to me on the way to apotheosis; I got the hots for Silver Salmon Sister. And because I fell head over talons and got fixed on her fishy-carnal image, her shy-narcotic sound, her very alder-smoked smell, I figured I'd better say my goodbyes to Dog Salmon Brother and finish up my business with Coyote, at least before retrieving my light-filled box and becoming a light unto Silver Salmon Sister's world.

So I went into action. "Hey, Dog Salmon Brother, I've been worrying about all this. I mean, what are you going to do? You and your village can't go on like this much longer."

"True." Dog Salmon Brother didn't look at me. He looked somewhere beyond. Maybe he was looking at the end. I didn't know.

"I mean, do you have a plan? Your sister doesn't look so good. Neither does anybody else."

"True."

"I hope I'm not speaking out of turn, but you seem a bit short on ideas. I've been thinking, kind of cursed that way you might say . . ." and I paused. I waited to see if Dog Salmon Brother would think me presumptuous. He didn't show anything, blank, so I continued, ". . . now the thing is, I might have a few ideas of my own. They're kind of half-baked at the moment, but maybe together . . ."

"I'm listening."

"Well, as I see it, you all need some gumption, maybe enough to renegotiate your contract, the one where everybody takes your bones back to the rivers so that you folks return next year."

"Too late."

"Okay, but see what you think anyway. The thing is, I've taken into my possession this light-filled box, you know, a little starlight on a new moon night, and I thought it might do your village a world of good."

Dog Salmon Brother turned away, and instead of me, he saw all the Old Growth Salmon turning to gelatin and dissolving into the Pacific. "Doesn't matter."

"Maybe not, but it's at least worth a try. How about we head out and retrieve my little miracle cure? It's worth a shot, right?"

"I'm not going. I'm done. We're all done. My folk are right. This is what happens to a promise betrayed."

BOOK TWELVE

ONLY OLD JOHN KNOWS

WAIT ONCE MORE

BAIE'S JOURNAL

Entry 45

Wait once more
to see atop
this cedar log
dear Mother's
gathering basket,
to hear her snip
a berry from
its child's finger stem,
to feel the blood pearl
roll between
my thumb and finger.
Our sun brings out
the raven highlights of
your hair, and
the gulls *kiau, kiau.*
Wait once more for
the lost's return.

Wait once more
to see against
the rain-worn barn
dear Father's
cranberry washing frames,
to hear him tap
the loose rabbeted ends,
their vows renewed
each to each.
Our well water washes
the weathered wood, and
the hummingbirds buzz.
Wait once more for
the lost's return.

As a child
I made
a rosary:
knotted,
braided
three strands of
twine;
chose,
stitched
ten cranberries in
a line;
knotted,
braided,
chose,
strung
ten three
times.
Our north wind

blows, and
the chorus frogs chirp.
Wait once more for
the lost's return.

Wait once more
to see in
Sesily's arms
dear Freya's
wandering daisy face,
to hear her coo
the jewelweed joy of
our kaleidoscopic world,
to feel the rise of
our newest moon.
Our Humptulips' flood
sweeps all away, and
the hawk moths whir.
Wait once more for
the lost's return.

ROADKILL

BAIE'S JOURNAL

Entry 46

Ruth Ann said to
all the wildsisters
—Wishin' an' waitin',
neither'll bring
baby Freya home.

Ruth Ann then led the way to
her idle Suburban.
We followed behind,
finding our seats on
the cracked vinyl benches.
Ruth Ann ground the starter, and
the black bear engine roused.
Once onto the highway,
we cruised into
the Humptulips fog,
navigating through
the wind-torn spruce.

So unexpected,
so out of nothing,
a heap appeared ahead.
I pointed and shouted
—What's that, dear Ruth Ann?
Stop!

She pulled
the Suburban into
the aimless gravel.
I swung open
the heavy door.
I entered
the headlights' beams.
I recoiled,
overexposed.

And there it was.
I knelt before

a doe, broken.
Her moonjelly eyes
returned our light.
Her body had been struck:
her skin torn away,
her hip bone dislodged,
her short ribs cracked,
her liver bruised,
her lung punctured,
her scarlet blood
oxygen-frothed.
I judged she had
not suffered long,
passed unconscious.
I imagined she had
flipped in the air and
landed on her jaw,
the shock ripping through
suddenly like
a thunderbolt.

A car then approached.
Coming from the Olympics,
heading to North Bay,
its headlights wiped
our shadows clean, and
we disappeared,
too much light.
Its headlights passed,
fading.
Its taillights appeared
ruddy,

dying into
the moist darkness.

I said a prayer,
dear Mother,
my heart-felt charm to
send the doe down
the spirit trail.
—Where is the panic grass
where you'll not want?
You will lie down in
Sitka spruce forests.
You will ford through
snowmelt streams.
Your life will be renewed.
You will walk the trails of
your ancestors that
walked before you.
Amen.

Finished, I got to
my feet, grabbed about
her head, dragged her beyond
the berm, and slid her down
the embankment.
Her wrong-angled head
came to rest in
tangled blackberry
heavy with
green fruit.

MORE ROADKILL

BAIE'S JOURNAL

Entry 47

After I returned,
Ruth Ann drove cautiously hard,
taking us further up
the Humptulips drainage.
She held the wheel fast and
boldly growled out
—What y' say 'bout
us jus' blastin' in?
I'm o' two minds, y' know.
One says we park outside, an'
when they come out,
the big surprise, y' know.
Th' other says t' me
Ruth Ann, y'ol' momma bear,
jus' shine y'r brights an'
blow a big ol' hole in
th' door. Jus' bust in with
y'r ol' Humpback.
Bring the hellfire, you know.

Peering intently out
the window, Dori cut loose
—Howdy J. Doody Christ,
I don't give a fly's shit.
Do whatever works, Ruthie.

Then Shasta Lynn offered
—Yass, yass, holed up, eh.

See the oxbow? I do.
It's twisted my bones.
Feel my brothers? I do.
They just came inside.
Smell John Tornow? I do.
He's mink mad as hell.
John's black retriever
snufflin' just outside, eh.
His dog's sniffed us out, and
he's fetchin' old John.
Hear the frogs? I don't,
not a sound.

And Dori snarled back
—Stop your babblin', Shasta!

Again Ruth Ann spoke up
—Hey, Shasta, y' know
th' ol' story, th' one 'bout
John Tornow? People called'm
Wild Man o' th' Wynoochee.
Story goes a posse
hunted 'm down like . . .

Then Ruth Ann went silent.
Instead we jerked right and
skidded to a halt.
—Looky here, Baie,
a dead porkypine.
Now, out y' go, girl.

Once more I stepped out,
stopped, and looked down upon

the decaying ruin:
body-hardened rigor mortis,
harelip and cheeks receded,
yellow beaver teeth remaining,
claws-extended vampire nails,
death quills sharply bristled,
eye socket maggots tumbling.

To avoid a piercing,
I reached out my shoe.
I contacted the belly.
I pushed again and again,
inching the carcass off
the road's edge, the remains
disappearing under
the evergreen salal.

And once more I prayed
—Presently you walk through
the mudslide's wreckage
fearing all evil
because all is absence.
Slash pile and bear claw
are no comfort.
Amen.

Finished again,
tears filled my eyes.
Yellow gnawed my ear,
gray tore my tongue, and
black ate my heart.

THE WILD MAN OF THE WYNOOCHEE

BAIE'S JOURNAL

Entry 48

Gunning the engine once more,
Ruth Ann propelled us forward.
We continued upstream,
driving straight for
the Humptulips Oxbow.

Placing her hand on
my shoulder, Dori said
—Y'all right? Y' look like
that critter stood up on
its dead ol' legs an'
called out y'r name.

—I hurt, dear Dori.
I just hurt.

—Sure's a mighty big load.
Y' know you're not alone.
I'm goin' t' make things right.
Y' know I always do.
Ruthie might take us t' hell, but
she'll drive us right back out.
So Ruthie, you were sayin' 'bout
long-gone John Tornow?

—Well, the way I heard it,
ol' John was born up by

Matlock, you know, jus' south
o' Beeville, 'bout 'round
th' late eighteen hundreds.
When he was only nine,
a dog tick bit'm, an'
he got th' black measles.
It addled'm some, an'
he took t' goin' off with
his best buddy, Cougar.
Ol' John lived all 'cross
the Satsop, Wynoochee, an'
this here Humptulips.
His daddy was mean, an
John didn't like bein' home.
One old-timer told me
John's thirty-thirty
had no sight. He shot by
feel, just shot from
th' hip. Hit a bear
three hundred yards in
th' right eye. Plunked it,
butchered it, made jerky.

Unable to contain herself,
Shasta Lynn broke in
—Yass, we're comin', John.
Soon we'll be—

—Shut th' hell up, Shasta,
sure as shit you're gettin' on
my nerves. John's been dead
long before you were born.
So Ruthie, you were sayin'.

—Well, loggers'd be cuttin', an'
hunters'd be trackin', an'
suddenly there's ol' John.
He's all scruffy-bearded, an'
he ain't seen a bath since
God only knows when.
Where'd th' hell he come from?
Well, nobody from 'round
here was surprised 'cause
this place's all tangled up
vine maple an' devil's club.
Y' can't see but five feet
most times, you know.
But like I was sayin',
one time an uncle
tricked John into
goin' an' gettin' help.
Turns out th' uncle
locked up ol' John in
a Portland nuthouse, so
you know what John did?
He busted hi'self out.
Then it gets really sad.
Later, his twin nephews
got shot an' killed.
It was a big myst'ry.
They was young bucks who
John really liked, an'
John didn't like much 'cept
ol' Cougar, you know.
Be that as it may,
folks fig'red his nephews
went trackin' John, an'
John killed'm. You know,

he wasn't goin' back to
no nuthouse, no way.

—It's the end, John Tornow.
I hear the—

—Jeez-us F'n Christ, Shasta,
if you don't—

And Ruth Ann jerked the wheel,
this time careening us onto
a Forest Service road turned
overgrown game trail.

EXCUSE ME, WHITE OTTER HAS SOMETHING TO SAY ABOUT RUIN

Orca,
ruin trails your wake, but
you are not ruin.
Ruin shadows you, but
you are not ruin.
You pursue and savage,
your smile meat-toothed,
your eye sun-sparked.
You are Earthquake,
Volcano, Typhoon, but
you are not ruin.

Ruin is coughed up by
this sick Pacific:
polystyrene floats
unnaturally orange,

pressure-treated lumber
copper arsenic green.
Ruin has poisoned the kelp,
both castle and cathedral.
Ruin has poisoned you,
all bloody gums and lost teeth.

Orca,
I've faithfully built us
a graywacke cairn, and
I cleanse our soul with
this life-giving prayer.
—Where is the eel grass
where we'll not want?
We will lie down in
bull kelp forests.
We will swim in
offshore waters.
Our lives will be renewed.
The safe currents will run
where we'll not be forsaken.
Presently we swim through
the riptide's strong flow
fearing all evil
because all is absence.
Steel scrap and gull skull
are no comfort.
We occupy a wasteland in
deadly profiteers' palms.
Heavy metals baptize our heads.
Our flesh melts away.
We pray that faith and grace
will steep our Olympics, and

we will reside pure and wild
hereafter.

Kyrie eleison.
Christe eleison.
Kyrie eleison.
Je ne suis plus un créature
de la terre
or the air.
I am a creature
de la mer.

EVEN MORE ROADKILL

BAIE'S JOURNAL

Entry 49

Finally we stopped.
—Looky out there, Baie. You see?
Now you hop on out:

bit my wrist; flesh in
my teeth in remembrance of
me; salt on my tongue

an owl, wings heavy and
sonorous against the damp
air, sounded somewhere

log truck barreling;
wheels smashing the snake's thin, now
papery body

the remains: Doug-fir
green, orange-striped, white-flecked; once a
rope, now a ribbon

peel the gravel-pocked
skin from the road; soul blown free
in cool ev'ning air

lay the papery
body to rest off pavement:
horesetail, spent foxglove

a breeze came up; a
prayer grew heavy in my
throat and fell asleep

MORE WILD MAN OF THE WYNOOCHEE

BAIE'S JOURNAL

Entry 50

While Ruth Ann drove on,
red cedar limbs
closed all about, and
we were quiet until
Dori whispered
—Baie, y' feelin' like
Freya's close by?

—I don't know, dear Dori.

Shasta Lynn sat, rocking;
then she mumbled
—Let me go, brothers.
Let that baby go, eh.
Why you pushin' down?
Yass, Old John's comin'.
He's there, right outside.

Dori threatened
—Somebody shut her up!

Then a terrible silence.
Blood crusted on
my wounded wrist.
Dori softened
—So, Ruthie, this John Tornow,
how'd it all turn out?

—Well, the way I heard it
there was a posse.
John plugged each one,
dead center forehead.
Didn't know what hit'm.
Covered'm over
shallow-like, you know, with
some dirt an' some moss.

All sarcasm and damnation,
Dori answered back
—Put all my cash money on
th' posse bein' th' ones who
killed John's cousins.

—Only ol' John knows.
Maybe it happened different.
Maybe his nephews said
they was takin'm back to
that Portland snake pit, so
old John gunned'm down.
Maybe John was like
his dog, Cougar; he smelled
his family had gone wrong.
Facts say th' twins got plugged.
Then facts say no more.

Dori snickered
—So is John right outside?
Shasta here says so.

And there was a thump.
Ruth Ann stopped the car on
the Forest Service road,
dead center middle.
—Now, Baie, what y' think?

I followed Ruth Ann's finger.

THE LAST ROADKILL

BAIE'S JOURNAL

Entry 51

A hawk moth's remains:
yellow-green glass splatter,
splayed fairy wings,

sacrificial angel.

I pulled the wings from
the windshield and
gracefully cradled them.
I entered the red cedars.
I joined the salmonberry.
A flutter brushed my cheek,
brushed my cheek again,
this time a tickle.

Holding beauty's remains,
I softly sang this psalm.
—Certainly
justice and community
shall be welcomed to
inhabit our home, and
we will abide in
joyous jubilee
here and now after.

Then a flutter tugged at
my wispy hair strand.
It pulled me along
the old logging grade.
We moved among
licorice and sword fern.
My wildsisters trailed behind.

Finally the tugging ceased.
The curl lay back against
my cheek. I stopped, knelt, and
gracefully settled
the hawk moth's remains.

WHEN THE SHOOTING STARTED

BAIE'S JOURNAL

Entry 52

Ruth Ann's mouth
opened
—The oxbow!

That's
when
the shooting
started.

Kyrie eleison.
Christe eleison.
Kyrie eleison.
Tout
est perdre.
Tout
est retrouver.
Now and
here,
wildsisters.

BOOK THIRTEEN

SHOT THROUGH

BERT LANCE VERSUS ANTHONY COMSTOCK

Well, well, well, I see you're back. You want to find out what happens when Petr wakes up. You want to know what Petr does when he looks down and finds the feeder to his transmitter antenna coiled about his sex. What exactly was up with all that biting, tearing, and feeding? And what was up with the "she" in the tree?

Before we get to those questions, I think it's helpful to stop for a moment and consider our frame of reference. We don't want to get all excited and head out from Humpnoochee Pass with our fancy pants chuck-bores in a kink. We don't want to be accused of any comstockery. Truth be told, like so many other ideological niceties, we here on the Olympic Peninsula don't take bets on damming up the river of desire. Sure, our rivers are full of log jams and have occasion to drop some precipitous waterfalls and hairy-assed rapids. And sure, they are subject to floods, but that's just all water under a Forest Service bridge. Fact is we like our rivers here to run wild and free.

"But not so fast," you say. "What about counterarguments like the value that's obtained from controlling desire? For example, what about the Wynoochee River, the one that the Army Corps of Engineers damned in 1972? What about the electricity generated by the dam's power station, and what about the property protected downstream because the river doesn't flood?"

Yes, yes, all valid points to be sure, but I think you're forgetting that our southern Olympics have been known to get winter and spring rains of four inches a day for three days straight, and when you string three of these three-day rains together over a two-week period, four inches times nine days equals thirty-six rain-soaked inches, an amount that's got Biblical proportions written all over it. Then consider that when we get this sort of rain, and we get it more than outsiders think, the Corps protects their dam by releasing water, so much water, in fact, that the Wynoochee Valley catastrophically floods. The Chehalis River Valley catastrophically floods. The Satsop River Valley catastrophically floods. Parts of Aberdeen city go underwater. Parts of Montesano city go underwater. Parts of Brady village go underwater. Parts of Satsop village go underwater. Parts of Elma city go underwater. This all happens because some folks, not pointing any flight feathers, don't like our rivers to run wild and free.

And if you're still not convinced, allow me to go at this river of desire thing in another way. Think of the Wynoochee Dam, wonder of the world that it is, as the 1873 Federal "Act for the Suppression of Trade in, and Circulation of, Obscene Literature and Articles of Immoral Use," authored by none other than Anthony Comstock, self-proclaimed "weeder in God's garden."

> Every obscene, lewd, or lascivious, and every filthy book, pamphlet, picture, paper, letter, writing, print, or other publication of an indecent character, and every article or thing designed, adapted, or intended for preventing conception or producing abortion, or for any indecent or immoral use ... is hereby declared to be a non-mailable matter and shall not be conveyed in the mails or delivered from any post office or by any letter carrier. Whoever shall knowingly deposit or cause to be deposited for mailing or delivery, anything declared by this section to be non-mailable, or shall knowingly take, or cause the same to be taken, from the mails for the purpose of circulating or disposing thereof, or of aiding in the circulation or disposition thereof, shall be fined not more than five thousand dollars, or imprisoned not more than five years, or both.

Clearly old Comstock knew how to build a considerable legal dam, but we on the Olympic Peninsula don't live by the Comstock Laws, we live by American sociologist Robert Merton's law of unintended consequences and former U.S. Dept. of Management and Budget Bert Lance's maxim, "If it ain't broke, don't fix it." And just between you and me, the Olympic Peninsula wasn't broke until some folks, not pointing any talon claws, tried to fix it.

So Petr's got a choice. Either he can go southeast along the West Branch of the Wynoochee River downstream to where it's all plugged up by the Army Corps' dam. Or he can go southwest along the West Fork of the Humptulips River downstream to where, if you've been paying attention, and I know you have, Baie and her wildsisters are moving upstream.

I don't know about you, but around here we like our rivers to run wild and free.

DOWNSTREAM

Licorice fern grew from beds of moss lying on the crotches of limbs. Horsehair lichens festooned the tree trunks. Sulfur shelf fungus popped from a downed log, mushrooms child-Petr had often poked. Very few knew of this place, and the few who did called this saddle between two higher places Humpnoochee Pass.

When Petr awoke, he uncoiled the feeder to the transmission antenna from his sex. He remembered the mystery of last night. He felt the biting. He felt the tearing. He felt the feeding. And then he did as he always did: he stood, stretched, collected his equipment, and started to move, this time walking west, walking down, down, down, entering into a damp, green temperate jungle, listening to the pop of chocolate lily buds, the knocks and clicks of an unseen raven, and the yelp and rattle of a Pacific giant salamander.

Petr found this to be little more than a game trail which he hoped would lead to a Forest Service road. He switchbacked once, twice, a third time, and finally once more, the path settling along the headwaters of the West Fork of the Humptulips River. He repeatedly crossed the river, first hopping from bank to bank, but as the stream widened, leaping from bank to stone to bank. More than once he scrambled over recent deadfall.

Soon springs and rivulets widened the channel, deepening it in places. Thickets of salmonberry, nettles, and devil's club arose from where mountain hemlock and silver fir had fallen and opened the canopy to sunlight. Petr had to fight his way forward, sometimes avoiding the trail altogether, choosing the river proper, wading with the summer but still-quite-chill current. He saw little percentage in bushwhacking through what some called Eden, and some called Hell, but really just Is.

At one point Petr stopped to rest. He scanned the steep valley walls, first to the north, then to the south. He judged these silver firs, most 150 feet tall, a few 100 feet taller, to be mature old growth. Though valuable, these gray-scaled giants were fairly inaccessible. It had always been cheaper to log downstream.

Petr imagined an old-timey timber cruiser walking and stamping these woods in his mind with dollar signs. He imagined the teeth of a dirty-orange chainsaw cutting into a ripe trunk. One machine soon multiplied into an army, their thirty-four-inch bars dripping with chain oil. He tasted the blue-sweet exhaust of their two-stroke engines.

MORE DOWNSTREAM

beaver dam, bear shit,
twenty-seven soggy fords;
twilight at trail's end

OPEN UP THE TRAILER, JOHNNY

Rattle. Clank. Rattle. Rattle. Petr awoke. A pickup and horse trailer had parked a hundred yards away. A man from the driver's side got out. Another man from the passenger side got out. A teenager followed. They were dressed more like Western ranchers than woodsmen: wide-brimmed hats, not caps; yoked cotton shirts with snaps, not hickory shirts; bootcut jeans, not high-waters; and tooled leather riding boots, not cork boots.

"Open up the trailer, Johnny. Me and Uncle Bob'll grab the supplies."

Johnny opened the trailer, reached inside, and led a roan out by its roper rein. Uncle Bob lay saddle bags across the roan's rump and checked over the blanket, saddle, bit, and bridle. "Looks good, Johnny. Okay brother Joe, first one to Campbell Tree Grove gets dibs on the sandwiches." Uncle Bob then took the rein and mounted.

Johnny reached inside and led a palomino out. Joe lay saddle bags across the second animal's rump and, like Uncle Bob, checked the animal's gear. Joe then took the rein, but instead of mounting, stood, waiting.

Johnny reached inside a third time and led a pinto out. He handed the rein to Joe. "Okay if I close the trailer up, Dad?"

"Sure, Johnny."

The young man closed the trailer door, dropped the lock mechanism into place, checked the pinto's gear, took the animal's rein, and then mounted, the cue for Joe to do the same.

"Let's head out boys. Fog'll be burnin' off soon. Fig'res t' be a beautiful day."

THE SEAT OF HIS PANTS

Now that the three horses were gone, Petr came off the trail that tunneled north into the southern Olympics, the one that Petr had walked south on the day before, the one where he had spent the night, the one he had stepped off of, sight unseen, while the horses passed by.

He walked into a gravel-covered clearing and focused his attention on a lone pickup. He approached the driver's side window and spied a bag of potato chips. CLICK. CREAK. He reached inside, grabbed the bag, unrolled the top, plunged in his hand, extracted a heap, and shoved the pile into his mouth. The chips, both starchy and oily, were instantly satisfying. He craved cracker crumb razor clams. He craved cola-barbecued venison ribs. He craved alder-smoked blueback salmon. But right now in this place, these pickup-dived chips were a kick placed squarely in the seat of his pants.

Petr crinkled the empty chip bag, tossed it into the back seat, reached again, and this time grabbed a ribbed aluminum container, the thermos that had been concealed, the one that hid behind the chips. TWIST. SWISH. He saw a steamy wisp and smelled the bitter coffee. One draft, five gulps later, his throat burned and his eyes widened, time to skedaddle.

BUT I DIGRESS, *SCHEMATO ERGO SUM*

Now that we've got Petr nicely down off the mountain and into the Humptulips' drainage, you might be wondering what ever happened to our old friend Coyote. Sure, you know about my hots for Silver Salmon Sister, and sure, you know about Mole and her hots for yours truly, but what about Coyote? you know, the one who puts the *trois* in *menage à trois*. What about Coyote the Shape Shifter, Coyote the Imitator, Coyote the Lord of all People? What about Schemer, He Who Makes Schemes, *Schemato Ergo Sum*.

Following from this maxim, you won't be surprised to learn that Coyote's *a priori* scheme was to fill his empty stomach, and you also won't be surprised that he wasn't shy about playing his ace in the hole, Mole, the one who always had something stewing on the home fire. No, she wasn't a gourmet cook; she wasn't the Lac Beetle Clan who once served Coyote ambrosial shellac, but she did always have something in her pot to get his mind off his belly.

Unfortunately, when Coyote awoke from his nap, returned home, and lifted the lid, he found this message.

NOTHING

NADA

RIEN

NICHTS

NANIMONAI

NICHEGO

KUCHH BHEE TO NAHIN

OHUNKOHUN

Seeing that his dinner was, as the old song goes, "plenty of nuttin'," Coyote couldn't help but question, "What?" and then again, "How?" Fact was the empty cooking pot shook old Schemer's worldview to pieces like the winds of November 1940 did to Tacoma's long gone bridge, Galloping Gertie.

Then to add insult to injury, Coyote's wife walked through the door not only glistening after a dip beneath an Olympic waterfall but also flourishing a mussel shell necklace. He wondered if his wife were some scheming Kushtaka, but rather than reveal his doubts, he fell back on stating the obvious, "Nothin' in the pot."

"No, I don't suppose there is," she deadpanned.

He thought her taller, her shadow longer. "What's goin' on with you?"

"Nothing. I'm happy; that's all," she smiled, taking a proprietary stance next to her wings, the ones in the corner that replaced the salmon bones that Coyote routinely discarded.

And, boy, did the glint winking off those wings' salmon scales catch Coyote's eye. "Sure are somethin'," he let slip.

"I like them."

"Don't suppose they work."

"I wouldn't know . . . dear."

"Didn't think you would. But, hey, if I can make them work, these'll get me off the ground, and if they do, I figure to fly off and visit the Old Growth Salmon. Folks've been complainin' that salmon aren't comin' back the way they used to. They say the ones that do come back are smaller. I think ol' Schemer might use these wings to solve this salmon problem. To hell with fish ladders, fish farmin', hatcheries, and all that.

"Yes-siree, stop treatin' the leaves and get at the root, right? Maybe me and the Old Growth Salmon can get together and strike up a new bargain, somethin' that will satisfy both our interests. People'll call me Salmon Restorer, maybe Redeemer, even Savior. Then I can take time off for good behavior!"

Now that Coyote's scheme was born and walking on its own four legs, he took a proprietary stance on the other side of his wife's wings. Standing firm, he snatched the wings with such force, "Don't mind if I do," that a rainbow of a scale came loose and fluttered down.

Followed by one of Mole's sparkling tears.

THE OLYMPIC SUN

Petr got off the trail, the one that was married to the river, the one that in Petr's experience had intercourse with the river twenty-seven times, and he walked past the GORGE BRIDGE TRAILHEAD sign and out onto Forest Service Road 2204, the one that was only kissing cousins with the river, not married, but cousins all the same.

The sun rose like a saint's aureole, and Petr walked. The sun hung overhead like the eye of a blast furnace, and Petr walked. The sun set like an atomic red huckleberry gone supernova, and Petr walked. And then FS 2204 came to a dead-end T. Either turn put Petr on FS 22, known to us on the Olympic Peninsula as Donkey Creek Road, an old Coastal Salish trail. Here Petr turned right, back in the direction of the West Fork of the Humptulips River.

As the sun disappeared, Petr began to forget himself. The rhythm of his walking put him into a gentle trance, one where he seemed to be sinking, at first treading ankle deep: step, step, step, then slogging up to his calves: step, step, step, and finally wading to his waist: step, step, step. If some local poacher had set his portable jacklight ablaze, Petr would have appeared to be half a man. The poacher would have thought Petr a thing passed over.

SORRY

Petr continued to walk in the dark, in the fog, off the road, and into the woods. Up ahead two appeared: one dark, bearded, unkempt, dressed in oil cloth; the other a black retriever, gray about the muzzle, an old companion. The two's gait was slow and purposeful.

Petr drew near and went with them. He chose his words carefully in the way a man should when entering another man's camp. "Name's Petr. I'm heading downriver a ways. You headed downriver, too? Mind if I join you?"

The darker one, not breaking his stride, not turning to acknowledge Petr, answered, "Round 'bout an' down. Always down, ol' boy. Never seem t' be goin' up. Always just seems t' be down for us."

Petr tried to stay on the friendly side. He knew he was close to the threatening edge. "I'm just passing through. You and your dog live around these parts?"

"Hmph, guess you ain't heard what's happenin' 'round here. Hey, Cougar, keep on up here, ol' buddy."

"No, can't say that I have."

"All 'bout bullets. Been bullets an' 'bortions. Nephews, both been shot, twins dead an' gone. Rusty knives an' blood. Nothin' but red an' black for my sister. Rot an' wrong, huh, Cougar? Good ol' boy. Ain't never deserved what he got, did you, boy? Bullet in the hip. 'Nother in the chest. Good boy, come 'long now ol' buddy."

"Sorry."

With that, the darker one stopped, his retriever at his heel. The darker one's gaze went off nowhere, inside the woods and out, neither here nor there, and then a grimace cut across his face, jagged like a wound left by devil's club. "Sorry? Hmph, sorry, did you say? Sure was sorry to make a man suffer the shootin' of his own kin. The ones he played with from when they was kits. To see them grown an' have them turn on you like some rabid 'coons. I can tell you there's no rest. Can you hear? Frogs been singin' since I was nine. They're uncommon quiet now."

"Yes, uncommon quiet," Petr agreed. A raven call went up, and a cone dropped from a fir. Another cone dropped. A mosquito whined, insistent.

Then the darker one, blank, the light snuffed long ago, took up walking again. Cougar, his old buddy, shuffled along behind. "Comin' near where we're goin'. If you're goin' further, you can be on your way."

The darker one's dog rubbed up against Petr's knee, raising his face to Petr's. The dog's moist mouth, open and humid, teemed phosphorescent. His eyes were sewn shut. Petr felt this retriever had seen something, a wholly unfortunate event, an abomination.

"My ol' mother's passed on. All nothin' on top of nothin'. Daddy, he was rotten before I was born. Sister's passed on, all razors an' blood. Nothin's worth a good goddamn. Twins, too. Everything's shot to hell."

Petr felt the darker one sliding under deadfall, a flow, and between tight columns. "Hey ol' buddy, duck right under this bent cedar. Now through these thimbleberries." Then the darker one stopped.

That's when the shooting started.

A RADIO PLAY

Cast of Characters
SHOT-THROUGH-THE-EYE
SHOT-THROUGH-THE-EAR
SHOT-THROUGH-THE-HEART

The play takes place on the West Humptulips Oxbow.
(One summer night. Inside a dilapidated shack. Three scruffy bodies lie dead, each with a bullet wound to the forehead. One, a male, an additional eye wound. Another male an additional ear wound. The third, a female, an additional chest wound.)

Shot-Through-The-Eye
(pitiful)
I am Shot-Through-The-Eye. So-o-o-o-o sorry.

Shot-Through-The-Ear
(interjecting)
I am Shot-Through-The-Ear. Uh, I, this . . . s'not funny.

Shot-Through-The-Heart
(clutching)
I am Shot-Through-The-Heart. Got it! My finger's itchin', itchin', and not givin' it back!

Shot-Through-The-Eye
(remorseful)
So-o-o-o-o sorry, all shit and bother. My feet're—

Shot-Through-The-Ear
(pointing)
Here! And here, too. Over there. Bone. Skull open. Chest open.

Shot-Through-The-Heart
(assessing)
Got it right here. Cold night seeping in. Damp and gloom. Lost in gloom.

Shot-Through-The-Eye
(reporting)
So-o-o-o-o sorry, considerable jumpy and worryin'. To shit. My feet're in a hurry.

Shot-Through-The-Ear
(observing)
On the dirt. Black moldy end days. Skipjack crawlin' across. Strippin' a carrion lug.

Shot-Through-The-Heart
(despairing)
Fast a hold of, grabbing, all desperate, inky.

Shot-Through-The-Eye
(conceding)
So-o-o-o-o sorry, plumb blood and suffer. To shit. My feet're—

Shot-Through-The-Ear
(going under)
Diggin' here, and on that there, and this. No.

Shot-Through-The-Heart
(hell-bent)
All slippery and quiet. Got it right here! Itchin'. Not givin' it back!

TABLEAU

Then the dust softly settled. Hanging from a single hinge, the shack door lay open. A man, greasy hanks of hair tousled about, was stretched out like roadkill. His feet were inside the shack, his bullet-pierced ear outside. Around his ankles were boxers streaked with blood, some of the stains old, others fresh as pain.

Further inside lay another man with one frozen, caught unaware eye. His skin was slick gooseflesh; the hair on his chest and arms stood, raised against the cold. Stung, a bullet hole blacked the other eye.

Back against an inside corner, a young woman sat, head bowed, hair draped, covering her bared breasts. The V of her dead legs shrieked, a chest wound not the only violation she had suffered.

All three wore an additional fairly clean wound, dead center forehead.

Having become a part of this horrific tableau, Petr heard a rustle, a hawk moth, beating its wings against a corner, the one directly across from so much ruin. Something moved. Something in a blanket massed upon the floor.

Outside passing among the trees, a raven quorked three times.

Chorus frogs stretched on their long toes, the air sacks on their chins aquiver.

Kushtakas tightly gathered around.

Petr fished in the blanket's folds and revealed something round, fleshy, with eyes, mouth, and tiny nose, yes, an infant, its cheeks tensing against the sudden slap of cold.

Petr felt anxious, as if caught in the crosshairs, and then from behind, he heard a cough. Startled, he turned. A woman stood in the doorway.

BOOK FOURTEEN

INTO THE DEEP BLACK

INK

Entry 53

I burn the coffee,
forget to make the bed,
neglect to pick fruit,
and make ink from skins and tears.
I make ink from skins and tears.

Moss rots the roof shakes.
Baneberries poison the wine.
Black spot stains the leaves.
I make ink from skins and tears.
I make ink from skins and tears.

Mother and Father are gone.
Freya's born and gone.
Misty's ruined and gone.
I make ink from skins and tears.
I make ink from skins and tears.

LOOKY RIGHT HERE

BAIE'S JOURNAL

Entry 54

I saw a man,
dear God,
standing in
the rotten cabin,
standing in
our shell-shocked presence,
standing with
our swaddled hopes.
I wondered silently,
then wondered aloud
—Who are you?

Looking up from
the infant's face,
he answered—Petr.

Ruth Ann growled
—What th' hell?

And Dori barked
—Jeez-us Shit's Ditch Christ,
Where's my lighter?

A flame jumped from
Dori's thumbnail.
Its flickering glow lit
tossed-about clothing,

two wishbone chairs with
broken caning, and
a three-legged table.
Salmonberry grew through
absent windows.
One body lay motionless;
this one I stepped over.
Another body lay motionless;
that one I went around.
A third body lay motionless;
this one I mourned.
—Where is the eel grass
where we'll not want?
We will lie down in
bull kelp forests.
We will swim in
offshore waters.
Our lives will be renewed.
The safe currents will run
where we'll not be forsaken.

Then Ruth Ann addressed us all,
this time not a growl,
this time a gentle,
uncharacteristic coo.
—Well, looky right here.
Don' that jus' beat all, like
findin' a wee bear cub in
a hollow log, and
a rotten log at
that. An' looks like
we got here none too soon.
This here baby could use

a feed, you know.
She's missin' her momma
somethin' gawd-awful.

I joyfully looked to
our redeemed newborn:
Freya full of grace,
Freya blessed among
these wildsisters,
Freya blessed among
our cranberry fruit.

Taking the infant from
this sudden stranger,
Sesily put Freya to
her lonely breast.
Blood dry-crusted
the child's soft hair.
Veining blue-tinged
the child's new skin.
Her eyes brightened,
two Oly oysters
just freshly opened.

Needing to see,
needing to believe,
Dori crowded closer.
—L'me look, Ses.
Yep, it's her all right, an
yep, she's a wildsister.

Sure as shit li'l critter,
you was born in
a crazy place an'
a crazy time, too, but
who's this no-account?

PETR

BAIE'S JOURNAL

Entry 55

chewed his bottom lip,
tugged at his taut backpack straps,
looking just beyond

cuchddu lambswool hair,
wet basalt spotted owl eyes,
present, possible

an ear, a flower,
an uncomfortable question mark
radio Petr

brewin' moon's drop punch
with my cran-strawberry jam,
spoon to lick spotless

FALSE DAWN

BAIE'S JOURNAL

Entry 56

So here stood Petr,
the one Dori
labeled no-account,
the one that Ruth Ann
presently addressed.
—Don' know y' from
a Doug-fir beetle, but
I do know these boys.
All us know this girl, too.
Ain't nobody, an'
I mean nobody'll
miss their coyot' hides.

After saying her piece,
Ruth Ann then kicked a dead foot.
She gravely stepped over
a just-killed body as
she made her way outside.
Sesily followed Ruth Ann,
Petr fell in line, and
I followed Petr into
an uncertain false dawn.

Still inside, Dori called out
—What should we do with
these kin fuckers, Baie?
We need to do somethin'.

I surely hate 'em, but
it's not right t' jus' leave.

I stopped and called back
—Bless you, dear Dori.

—Somethin' should be said.
You know I'm no talker.

So I returned inside,
traveling back to
more innocent days,
traveling back to
my Catholic monastery for
holy inspiration.
—Sing to the kelp
a new song,
the waves rolling across
the Pacific.
For a long time
we have been exiled.
We have been marooned.
We have silently closed
our nightmare eyes like
violated children.
We have counted the hours.
But now the kelp
is renewed like
an antique forest.
It nourishes fully
even the wasted.
It envelops lovingly
even the tormented.

It harbors gracefully
even the storm-tossed.

—Damn, Baie, you say
th' weirdest stuff.
I guess that'll do.
Now, you go on out.
I got my own ideas.
I'll be out shortly.
Might make some noise.
Jus' doin' what needs doin'.

EYES SEALED SHUT

BAIE'S JOURNAL

Entry 57

As we followed Ruth Ann into
the damp deep black,
what was it, dear Mother?
What sealed shut my eyes,
the spruce pitch smell?

Then came the lifting,
my weightless stomach.
Then came the thudding,
a hard wood floor.

I was overpowered,
the red cedar smell,
the wood smoke smell,
the charred salmon smell.

I heard a mumbling,
maybe someone singing,
no, raven chatter,
then something familiar,
something I love,
a voice looking for
a fairy frog,
no, for
something more uncanny.

RADIO SXWAYO'KLU

BAIE'S JOURNAL

Entry 58

—So, Sxwayo'klu, good to see you again. Our listeners may recall our last visit when we set up a live remote at your home, and we got to meet your children.

—I can still see their faces. I remember a nervous one and an exhausted one, too. And I remember the absent one. We learned they were all battered, stolen, or murdered. Some were all three.

—While we were there, they came through the roots, and we shared a plate of your home cooking. We had salmon with spring beauty bulbs in black huckleberry sauce. I will never forget the meal you prepared and shared.

—And as I imagine their faces, I want our listeners to know about your work. You not only do search and rescue, but you also care for these lost children. Let me say from all of us on the Peninsula, thank you for all that you do for kids. I know it's cliché, but without you, these kids would have perished forgotten.

—Which brings us to another point: most of us only know the forest legends. If we know anything, we've heard that you hide in the woods and steal people's kids. The way it's told around here, some hero saves the little ones by pushing you into your own campfire.

—I also remember you told me you don't mind a little bad press in support of a good cause. All the same, you are with us tonight because of this evening's tragic events. Our listeners would appreciate hearing your thoughts. Isn't this sort of thing—rape, murder, and child abandonment—becoming the rule instead of the exception?

> —rustle
> beech grass
> dry
> —skitter
> locust shells
> breeze-blown
> —whir
> hawk moth wing
> frail

—I couldn't agree more. But don't you think, Sxwayo'klu, that this evening's events were particularly terrible? There was a newborn involved. Was it murder or retribution? And as you know, no one really saw what happened. Often I think depravity slaps hardest when we are taken by surprise.

> —blow
> low sand dunes
> loose

—Yes, you're right, of course, I didn't mean to say no one. Only to say . . . hmm . . . no one like me, hmm? It's true that there are some around here who do nothing but notice. Old Bernard Huelsdonk seems to be everywhere all the time. My theory is he tipped off John Tornow. Just a theory. And we all know John's got a belly full of pain. His patience was used up long ago. And then there are the Kushtakas. What about them?

—wheel
   bone ash
      dust devil

—Down by the Humptulips, you say? Of course, they don't stray too far from water. I'm sure they heard all the shooting. And what about Raven? He's always about, hmm?

—creak
   Sitka spruce
      wind-woven

—Yes, I know better. Silly question.

EXCUSE ME, WHITE OTTER HAS SOMETHING TO SAY ABOUT VIOLATION

Razor Clam,
the tide is low, and
you are vulnerable.
Sand-encased, you stand.
Open, you stretch.
Exposed, you rise.

The sun is high, and
Gull sails a stiff breeze.
He knows the tides.
He knows your flesh:
opalescent, sweet, and
oh, so succulent.
He hangs and waits for
your muscular spasm to
expel its watery jet.

Seeking salvation,
you desperately rub
a starfish's foot and
fervently pray to
break Gull's bill, to
sever Gull's talon.
You fervently pray to
plant your foot in
sand unfamiliar, in
sand not tasted.
You fervently pray to
write your history into
an analgesic prophecy.
And since you cannot forget,
you fervently pray for
your prophecy's fulfillment.

But it is not enough.
GULL HAS HIS OWN GOD
He sharply dives.
HIS OWN BAYONET BILL
He shatters your shell.
HIS OWN PROPHECY
He gives a fierce headshake,
roughly separating
your hard shards from
your velvety meat.
HIS OWN PROPAGANDA
—DEATH IS MY GENEROUS GIFT
He swallows you torn.
He swallows you whole.

Kyrie eleison.
Christe eleison.
Kyrie eleison.

Je ne suis plus un créature
de la terre
or the air.
I am a creature
de la mer.

GRAVITY

BAIE'S JOURNAL

Entry 59

I felt a tumbling out,
a thud shiver through
my surprised body,
the ground cold and damp.
Someone grabbed the spruce pitch
near
my right eye and
stripped it free.
Early light,
my eyes overwhelmed.
Familiar sound,
my ears cheered.

BURNING THE CANDLE

BAIE'S JOURNAL

Entry 60

Alarmed, Dori called
—Baie, is that you?

Jeez-us, it's you and
what's his name.

Coming from her Suburban,
Ruth Ann joined Dori.
—Thought we lost y' both.
Don' wander off like that.
We called an' called an'
beats me how y' got back.
These woods're crazy.
I quit wonderin' 'bout
all the weird stuff
that happens 'round here.

Returning to the Suburban,
Ruth Ann started the engine.
Gravity pulled us and
the Humptulips home.

Soon familiar shapes emerged:
our weather-worn Sitka spruce,
our familiar farmhouse,
our cranberry bog
lushly attired on
twisted twigs,
our Wildsisters' barn.

I led Petr amidst
the ripening cranberries.
The first fruit was on.
I imagined busy fingers.
I imagined baskets full of
hard, red, piquant fruit.
I deliciously ached to

run my fingers through
his midnight fleece, to
turn back the quilt.

That's when Ruth Ann sent
us wildsisters to bed.
—Guess that's that, you know.
You lockin' up, Dori?

—Sure thing.

Then Sesily yawned
—Well, it's way past
me and Freya's bedtime.
Goodnight. Or I should say
good morning.

And Ruth Ann teased
a benediction
—Don't burn th' candle at
both ends you two.
Got a feelin' we're goin'
t' need more wick t'morrow.
Get some sleep, you know.

With that Petr and I
found ourselves alone.
As we crossed the farmyard,
I smiled at dear Father's
red-rusted wheelbarrow.
As we entered the kitchen,
I smiled at dear Mother's
blue-splattered mixing bowl.
As we shared a meal,

I twirled around my tongue,
a sugar kelp blade
held fast within.

Kyrie eleison.
Christe eleison.
Kyrie eleison.
Tout
est perdre.
Tout
est retrouver.
Now and
here,
wildsisters.

BOOK FIFTEEN

CONFLUENCES

HUMPTULIPS

Now that Baie and Petr have come together, let ME welcome YOU to Wildsisters, the women's roadhouse situated on OUR Humptulips River. Yes, I know, you've already spent a good bit of time here, but that's been without yours truly. And that's been without Petr. So now that our different experiences have come together, you might be feeling a bit of omniscience. Or is it omnipresence? Fact is you've been inside a number of different consciousnesses moving through a number of different places in time. You know, all that philosophical and literary blah, blah, blah. Those sorts of things.

So here we are: Baie, Petr, you, and I.

Speaking of here, the word *humptulips* is a curious word, isn't it? A few people, those who claim to know something about the word's history, joke that it is derived from some sort of manic violation of the nether lands. But all such Eurocentric nonsense aside, *humptulips* is a Salishan word whose origin stirs up a bit of trouble, even among folks who truly know something about Salishan dialects. Some knowledgeable folks claim humptulips means "hard to pole," as in the river is so choked with downed logs that it is unnavigable. And given the number of trees in the Humptulips, the ones washed down by winter and spring floods, such a claim makes sense. Other knowledgeable folks claim humptulips means "chilly region," as in this place is always dark, damp, windy, and cold. And given our foggy, temperate rain forest climate, the one that the Alaska Current blows over this terrain, such a claim also makes sense.

Be that as it may, everyone agrees that there once was a well-defined Humptulips group of Lower Chehalis natives, and everyone agrees that these Humptulips natives were not interested in signing anything Washington Territorial Governor and Superintendent of Indian Affairs Isaac Stevens put in front of them. Then in 1864 with Stevens dead and gone, the United States Secretary of the Interior John P. Usher signed an executive order creating the Confederated Tribes of the Chehalis Reservation. The Humptulips and other nontreaty, "fish-eating Indians" were not parties to this action. They were not invited to any signing ceremony out in Washington, D.C. But they were told that if they didn't want trouble, they needed to move. Their home was now the newly created and ridiculously small reservation at the confluence of the Black and Chehalis Rivers.

So as I said, here we are: Baie, Petr, you, and I.

If you like, you can think of our current experience as many streams of consciousness coming together to form one wild and free Humptulips River of consciousness, after the shooting stopped, after Sxwayo'klu and Ruth Ann brought Radio Free Olympia to Wildsisters. A pretty novel idea, don't you think?

IN BAIE'S BED

Waking with early afternoon Humptulips' fog in her head, Baie blinked, blinked again, and then opened wide her eyes. A man, one wrapped in her blue-checked bedsheet, lay next to her. She shook her head to clear away the mist, and then she thought about prayer.

Baie thought it wrong to say prayers to fulfill selfish wishes. Prayer was for God's will. Then she thought about the religious education she received while she was a postulant in the monastery. During her short stay, the nuns taught her that Saint Thérèse had struggled with separating her personal from her religious passions, a struggle Baie certainly could identify with. After all, Saint Thérèse had once been like her, a maturing young woman.

Baie then thought about another struggle. She thought about the way child-Baie had confused the Olympic Peninsula with the monastery her dear

Father told her about. Sure, she knew the peninsula and monastery were geographically different, but her dear Father talked so often about his monastic experience that she made the two places spiritually one. For example, he told child-Baie that the nuns taught him that *"observer le travail de Dieu est un grand plaisir,"* which she understood as "doing God's work feels good." He told her that the nuns gave him the name *"le petit ange,"* or "the little angel." He nurtured in her, the one who was new, the one who was his daughter, a passion for great spiritual experience.

But her dear Father did not nurture in his dear Baie an equal passion for obedience, and therein lay the struggle. Anyone who bothered to get to know Baie—and no one other than her parents and her good friend Dori ever had—would have said that she was spiritually wild. Not that she was rebellious and incapable of self-discipline, because she wasn't. It was just that her experience, the two years she spent in the monastery, had taught her she was no domestic blueberry, no mechanically harvested cranberry. Instead, she was a wild cranberry bush, and like this wiry evergreen shrub, she did not transplant well. She was of a Humptulips bog, and if she intended to nurture her passionate spirituality, she needed to fix her roots deep in Humptulips soil.

Now safely in her bed, Baie stopped thinking and looked upon Petr. She remembered his face, the one she saw in the doorway of last night's shack. She remembered the two of them walking to her sunrise farmhouse. She remembered her hands working on a meal, filling a large mixing bowl with flour, baking powder, sugar, a dash of her cranberry and vanilla bean infusion, shortening, milk, and eggs. She imagined dipping an old steel ladle into the mixture and pouring out one, two, then three, and finally four ladlefuls onto the hot-sizzle skillet. These hotcakes, made from a mother-blessed recipe, fried in Ruth Ann-blessed bear grease, and eaten with father-blessed cranberry syrup, were an intimation of heaven.

Baie also remembered laying the meal before Petr. He ate, hungry like a man who did not know abundance. She then remembered her own plate and heard her own words, the ones she spoke to him. "So what brings you here?"

"Don't know."

"Okay. So where'd you come from?"

"My daddy, his name's Bear. He's dead now."

"I'm so sorry. I grew up here. My dear Mother and dear Father passed away. They left me this place. My dear sisters, they're not my real sisters, I don't have any of those, but they're my dear sisters all the same, well, they're helping me run this place. We call it Wildsisters."

"Okay."

"So what about your dear Mother?"

"Don't know."

PLEASED

When Petr opened his eyes, what he saw pleased him. The fog-filtered sunlight brought out subtle highlights in Baie's cinnamon bear hair. He liked her lips. When she smiled at him, he liked her teeth, the way they were set up, the way they were bunched. He especially liked the river otter sparkle of her eyes.

Petr couldn't find words to say, so he became anxious. He recalled the sound of this woman's voice in the night and then later in the morning, but he couldn't recall her words. He mostly recalled that he had been tired and hungry. He then tried to make his eyes smile, the way Bear did, but the expression felt unnatural, and because it felt conky, he figured she must think she was getting the snotty end. His anxiety remained.

Then Petr heard her say, "Cougar got your tongue?" and he felt her burrow into the hickory shirt, the one he got from her, the one she said was her father's. "I'm glad you're here, but I don't . . . know. You, you probably have places to go. Why don't I take you across to Wildsisters? It's the little roadhouse I told you about. I'll show you around. Dear Shasta Lynn's been up for hours. She gets coffee going for the early traffic. Oh my goodness, look at the time! I'll bet it's way past lunch. I'll bet it's even past nap time."

Petr continued to be pleased. He liked the way she rose from the bed; the way she busied herself, straightening the curtain, folding a blouse, pulling a brush through her hair; the way she looked in the mirror and pursed her lips, one side in a smile, the other in a frown. He liked the way she said, "Guess it'll have to do. Now, I have a feeling…" and he liked when she turned toward him, he who was brought to her home, he who was in her bed ". . . that you will like Wildsisters. Just a feeling. I'll bet you could use some coffee. I know I could."

Petr was surprised when Baie approached, firmly grabbed his hand, pulled him from her bed, and led him through the house. They stopped in the kitchen, his backpack resting on a chair. Again he was surprised when she swung his backpack up into his arms. He needed to stay on his toes, and this pleased him, the way she was assertive, the way she was a jerk wire to his donkey whistle.

Once more Petr felt Baie grab his hand, this time pulling him outside the farmhouse. Here he tasted the salt astringent breeze, heard an incessant Doug-squirrel scold, saw the ragged towers of Sitka spruce. Here his memory went back to Bear's dented aluminum percolator, his child-hand pouring their coffee grounds slurry into two enameled tin cups. And here he recalled his child-sips, his child-dash outside their shack, his child-shouts at the fritillaries and anglewings dancing in the dappled sunlight, "GO-O-O-O-OD MORNING . . . SHI SHI BEACH. OLYP weather is hot and steamy with periods of coffee."

And out of these further memories came his must-have-been mother, the one who appeared only in dreams. He remembered cracked bleeding fingers encircling a chipped bone china cup. His tongue was bitter-scalded, then his throat. She seared all the way down.

GRAY-WEATHERED

ocean damp on moss,
corpse among the split firewood,
three years memory:
ancient Douglas-fir witness,
ancient Douglas-fir wisdom

Doug-fir barn siding,
red cedar shake roof shingles,

bigleaf maple door:
old native scout Sitka spruce,
old Humptulips Sitka spruce

GHOST BARN

BAIE'S JOURNAL

Entry 61

Transplanted French man
renovates the cow stalls
into some fruit bins.

Skilled Quinault woman
brings in red cedar baskets
of ripening fruit.

Strong Olympic child
deftly climbs from the fruit bins
into the rafters,
converses with some peeping,
ravenous baby swallows.

INSIDE WILDSISTERS

After Baie used her left hand to open Wildsisters' bigleaf maple door, and after she used her right hand to lead Petr into Wildsisters' great room, Petr's awareness crystallized like a many-faceted geode.

A pair of millwrights stood at the counter. They wore jeans, flannels, and work caps. Their jaw lines were soft. They were placing a to-go order.

Two others sat at a far corner table. They were making love across a single oversized cinnamon roll. They were buttery and sweet. They had their own wound-about-themselves reality.

Two more gathered about an infant. One was nursing. The other was drinking from a heavy mug, a vessel that had been fired to pound nails.

Beyond the people, a mural started behind the bar and continued around the dining room. The mural was black outlines with red fills, stylings handed down from Old Growth artists.

Studying the mural, Petr made out a child's face. He made out a few salmon spawning. And he felt a deep and pervasive wound.

Then Petr began to hear a diaphonous prayer, no, a gossamer song, or maybe a disturbing call; an echo of chick-raven chatter; an echo of otter chuckle swirling in the Humptulips; an echo of salmon bodies, spent and torn, dragging over gravel; an echo of a hawk moth whirring, no, Petr's ghost mother, the smell of mold spore swirling through falling cranberry leaves.

SPIRIT MAGGOT MUSES

Baie led Petr farther into Wildsisters. This time she softened her excitement. She thought it better that her gestures be less of an insistence and more a suggestion. She brought Petr to the one who was painting the mural. "Dear Shasta Lynn, do you remember Petr from last night?"

Unnerved, Shasta Lynn put down her brush and then her palette. She put them on a step leading upstairs. "Yass, yass, they got a hold of my hand. Can you feel them? I do; it's spirit maggots. Who does the paintin', eh. Not me; they do it. Know where they live? I do; live in the mountains. They hole up in the rocks mostly. Can you smell them about? I can. They're born when the white fungus sets in, when the spirit comes loose from the flesh, eh."

"Dear Shasta Lynn . . ." Baie said reaching out her free hand. Her fingers intertwined with the painter's. The three, Petr, Shasta Lynn, and Baie formed a triangle with Baie the vertex ". . . have you been painting all day?"

Shasta Lynn didn't answer. She gently rocked back and forth, a leaf in the breeze.

"Last night you never got out of the car, did you? You remember the roadkill and the prayers I said? You remember all the shooting? You stayed in the car and didn't get out until everyone went to bed. Am I right?"

Shasta Lynn remained silent. She continued to sway. She was a child's mitten caught on a branch pulled by muddy floodwaters.

"Okay, dear Shasta Lynn, I'll let you paint. I really like what you're doing. I feel a prophecy coming on, so you keep painting as long as you like."

BUT I DIGRESS, OH, HONEY MOUSE

Hey you, I'm up here in this Sitka spruce, and by the look of things, I'd wager you're intrigued by Wildsisters, you know, the whole berry-worshipping, women's commune sort of thing. I'd also lay down even money that you're all sexed up over the way Baie and Petr are coming together. *Oo, la, la* and all that, right?

But before we get back to that, and I promise you we will, don't forget that you and I have our own narrative tributaries to join. Don't forget that Dog Salmon Brother, Silver Salmon Sister, and the Salmon Village have become resigned to a gelatinous future. And don't forget that I found all that pretty depressing.

Luckily I'm not one to worship at the altar of Judas Thaddeus, the patron saint of lost causes, so my story continues when I decided to fly out of the Garden of Oceanic Delights. From there I caught a tailwind, a breeze so stiff that it propelled me into the Chehalis Wind Gap, shot me across Blue Slough, and blew me clean past the Chehalis–Wynoochee confluence. Then after banking a hard left, I headed straight into the Satsop drainage, and as it turned out, I spotted Coyote carrying Mole's salmon bone and scale wings. I really couldn't miss him, so I pulled up on a large erratic and called down, "What you got there, mate?"

"None of your business."

"Hey now, what about that little bit of business you pitched my way a while back?"

"That was then. Right now I got a new scheme. I figure these wings are my ticket to fame and fortune."

"Not so fast Top Dog. You ever flown before? Take it from one who's logged more flight time than you have dinner time, you don't want to start out solo."

"But I . . ."

"No buts about it, unless you're aiming to get into the resurrection game. What you need is a flight instructor. Why don't we go back to your place. I'll bet your wife's got something in that cooking pot of hers."

So that's what we did, and soon "Honey Mouse, we're home" became "Gee, Honey Mouse, you've outdone yourself!" which led to my buddy Coyote asking, "Have you heard the one about my scheming cousin Jackal?"

"No, can't say that I have," although I was pretty sure I had.

"Well, one time Jackal was really sick of being famous for giving dead people a helping hand. He didn't like being typecast, you know. He was also really sick of everyone going on about Salmon, about how wise and powerful Salmon was. So in an effort to expand his brand, he made a magical net. And you know what he did?"

"No, can't say that I do," although I was pretty sure I did.

"Well, my cousin Jackal took the net, caught a school of salmon, and threw that net and all its contents, sparkling scales and all, up into the night sky. He wanted to bring a bit more light to the darkness and break free from everyone calling him Death Dog. He wanted everyone to call him Sparkle Pup. And now you know how some of those stars got up there."

"Wow, that's really something. Who knew? And while you're at it, pass me some more of that beetle grub and salal berry cobbler."

"Sure. Thing is, I think I can outdo my cousin. I've got this plan to save the Salmon Village."

"Oh, how's that?" I asked. Now we were talking.

"The way I see it, I can take those salmon wings and fly up to Jackal's net."

"Go on."

"Then I'll cut a hole and let all those glittering salmon fall back to the Pacific. Yes-siree, with just flick of a knife, all those starry salmon will return to the rivers of their birth! Praise be to Salmon Redeemer!"

Although it was a pretty crazy idea, I thought it might have some entertainment value. What I didn't understand was Mole's role in all this. I mean, it was my understanding that she was the ever-supportive wife, but as my right eye followed Coyote's antics, my left eye watched her fade into the shadows.

CONVERSATION AT WILDSISTERS

After sending Shasta Lynn back to painting, Petr and Baie walked toward the center of Wildsisters and stopped by the two with the infant. The one not nursing said, "Hey, Aces, get off those stairs an' come over here. Shasta won't bite. She might turn you int'a a paintin' if y' hang 'round the stairs too long."

Petr didn't remember seeing the boy. He thought the boy had come from upstairs, but no sooner had the boy been scolded, than he dashed down the remaining stairs and between this table and over that chair. When he finally came to rest, the one not nursing started up again, "Jeez-us, get over here. You're disturbin' everyone in the place. I'm sorry, Baie, he's that age, all run, no talk. He's like some dragonfly high on Shasta's coffee. Sure as shit, isn't any use tryin' t' calm him down. You know what happens when y' pack powder too tight. Boo-oo-oo-oom!"

The boy, huffing, puffing, and all-the-while grinning, reined himself in and joined the circle around the infant. His long bangs hung in his eyes. Then, the one not nursing, the one Petr judged to be the boy's mother, said, "So, Baie, how 'bout makin' some plans."

Petr was aware that Baie looked to him. Her look made him uncomfortable. Apparently, he was now someone for whom plans must be made, a characterization that hung on him like a rumpled shirt thrown on the floor, careless, and then taken off the floor, nothing to be done but to be put back on.

"I don't know, dear Dori. What do you think?"

"First thing we need t' do is get these kids settled. Ses, you hand your baby t' Baie. Give yourself a break. There, that's better. Now, I'll put Aces right here on my lap. How's that?" The boy nestled into his mother's blue-flannel shirt. He grinned wider, his face a childish drawing.

Then Dori continued, "Now, Baie, y' know I'm no good at bein' polite, but here goes. My name's Dori, and this new momma's Sesily. Her baby girl's name's Freya. My boy here's Aces, because he's th' luckiest card I ever drew. I expect you're well acquainted with Miss Baie by now. Okay, so now it's your turn. Who are y'an' where'd y'come from? An' sure as shit, what were y' doin' last night in the middle of all that butt rot blowdown?"

"Name's Petr."

"We got that last night. Where'd y'come from?"

"My daddy's Bear Bauer, but he's gone. Died chopping wood, and I found him, and I buried him, and I left."

"That's a start, but it don' explain where y' come from last night. Come on now, y' got some explainin' t' do," and then softer, "if y' plan on stayin', that is."

"Well, you see . . ."

Petr felt Baie, one arm still cradling Freya, reintroduce her free fingers to his. "Take your time, dear Petr. You know I'm your friend, and we're all wildsisters. Even you, if you'd like."

"Well, uh, I got this pirate radio station. It's in my backpack, and, uh, I started up the Dosewallips. I started broadcasting. I do interviews. I met up with Sxwayo'klu. We talked a bit."

Dori interrupted, "Who's Swa . . . oh, good gawd-damn."

"Sorry, I talked with Basket Woman."

"You interviewed Basket Woman? The one in the kids' book? On the radio? Good-gawd!"

"It's okay, dear Petr." He felt Baie's fingers tighten. "Tell us more."

"Well, I went over Anderson Pass. I met Bernard Huelsdonk."

Again Dori interrupted, "Y' don't say? I know 'bout him. Suppose y' interviewed him, too?"

"No, we just talked on the trail. Couple of times."

"Heard he's long dead, but he ain't in no kids' book. So go on."

"Well, okay, then I came down the Quinault. I was heading for Shi Shi Beach, I guess. I don't know. That's where I grew up. But some weird stuff happened, and I turned south instead, down the Humptulips."

Dori interrupted a third time. "Weird stuff, y' say?"

"Yeah, weird stuff, well, uh, as I was saying, I turned south, and I met this guy. We took to walking together. He said his name was John Tornow. He had a dog. I think he called him Cougar."

"Ah, come on, everybody knows 'bout John Tornow. He's been dead goin' on seventy years. We can take a drive an' visit his grave tomorrow, if y' like. Why, Shasta over there makes all kind o' noise 'bout ol' John Tornow, an' me an' Ruthie's been talkin' 'bout him, isn't that right, Baie? You expect me t' believe y' been talkin' t' John Tornow? You're crazy as the one paintin' over there. Hey, Shasta, we found y' someone who talks with all your 'maginary friends. Y' two can have a regular seance!"

Petr felt Baie release his hand. She used it to shift Freya's sleeping weight. "Don't mind dear Dori. She doesn't talk to spirits, but she does talk to her tools. Don't you, dear Dori?"

"Sure as shit do. But they sure as shit don't talk back."

"So go on, dear Petr. Dear Dori may not understand, but she's got all our backs. And you're a wildsister, too. Like I said, if you want."

"Okay, well, John, he was pretty upset. He said his mom and sister, and, oh yeah, his two nephews, John and William, were dead."

"Jeez-us I. G. an' A. Christ."

Aces, bored by all the adult talk, hopped off his mother's lap, dashed through Wildsisters, and disappeared out the door.

"Now, dear Dori," Baie said, "Wildsisters isn't a courtroom, right? We certainly wouldn't want that."

"No, surely not. I'm no fan o' no courtrooms. An' just for th' record, I'm no fan o' good-for-nothin' men neither. But you're right. It's not like I got room t' judge. There's been a baby born an' a kidnappin'. There's been racin' off t' th' oxbow. There's been a shack full o' dead bodies, an' I'll tell y' one thing, your boyfriend makes 'bout as much sense as anything 'round here. Hell . . ." and Dori turned from Baie to Petr, "so, tell us 'bout your momma. Mine was a hellcat. Tore up more men than, well, than . . . let's just say she was so busy tearin' up men she never got 'round t' me."

"I didn't exactly know her."

"Not surprised. Maybe Baie's got somethin' for you. I sure don't, but I've had 'bout 'nough o' this talkin', an' I need t' be doin'. Baie, I'll bet you an' Ses can take care o' this place, an' I can get out in th' bog an' make some progress."

TONIGHT'S MENU

WildsisterS

*sanctified and sainted
for you who love women*

hominy crumb salmon with
nettle shoot-cran ragout

coolest crop with
pickled cran salads

métis fries with
antique apple-cran dressing

razor clam cakes with
wild 'shroom-cran reduction

MORE CONVERSATION AT WILDSISTERS

After the kitchen closed, Wildsisters received new patrons. The two were clad in biker leathers. Skin tanned, hair wind-tangled and gray-streaked, their boots resounded upon the bastard-sawn Doug-fir floor. They pulled up at the counter, ordered coffee, and then one, speaking words silty as the Humptulips floodplain, said to the other, "Heard what come off in th' woods?"

"Nah."

Petr listened.

Baie listened. She put her hand on Petr's shoulder.

Sesily listened. She turned in her chair, putting her back between Freya and the two at the counter.

"Found bodies up th' Humptulips. Two dudes an' a chick."

"Huh."

"Brush pick'r found a just-burned shack, and when the sheriffs come in, they found the bodies. They weren't so charred they couldn't tell they was fresh-killed. Six bullets."

"Huh."

"Shootin' from th' outside. Some kind o' ambush. Dudes're brothers. Chick's their sis."

Shasta Lynn brought the coffees.

The knowledgeable one continued. "Heard 'bout th' missin' kid?"

"Nah."

"Got a radio transmitter. Been hidin' out. Been broadcastin', too. Kid's a suspect."

"Huh. Finish these outside."

"Sure."

OUT IN THE CRANBERRIES

Baie was upset by what the patrons said. She thought Petr also must be upset. As she thought some more, she prayed to both the Christian and Cranberry God. Cranberry God? She smiled. She prayed that Wildsisters would continue to be a part of God's plan.

With her upset fading, Baie thought to do the same for Petr. To this end she devised a distraction, one that explored her passion. She thought to take Petr into her cranberry garden of earthly delights and play with him. She thought it delicious.

"So, dear Petr, dear Shasta Lynn's called it a night, and dear Sesily and dear Freya have gone to bed. That means just one thing, that it's time to pick moon berries."

Baie gazed deeply into Petr's slow-blinking eyes. His irises were wet sphagnum brown. His pupils were new moon black. She was drawn to his eyes the same way she was drawn to peat bogs, each step toward the central open expanse more precarious. Step, her bare feet submerged but supported. Step, her bare body not fallen through. Step, her bare soul plunged in mushroom ink, shadowless, only the fairies would know.

Baie pointed across Wildsisters' empty dining room. "Look out that window, dear Petr. There's no fog, and the moon, see, it's full. My dear mother used to tell me, 'Baie, the berries, they are powerful.' And my dear father used to say, 'Baie, tonight you pick *par la grâce de Dieu*.'"

As Baie led Petr out into the moonlight and down toward the cranberry bog, a raven quorked. She watched it move among the Sitka spruce and then pull up on a nearby branch. She judged it to be a young raven, one with no place to go; maybe its parents had roosted in the same tree, and now it was chattering to itself in the way young ravens often do, a good way to end the day.

When the two reached the bog, Dori, who had been picking since before dinner, greeted them. "So I see y' got some sense. Here y'are, stopped talkin' and gettin' t' doin'."

"Yes, dear Dori, tonight we'll pick moon berries. Hail berries full of grace, the Lord is with thee. Blessed are thou among bushes. Blessed is the fruit of thy flowers, cranberry. Holy berries, children of Moon, pray for us wildsisters, now and at the hour of our grace. Amen."

"Well, that sure makes a hell o' a lot o' difference. Now grab a basket an' get to it."

Baie did as Dori said. She grabbed two baskets and then handed one to Petr. She was pleased to see him wade directly in among the bushes. At first his picking was clumsy. It was not at all skilled. It was not fluid. But over time he fell into a rhythm, one berry and then another and then another.

In contrast, Dori's picking was mechanical, efficient. Her thumbnail sliced each berry free from its stem. She was a reaper, delivering the burden to board, bringing the harvest to market.

And then there was Baie. Unlike Dori, her picking was gentle, compassionate. Her fingertips rolled each berry free from its stem. She was a midwife, helping these berries separate from one world into the next. As she worked, Baie recited a lyric written by Saint Thérèse de Lisieux, her patron saint.

> *En toi, j'ai canneberges délicieuses,*
> *Les libellules gracieuses,*
> *La forêt viege aux fleurs mystérieuses.*
> *J'ai les londs petits enfants,*
> *Leurs chants.*

Then she recited it again, this time in English, this time for dear Petr.

> In you I have delicious cranberries,
> The graceful dragonflies,
> The old forest with mysterious flowers.
> I have great little children,
> Their songs.

BAIE'S VOICE

Petr, out in the bog, beneath the outsized moon, among the ready, hard, crimson berries, felt Baie's voice.

Her resonance was like the Kushtakas, a pool rippling to him, attractive, an inviting question.

And her resonance was like Wildsisters, a wave swelling around him, pleasurable, a welcome promise.

But her resonance was nothing like his mother, a chasm frozen inside him, gagged, a blank page in a bottle.

BOOK SIXTEEN

DREAMT AWAKE

DREAMT AWAKE

BAIE'S JOURNAL

Entry 62

I dreamt awake one, two,
three and four, five and six
spirit-barren explosions.
One, two, and three
bodies broken for
no one, limp, forgotten.

I dreamt awake a man.
He followed me home.
We went upstairs.
We went deeply into
my mother-quilted bed.
He lingered under
the spruce sentinels,
the watchful moon.
He lingered while
Wildsisters' walls took
dear Dori's nails, while
dear Shasta Lynn simmered

boletus chowder, while
dear Ruth Ann vanished in
the fog that rolled through like
sunrise woodsmoke.

I dreamt awake children,
skittishly sitting on
our red cedar stumps,
furtively peering from
the salmonberry stands.
I heard one talking,
its tongue an angel wing.

THE CHILDREN WE SAW

BAIE'S JOURNAL

Entry 63

This morning
I asked
—Did you see
the children?

He answered
—Uh huh.

Again I asked
—Are they yours?

Again he answered
—No.

I pointed out
the storage bins
—I, ah, we really
appreciate your help.
We certainly do.
Let's pick berries, and
after they are stored,
we'll take a break.

After berry picking,
we entered the farmhouse.
Here I found ripe lemons,
a mini-chef's knife, and
our use-worn juicer.
I halved the tart lemons,
firmly turning them against
the swirl-fluted glass.
The sharp liquid ran, and
when only rind remained,
I poured the juice into
a tall tumbler with
sweet, sweet sugar and
clear, cold well-water.
With a long-handled spoon,
I stiffly stirred and
generously iced.

Then I took the cup, and
when I had given thanks,
I gave it to dear Petr
saying these words
—Blessed are the fruits,
their flesh will nourish.

Petr found a napkin.
He slowly tore
one piece, unique, from
another and then joined
one piece, singular, to
another.

And I continued
—Blessed are the children,
their souls will be nurtured.

Petr drank, his eyes closed.
His lips accepted the sweet.
His lips accepted the sour.

Has Petr dreamt awake?
I think so because
next he softly said
—They . . .
those kids . . .
they're Sxwayo'klu's.

OURS

BAIE'S JOURNAL

Entry 64

Rough
with
berry picking,
rough

with
constant living,
our fingers
slipped
between.
Mine were
small,
strong:
a fetus.
His were
round,
cleaving:
a womb.

WHITE OTTER AND THE STARFLOWER

BAIE'S JOURNAL

Entry 65

I said
—Let's take a walk.

And we walked into
a diaphanous fog.
We walked beneath
the descending sprays of
a buttressed red cedar.
We walked onto
the west bank trail
leading north along
the Humptulips.

Under a red cedar shrine,
four-and-twenty along
the bank, a cathedral,
I softly sang this prayer of
Saint Thérèse de Lisieux.
—*Par mon amour je veux te réjouir.*
Tu le sais bien, à toi seul je veux plaire.
Daigne exaucer mon plus ardent désir.
Pour te charmer et consoler ton coeur,
Mais en amour change toutes mes oeuvres.

Then again, this time in
English, I sang for
dear Petr.
—By my love I want to make you happy.
You know it, I want to please you alone.
Deign to grant my most ardent desire.
To charm you and console your heart,
But in love change all my works.

Here earth tongues sprang from
damp, crumbling logs.
Blood-spattered beard-festooned
bigleaf maple branches.
A ripe boletus looked
every bit a child's stool.

Petr ducked under
a downed Doug-fir and
helped me after.
He then leaped to
the loose outwash of
an exposed gravel bar.
I dutifully followed,

a salmonberry sprig in
my tangled hair.

Downstream stood
a congregation of
four river otters:
three pinedrops brown,
one ghost plant white

The three moved into
the stream and slipped beneath.
The one, a spirit otter,
caught Petr's eye and
curiously lingered.
Then it too moved into
the stream and was no more.
In this otter's place
grew a very delicate,
quite-blessed starflower.

Right there and then
I reverently knelt and
blessed this *fée vert,*
this green fairy, with
Saint Thérèse's words.
—*Jeter des Fleurs, Jésus, voilà mon arme*
Lorsque je veux lutter pour sauver les pécheurs.
La victorie est à moi . . . toujours je te désarme
Avec mes fleurs!!!

And once more, again in
English, I recited for
dear Petr.
—Throwing Flowers, Jesus, that's my weapon

when I want to fight to save sinners.
The victory is mine . . . I always disarm you
with my flowers!!!

Then I dug,
worked loose the soil, and
lovingly lifted
the tuberous root.
I recalled the time when
you, dear Mother, said
—This starflower dreams awake.
If faithfully prayed over,
the starflower opens.
If gracefully transplanted,
the starflower offers
blessed conception.

So I returned to you,
dear Petr, my love, and
as we started our way back,
I felt you weightless.
I felt you float beside.
Then you crossed into
my dreaming, and
we crossed into
the spirit otter's eye.

EXCUSE ME, WHITE OTTER WANTS TO TRY ON MR. ELIOT'S WARDROBE

Let's go Raven, you and I,
under a Pacific blood-red sky

like some ghostly broadcast that has our
ear.
Let's go, along detritus-strewn beaches,
the cormorant speeches
of strangulation by plastic beverage rings
and cancerous tumors, among other things:
a call that sounds like a stifled plea
of fateful prophecy
to open your ears to all that's denied.
Oh, please, beg the question, "Why us, dear?"
Let us listen and shed a tear.

In the swell the gray whales dive amused,
singing of St. Thérèse de Lisieux.

The red tide that winds itself among the forest kelp,
the red bloom that winds itself through the forest kelp,
catches starlight in the moon of its eye,
pauses spellbound by a chance eclipse,
releases from its mouth a mist lost in the fog,
turns into the current, drops into a weightless dive,
and feeling buoyed by the depths below,
closes the circle once begun, and feels alive.

And now I require faith
for the red bloom that's carried by the stream,
passing unseen among the forest kelp;
I require faith, I require faith
to conjure a prayer to dream the prayers that you dream;
I require faith to forget and play dumb
and faith for every word and spasm of the lips
that releases the question from my tongue;
faith for me and faith for Raven,
and faith now for every little destruction

and for every little construction and instruction,
offering a secure and safe haven.

In the swell the gray whales dive amused,
singing of St. Thérèse de Lisieux.

But I worry they will not sing for me.

I can hear them sound my soul
rolling the crests of the deep Pacific swell
delicately balanced between Heaven and Hell.

Raven, we are living on this knife's edge
among the chaos left by the stormy surge
'til the earthquake shakes us, and we're purged.

Kyrie eleison.
Christe eleison.
Kyrie eleison.
Je ne suis plus un créature
de la terre
or the air.
I am a creature
de la mer.

PLANTING FLOWERS

BAIE'S JOURNAL

Entry 66

We stepped off
the Humptulips' trail,

walked into
Wildsisters' yard, and
stopped by
an old hemlock stump.
From its crumbled wreck
sprouted a leggy bush,
a red huckleberry.
Again I knelt and
again I burrowed,
parting the soil,
fragrant, loamy,
placing the starflower,
its healthy tuber
gently down.
Only then
did I recite
these words of
my patron, my sweet
St. Thérèse de Lisieux.
—*Jeter des Fleurs, c'est t'offrir en prémices*
Les plus légers soupirs, les plus douleurs.
Mes peines et mes joies, mes petits sacrifices
Voilà mes fleurs!

And as has become
my steadfast practice,
again I translated for
my dear Petr.
—Throwing Flowers is giving yourself first fruits,
the slightest sighs, the least sorrows,
my pains and my joys, my little sacrifices.
Here are my flowers!

AMPHIBIOS

BAIE'S JOURNAL

Entry 67

time to welcome him
into my womb, cold water,
splash zone waterfall

A GOOD TIME

BAIE'S JOURNAL

Entry 68

Later that evening,
dear Dori greeted us at
Wildsisters' door.
—Hey y' two,
'bout time y' showed.
Berries been stowed.
Aces been tucked in.
Let's get workin' on
havin' a good time!

I watched dear Petr
shift his shoulders,
toe the floorboards in
an anxious circle, and
then erase his figure.
I thought he might bolt
our Wildsisters,

but he did not flee;
he did not vanish;
instead he said
—My backpack,
we left it in
the farmhouse, right?

I nodded, shy.

—Okay then,
I'll be right back.

I nodded again
reassured, and
then dear Petr left.

I turned my attention to
Wildsisters, busy,
the kitchen closed, yet
still a crowded house.
Musicians stood near
the stairway under
dear Shasta Lynn's swirl of
children's faces and
salmon spawning.
One musician readied
her red cedar drum box.
She began slowly,
a broken triadic dance.
I felt the flow of
the muddy Humptulips.
The other readied
her moist-muscle voice box.
She joined harmonically,

an old-growth tremolo scat.
I felt the laugh of
a lake-bound loon.

Then dear Petr
tapped my elbow and
gently led me to
a vacant table.
Here we sat, and
here dear Petr
married the parts of
his transmitter and
broadcast the sounds of
our Wildsisters.

Tell me, you, whom my shy soul adores,
where you catch our planet's lofty draft
proceeding directly to the sun.
Why should I be marooned behind with
only dreams of common horizon?

I'm a stand of flow'ring bleeding heart,
my petaled soul bloomed for you alone,
my ripened soul swelled in confession.
Foolishly I live in dank shadows
and await the caress from your sun.

Your lips are bold blooming springbeauty,
twin petals on a far rocky crag
which christens in sun while white ice flees
from meadow satiated with paintbrush
and suffused with blushing fawn lily.

Whither have you hastened my beloved
born again in sun-fire to my eye,
converted in aether to my ear?
Whither have you vanished my beloved?
Transfigured to starlight. Gone to tears.

And when the music ceased,
the wildsisters gone,
dear Petr and I,
co-conspirators two,
went reeling ripe among
our swelling berries.
The ocean roared my ears.
The clouds sailed my eyes.
My breath upwelled,
my flesh a riptide.
I howled, dear Petr.
I stretched, torn open.
I gripped cranberry wood.
The hard growth cut my soles.

Then from between
the pitch-sweet trees, from out
the cane-tangled thickets,
the children came down,
fay-fire eyes aglow,
night-dew bodies wet.
They came and enveloped us.
We were wrapped in
ocean kelp and lady fern:
our child swaddled green,
our child swaddled deep.

Kyrie eleison.
Christe eleison.
Kyrie eleison.
Tout
est perdre.
Tout
est retrouver.
Now and
here,
wildsisters.

BOOK SEVENTEEN

CAIN'T JUS' HAVE TH' GOOD

THE PORNSTAR VERSUS
THE BUCKINGHAM PALACE GUARD

My goodness, you've got to admit that was something. All that ripe fruit. All those desperate berries. Gripping onto that wood. Riptides of flesh. Mmm, mmm! the power of suggestion.

Which leads me to wonder about the difference between tourism and voyeurism. I mean, we have been keeping a wandering and prying eye on Petr and Baie, so I wonder if you and I are sightseers or peeping toms. For example, you and I watching Petr ecstatically transmit or Baie fervently pray is something like you and I watching the Buckingham Palace Guard dutifully change—tourism. But you and I watching Petr and Baie get it on among the swelling berries under the manic moon is an awful lot like you and I watching a pornstar performing, well, you know—voyeurism. OR is it less about what we're watching and more about what we're feeling? For example, you and I masturbating to Petr assembling his transmitter or Baie writing a journal entry is disturbingly like you and I masturbating to the changing of the Buckingham Palace Guard—again, voyeurism.

But let's just stop counting the number of fleas that can dance on the split hair of a mountain beaver. Fact is we here on the Olympic Peninsula only want to know if all this excitement does any harm, and since I'm a bird-brained fictional character, no harm, no foul.

So I'll just stop knocking my beak, and let's get back to taking a corvid's-eye view of all that gripping and stretching.

THE CHILD-OTTER'S EGG

Petr awoke with Baie spooned against his hip and shoulder. He felt Baie's last night's sex upon him. He felt her damp morning saturating his chest and belly. He felt her citrus, her sweet onion, and just a hint of her green olive.

He remembered Baie's ear lobe between his teeth, stiff yet pliant, sweet like Sitka spruce gum, salty like a razor clam foot, sinewy like venison-stewed blacktail tendon.

He remembered Baie's breath within him, unfurling his sex, swelling his spirit, teasing like an insistent hawk moth, resonating like gray whale song, murmuring like Kushtaka whispers.

Then Petr felt watched, so he opened his eyes and saw the same children Baie and he had seen the previous day and later that night. These children wore garlands of maidenhair fern woven loosely in their hair as they crept cautiously in from the trees.

But one of these children was different. The different one was a white otter, but not the white otter Baie and Petr had seen before. This one was smaller, more like the other children, a child-otter. Petr imagined the child-otter draw out a brown egg of densely packed maidenhair fern rhizome and present it as an offering. This child-otter then tipped open its forepaws and set the egg to roll, the egg slowly spinning toward Petr, his naked body lying among the cranberries, Baie's naked body still sleeping tightly against him. The egg rolled over Petr's hip and came to rest where his butt kissed Baie's belly. Then the egg burrowed, and the egg was enveloped. And when the egg was taken within, the fog burned away, and the children burned away, leaving individual Sitka spruce and red cedar tops etched against a vivid cerulean sky.

Petr felt Baie stir, and in her half-sleep she said, "Umm, this is . . . oo oo oo . . . delicious. You're warm. I want to roll with you in the bog, dear Petr, and I . . . I'm a forest. I'm a kelp forest. I'm a green, ripe, fertile kelp forest of God."

UNWINDING THE CORD

ey, Baie, what're y' doin' down here? Jeez-us, grabbin' a stranger out o' the woods an' lettin' him have his way. What would your dear departed mother an' father say? My weasel crazy mother would've said, 'Dori, y' nasty little whore! I ain't feedin' y' no more. Now, get out, an' don't let th' door hit y' on th' ass!'

Then Petr heard Dori soften, "But okay, y' two get untangled an' get inside. Shasta's got the coffee goin'. Somebody's goin' t' drive in here soon, an' sure as shit, they'd get an eyeful. We already got a reputation 'round here. We don't need t' give anybody more t' chew on."

When Petr tried to move to satisfy Dori, he discovered that Baie and he were wound up in his microphone cord, the microphone at their heads and the transmitter at their feet.

"If y' two aren't the sorriest . . . whose idea was all this wire? I'm all for if it feels good, do it, but whose bright idea was . . . I mean, Baie, this wasn't your idea, was it? Boy, if this was your idea! This ain't no way t' show a girl a good time, 'specially on the first . . . Jeez-us I. O. U. Christ!"

"Don't be so hard on him, dear Dori. We don't know how all this happened. One minute dear Petr and I are out talking in the cranberries, and the next thing it's morning, and you're yelling like your dear mother."

Petr could see Dori clench her teeth, and then he heard her unplug the microphone cord from the transmitter. This action allowed the two to roll out into the cranberries, stand, run for the farmhouse, dash through the kitchen, fly up the stairs, and disappear into Baie's parents' bedroom.

Once there Petr watched Baie go through her father's outsized hickory shirts and jeans. From these she chose for herself an outfit, slipping it on and rolling up the legs and sleeves. Next she chose for Petr an outfit from her mother's work shirts and pants. Petr found that they fit him surprisingly well, only the pant legs a bit short.

Now fully clothed, Petr felt Baie grab his hand and heartily intertwine her fingers with his, an action that allowed Baie to sweep Petr out of the bedroom, down the farmhouse stairs, through the kitchen, past the cranberry bog, and into the roadhouse, the one that she owned, the one known as Wildsisters.

THE GRASS CREEK BLACKBERRIES

Once inside Wildsisters, Baie immediately became aware that someone had placed four tin cans filled with blackberries on a center table. Baie thought these berries might be dried clots of blood fallen from the crucified Jesus. She wondered who had collected such remarkable berries, was it Mary Magdalene, or was it Mother Mary, the one who bore the child who died and then rose in a few days' time forever.

She received her answer when Sesily, who sat nursing Freya, spoke up. "I took a walk to Grass Creek this morning. A man was selling oysters in potato sacks out of the back of his pickup. He also had these berries. I couldn't carry Freya and the oysters, but I could carry the berries. He put them in an old grocery sack, and I carried Freya and the berries back."

"Why, thank you, dear Sesily. They will go so well with dear Shasta Lynn's coffee, don't you think?"

Baie watched as Petr plucked a berry from its container, popped it into his mouth, and crushed it with his teeth. She felt him overwhelmed by tart, and out of that emotion, and out of that goodness, Baie spoke again, this time her words a poem, this time her words an epithalamion.

> Good morning Aces and Freya,
> your eyes are all aglow.
> Your cheeks like berries
> or red, ripe cherries,
> and like a ring they're born
> in circles of promise.
>
> Good morning Shasta Lynn,
> your coffee smells so good.
> It opens our eyes
> as the darkness dies,
> and like a ring it's poured
> in circles of promise.

Good morning child-otter,
you came to us this morn'.
Forests of kelp will
harmonize ourselves,
and like a ring they thrive
in circles of promise.

Good morning dear Petr,
I give myself to you.
You a wildsister,
now and forever,
and like a ring we're pledged
in circles of . . .

"Jeez-us, Baie!" Dori exclaimed, twisting her lip and squinting her eyes, "I guess y' think you an' Petr are gettin' married, huh? And I don't suppose y' gave him a chance t' say no. Judgin' from th' way he's standin' there with his mouth open, that's a good thing. Now, let's get down t' these berries an' coffee before th' one gets moldy an' th' other gets cold."

Assisted by the other wildsisters, Baie went about piling the berries into small china bowls, each uniquely chipped, each of various design. Then she poured thick cream from a glass bottle. "Doesn't this cream come from the dear Toenniessen family up the Wishkah?" Baie said as she uncapped the bottle.

"Sure does," Sesily returned, dipping her finger in the sweet liquid and painting the cream on Freya's eagerly thrusting tongue. "They're having trouble staying in business. They got a lot of hoops to jump through. You know, with all the licenses and paperwork."

"Yass, yass, evil, the devil's makin' them sign their name in blood, eh," Shasta Lynn broke in. The coffee she poured splashed out of a wash-worn mug onto the table.

"Oh, I like them, dear Shasta Lynn. I do. I don't think the devil would ever come near their dear cows. I'm sure we could taste it in their milk."

"Devil's not in the milk; devil's in them papers. John Tornow knows. He knows somethin's up, eh. Somebody's not keepin' the bargain, and the devil will come a callin'."

"Now calm the hell down, Shasta," Dori jumped. "I say less yappin' an' more eatin'. These berries an' cream are so good they ought t' keep even you quiet."

With that, Baie served Petr last. She smiled to see him scoop up the berries with the cream, and when the bowl was empty, she heard him ask, "So, maybe I can stay a bit?"

Baie's smile moved from her mouth to her eyes, "Silly Petr."

"Well, that settles it," Dori said clapping her hands on her thighs, standing up, and looking to all the world bored. "Sure don't need no man 'round here tellin' us what t' do," and off she went, leaving Wildsisters in her wake.

"Don't mind her," Sesily said. "See, Freya's asleep. I think I'll put her down and clear these dishes."

"Dear Sesily, you don't mind if I take dear Petr out to pick cranberries?"

"No, not at all. Once Freya's down, I only have these bowls, those spoons, and a few mugs to wash. You go ahead. Our cranberries don't pick themselves."

PICKING UP ON THE CURRENT

As Petr and Baie picked, one basket became two and two baskets became three until the morning became afternoon. Then the two took a break.

Shasta Lynn had salmon cake sandwiches on the menu. The bread was a sourdough of her own devising, new Olympic yeasts falling into her mother culture, all coming together into individual sourdough barm-cakes, each cake the foundation and the roof for a sandwich. The salmon was Quinault River blueback delivered from an ice chest stowed in the back of a primer-spotted '66 Caprice wagon. The side dish was home-raised cabbage shredded into a slaw and pickled in Shasta Lynn's signature cranberry vinaigrette.

Well satisfied, Petr and Baie returned to picking, and as the afternoon became evening, Petr fell into a rhythm, his fingers moving among the little leaves and twigs. He felt at home filling one basket, then another, followed by one more, and just when the Sitka spruce and red cedar stretched their shadows into the cranberry bog, he paused, and in his stopping, he fell in love with Baie: her face touched by the tangerine sunset, the breeze lifting a wisp of her hair, holding it just so, and laying it softly down on her peat-dusted cheek.

Petr then turned his head, and from this new vantage, he fell in love with the children, the ones who had been with the child-otter that morning, the same ones who had been with Sxwayo'klu up in the Olympics. Some had settled low in the darkening places. Others were roosted high in the sunset-gilded greenery.

Petr and Baie continued picking in this tableau until Wildsisters emptied of its customers. That's when Baie brought her basket to Petr and lifted her mouth, placing her soft, moist, cool lips on his. He drank in her slow, long kiss and then watched her walk away to the farmhouse, leaving him among the cranberries.

Petr decided not to follow. Alone, he retrieved his broadcasting equipment and walked in a different direction, away from the farmhouse, away from Baie, and down to the Humptulips River. Then he turned north and walked a ways up the trail until he came to a red cedar stump, venerable, companioned by living red cedars, the association constituting a red cedar grove, a family. Here he stopped, and here he reconstructed his charger, transmitter, and antenna. Here he set to broadcasting, picking up on what the current brought his way.

HUGH SUDDERTH

Welcome back. You are tuned to HOO HOO FM, voice of all you water pups who know we must, indeed, all sprint together or, most assuredly, we shall sprint separately. And if you don't know that sprint is water pup for shittin', then now you do.

"Today we have a very special guest. He was born right here near the Humptulips River on New Year's Day 1890. Welcome Hugh Sudderth. It's a pleasure to finally meet you."

"Uh, hello."

"Never mind this thing I'm talking at. It's called a microphone. Act like it's not here. Just talk to me."

"Oh, okay."

"So tell me about the homestead you were raised on. What was that like?"

"Well, Daddy said he filed on the claim sometime in 1885. That's before I was born. He built a log cabin, two rooms downstairs with a hallway in between and two rooms upstairs. Some call that a dog trot."

"What sort of improvements did your daddy make?"

"He dug a well. It was forty-four foot deep. Momma used to send me out to haul up water. I didn't like lookin' down into that thing, so I didn't."

"What else?"

"Oh, we had chickens. And Daddy planted a considerable number of fruit trees. And berries, too."

"So your homestead was successful?"

"We got by 'cause everybody pitched in any ways we could."

"For example?"

"Well, Daddy, and later us boys, picked up loggin' jobs. Daddy also had a haulin' business bringin' wagon loads from Hoquiam and New London up here to Axford and further up north to Humptulips. We had a horse and a wagon. There was always somethin' to haul in or out."

"I hear your daddy had a war record."

"Yeah, Civil War."

"What can you tell us about that."

"He told us he signed up in South Carolina when he was sixteen. That's a year younger than me right now. He fired cannons in Longstreet's Division."

"Was he in any famous battles?"

"Whole bunch. He said he fired the first cannon at Lookout Mountain, and he was with Lee at Appomattox."

"Was he ever wounded?"

"Daddy always said he had an angel watchin' over him 'cause his only trouble was bad feet. He said all the cold and the marchin' made it so he needed those angel's wings to get around. He never complained much, though. Said he got used to marchin' no matter what."

"Your daddy sounds pretty hard-nose."

"Yeah, you could say he was a regular saddle blanket."

"But what about your momma. What can you tell us about her?"

"Well, you know, she had it rough. She had eight babies. The first one died in Olympia. She told me she carried that baby from Texas to Oklahoma to California to Seattle to Olympia. After all that, the baby died."

"It must have been terrible."

"Yeah, but she kept on goin'. She had my older sister Eoline and then my older brother James. He went by Bon. He and the rest was born in the Axford cabin. Then come me, and then there was the twins Earl and Pearl. Later come William and Ernest."

"Goodness."

"She wasn't hard-nose like Daddy, but she was hard-nose all the same. She used to say, 'Hugh, y' got t' take th' good with th' bad. Y' cain't jus' have th' good. T' have some good, y' got t' take th' bad'."

"No truer words've been said."

"Take my brother, Earl. When he was three, Daddy sent Bon and me out to cut some old vine maple. He didn't like where it was at. Now, vine maples ain't big like hemlocks and firs, but the old ones, well, they get so you cain't put your hands around them. So Bon puts Earl up on our fence to watch, and then we commence to cuttin'."

"This doesn't end well for Earl, does it?"

"No, it don't. You see, vine maples grow twisty, so you cain't always tell how they'll fall. This is true of any tree, but 'specially for old vine maples. Well, Bon and me were workin' a whipsaw, maybe more saw than we needed, but hey, we wanted to be real timber beasts, and when that trunk snapped, it twisted and bounced off another tree and fell right on top of Earl. Squashed my little brother. Squashed him dead. Didn't stand a chance."

"I don't know what to say. It couldn't have been easy to tell your momma."

"No, no it wasn't."

"What did she say?"

"Nothin' much. Cain't jus' have th' good."

"I guess not. And then, of course, there's your story."

"Oh, I caused Momma considerable heartache. Not that she'd ever show."

"I see your gravestone says you drowned. How'd that come about?"

"Thought you might get around to that."

"Well, it is why you're here."

"Suppose so. Well, like I said, we all pitched in any way we could, and I got this job blastin' on a neighbor's stump farm."

"Our listeners might be interested in finding out exactly what a stump farm is."

"Well, a stump farm is when a timber company logs off some stumpage and don't want to wait for the timber to grow back. You see, once the cuttin's done and they got their money, they sell the land for cheap, usually to somebody who thinks farmin's easier than loggin'. That's a stump farm. Some call it a stump ranch."

"But how do you figure in on this particular stump farm?"

"So my job was to help the stump farmer remove the stumps, and as you can imagine, old-growth stumps is a bitch. We often joke that dynamite's too good for these barber chairs. So as I was a sayin', we gopher holed a load of stumpin' powder under a bunch of stumps. On the last one I set a short spitter of a fuse and didn't catch enough cover 'cause I got so stove up I couldn't tell up from down."

"That's some hard luck, a chippy trick I'd say, but obviously the shot didn't kill you."

"No, not the shot. What happened was I wasn't so hurt that I couldn't walk home, but it was gettin' dark, and I lost my way a bit, and I stumbled into some slough. My head was too addled to get my way out. I struggled somethin' fierce, but in the end I drowned."

"That's some hard rub."

"Yeah, it's grieved me all this time, all the heartache I caused Momma. Like she said, 'You cain't jus' have th' good'."

COPS'RE COMIN'

Broadcasting from the red cedar stump next to the Humptulips, Petr saw the glare of headlights. He heard the crunch of wheels followed by the opening of a car door. He was close enough to recognize Ruth Ann's voice. She was shouting, "Hey now, cops're on th' way! We need t' get up an' movin!'"

Petr, still holding the microphone, froze in place. He thought that now wasn't the time to break cover. It wasn't the time to show his hand.

But it was time to be attentive, so he saw and smelled and felt and tasted and listened, and from his listening, Petr's ears brought him a muffled buzz. Then from out of this fizzle, he heard Ruth Ann again, "Cops're comin' all right! They got a posse out t' find who killed Misty an' her bunch up th' ox-bow! Somebody put two an' two together an' come up with Petr. We best flush'm out, so he can skedaddle!"

And that's when the earthquake came. Something broke loose out in the Pacific. Something rerumpled what someone called Olympia. Something dreamed awake what Baie called Wildsisters.

BUT I DIGRESS, WHERE COYOTE LEARNS TO BE ALBATROSS

So how about that earthquake? Fact is we here on the Olympic Peninsula don't bother much with the Rapture or worry about Jesus' Second Coming or even agonize over the Apocalypse, but we do concern ourselves with the Pacific Ring of Fire and especially with the Cascadia Subduction Zone. We truly do. And we also think a lot about a bigger-than-life earthquake-driven tsunami. Kind of puts the cata back in cataclysm, doesn't it? You know, the big flood, the colossal cleansing, the time when Gus and Barbara shouted out, "Holy shit, Babs, who drove the freight train right through the kitchen?" "Don't know, Gus, but felt like someone cut the elevator cord." "Hot damn, I think I should've listened to that voice in my head and bought us that pleasure barge!"

Given all that, maybe you thought I'd forget about my own story and just turn all this over to Baie's journal. But have no fear, I haven't forgotten. No sir, I think it's time for Coyote and me to finish our business, and not only that, it's also time to get back to that cataclysm story I started when I said, "And He rested from all the gambling and decided to cash in His luck, collect the story whose cataclysm He already knew . . ."

Keeping all that in mind, you may remember that I left off just before I signed on to be Coyote's flight instructor, and I got to say, getting his four-legged arse airborne wasn't easy. It all began with him hopping and flapping like a wounded sea gull, and it really didn't matter how hard he tried, he just couldn't get enough air underneath those wings. But he kept at it, and he kept at it some more, and eventually he got off the ground. Then he had to maneuver up through the trees, and when he finally got lucky enough to clear the lower branches, he still had to avoid sailing snoutlong into the trunk of some five-foot-wide hemlock or Doug-fir.

As for me, my challenge was to avoid criticizing his oh-so-obvious short-comings. I needed to stay positive, so with this in mind, I encouraged him with stories about Swan and Albatross, stories about how awkward they were on earth, yet how magnificent they were in the air. I reminded him that these particular wings were not of the terrestrial world. I reminded him that once he got into the air, these wings would work for instead of against him.

And let me tell you, once he got above the treetops, Coyote got caught up in the panorama of it all. He really was thrilled by the change of perspective. Oh, he didn't understand it, but he was thrilled by it. I watched him stretch out his paw and erase Mount Olympus. It's pretty heady stuff when you think your paw can omnipotently rub out an entire mountain. I also watched him wipe his paw across the entire Olympic north shore and eliminate the Strait of Juan de Fuca. At one point he flew so high his paw obliterated the entire Olympic Peninsula.

Yeah, I know, I know, all you psychology experts out there are screaming that this puts Coyote in the preoperational stage. It's like he failed third grade, so it should come as no surprise that when he came back to earth, he said to me, "Hey, Raven, now that I've got above the clouds, it's time for me to aim higher."

"You think?" He really was yipping into a strong headwind.

"Come on, Raven, at first I could hardly get off the ground. Now I'm makin' mountains disappear!"

"I hear you there. And if I remember correctly, your plan is to do some star flying, right?"

"Yes siree, I figure these beaut's will take me there and back."

"That would be something, wouldn't it? You thinking about tonight?"

"Why not? Wise Canine say, 'Practicin' the same will only get you the same.' I'm sure these wings'll take me higher."

"So," and I couldn't help myself, "if you get all the way to Jackal's net, how do you intend to cut loose all those starry salmon?"

In response Coyote pushed a small tule-woven basket my way. "Bird, you better tune your frequency."

"What's this?"

"Oh, I don't know; let's see," and he gingerly opened the basket's lid to reveal a wondrous thing, a barracuda jaw with razor sharp teeth. "Found it when I was scavengin' along the beach a while back. You're not the only one who can spot somethin' valuable, you know."

"It would seem so."

Right after the sun set, my mind took a turn. No, I didn't desert my post as flight instructor, but I got distracted because a lot of his plan reminded me of an earlier event: that time I caught an updraft, that time I left my father behind, that time I went for the sun, that time I hit the apogee, turned brilliant as magnesium flame, tumbled earthward wings akimbo, and splat-plunged into the Hood Canal.

I've got to admit that I was so-o-o lost in that memory that I didn't notice my buddy strap on those wings, and when I crawled out of my recollection, he was gone. I looked left. I looked right, I looked behind, and when I looked up, there he was, just a bit of moonlight reflecting from those marvelous wings and climbing without the aid of an updraft, his daytime escalator.

Then he surprised me. He really did. Instead of trying to talk his way out of doing the work, he dug deep and found sinews he didn't know he had. He strenuously stroked those wings through the cold night air. He paddled and pulled some more until something pliable, something elastic, but also something quite solid, stopped his progress. But even that didn't stop his effort. First, he twisted. Then, he turned. And finally, of course, he became exhausted, so wasted, in fact, that he panicked, and in his terror, he gave up.

You'd think that would've been the end of my buddy Coyote, but as it just so happened, giving up is what saved him. Giving up allowed his mind to refocus, and inside this new perspective, he realized that he was caught in Jackal's net. He had reached his goal. Jackal's starry salmon were just on the other side.

Armed with this new insight, Coyote went straight for his barracuda jaw knife and sliced through the threads of Jackal's net. And let me tell you, my buddy Pasture Poodle surely achieved his purpose. But what he didn't realize was that his cousin's net not only kept the starry salmon in place but also held back the cosmic winds, so that when he cut through the net, he let loose a celestial tornado that sent him earthward, the astral whirlwind corkscrewing up his nose, scouring his soul, and blowing out his arse.

And as a result, Coyote tumbled down, down, down, and when he hit the surface of the Pacific, some of his fur unglued on impact and scattered in the current. But this current was no run-of-the-mill Pacific current. Oh, no, this current was different, singular. One might even say this current was spectacular, so much so, in fact, that this swell turned out to be the tsunami generated by the Cascadia Subduction Zone Quake, the cataclysm we've been waiting for since "IN HIS BEGINNING."

BOOK EIGHTEEN

YOU GOT NO TIME

CRACK

BAIE'S JOURNAL

Entry 69

CRACK, a loosed terror
BANG, irresistible shock
BLAST, panic expelled

cracked after sunset,
splitting and spilling like so
much ripe fireweed fluff

Wildsisters shaken,
farmhouse cracked and fallen,
cloud puffs rushing by

cracking and crumbling,
shaking off these shattered shards,
these fissured fractures

my virgin heart cracked,
its green sea raining showers
of angelic kelp

FROGGING

BAIE'S JOURNAL

Entry 70

I recall,
dear Mother,
you never dropped
a stitch,
but
I must confess,
I cannot continue
in pattern.
I cannot join
new yarn.
I cannot tink
back.

THIS WAS OUR WORLD

BAIE'S JOURNAL

Entry 71

When the minutes that
shook Wildsisters, that
felt an hour, that
felt a day,
felt a lifetime,
ended,
I called, and
I called again

—Dear Petr,
dear Petr, dear Dori,
dear Dori, dear Aces,
dear Aces, dear Freya,
dear Freya, dear Sesily,
dear Sesily, dear Shasta,
dear Shasta, dear Petr,
dear Petr,
oh, dearest Petr!

Then I listened.
I received nothing:
no voice, no sound.
After the shaking,
our Humptulips,
these dark Olympics,
the vast Pacific,
possessed not a tongue,
only an ear . . . except,
settled upon
a fallen red cedar,
a silhouette against
a waning moon,
a solitary raven
spoke, but to whom?
—Quork, quork, quork.

And I began to cry,
first a shudder,
a tear running from
eye to ear,
then a convulsion,
a spasm, delivering up
an ache.

This was our world
broken for us:
I, Baie, among
the fallen berries,
this raven atop
a fallen red cedar.

JUDAS NIXON HELL

BAIE'S JOURNAL

Entry 72

—Holy Jeez-us
Mother Fuckin' Christ,
what the hell?
Get off o' me wall!
Damn, that hurts!
Maybe cracked my ribs.
I sure as shit don't know.
Gawd-damn, dumb-ass wall,
I can put you up, an'
I sure as shit can tear
your stupid-ass down!

And then a glorious sight.
Dear Dori, mouth full of
blood, stood up out of
the farmhouse wreckage.
—Baie, that you down in
the bog? Damn it all.
Damn it all t' hell, an'
thank gawd I found you.

You okay out there?
If I can sure as shit walk,
I'll be sure as shit fine.
That makes two, you plus me.
What the Judas Nixon hell?!

—Earthquake, dear Dori.

—No shit Charlotta! but
where's my Aces at?
He's got t' be 'round? An'
where's Freya at?
Where's Sesily? An'
Shasta an' Ruth Ann, too?
Where'd that Petr get to?
Just like a man t' disappear
when there's work t' do.
Now, get your head 'round
this mess, Dori-girl.
Got t' rise 'bove all this.
Got t' find my Aces!

WHAT BERNARD AND JOHN SAID

BAIE'S JOURNAL

Entry 73

I heard two men.
They stood where
the river bank had been,
their waists now cut by
the water's surface.

Then I saw both turn and
meander our way.
They continued talking.
—Now you listen here,
John Tornow,
this was comin' for
some considerable time.

—Sad, Bernard, ain't it?
Hmph, all nothin' on
top of nothin'.

—I'm tellin' you,
I've been up with
those whisky jacks, an'
they keep bringin' back
queer, rotten tins an'
weird, mangled bits.

—Everythin's slipped away,
Bernard. There ain't no rest.

—I know, John Tornow,
salmon are stayin' home.
The ones I find, they
all got tumors and such.

—All razors an' blood,
razors an' blood.
Sis passed on, an'
damn, John an' William,
my ol' mother, too.
Her name was Louise.

Hey, you got a mother
to go home to, Bernard?

—No, her bones are back on
th' Skagit down below
th' Cascade foothills.
Her and th' salmon,
they aren't comin' back
unless, maybe, that
earthquake shook 'em and
woke 'em all up.
What you think, missy?

Numb,
I chewed my hair's loose ends.
Chilled,
my useless hands trembled.
Faithful,
I said a desperate prayer.
—Our dearest kelp
who covers the Pacific,
luxuriantly flourish.
May your holdfasts grasp firm.
May your fronds stretch sunward.
Nurture us; grant us grace, as
we, too, grant others grace.
Do not broach hazard, but
resist the destruction.
Yours is our home and
our love and our peace,
here and now.
Amen.

—Well said; well said.
So tell me, missy,
you feel it buildin'?
Not so far out,
it's for sure comin'.
Time's a wastin'.

—Hmph, all razors, I say,
razors an' blood.

—Don't mind ol' John, missy.
He sees what's behind, but
I see what's ahead, an'
you and your friend there
best be headin' on out.

Moth-eyed with
terror, I answered
—Our friends are gone.
Where would we go?

—Missy, you got no time.
Do you see those cedars,
the ones that are standin'?
Can you see out beyond?

Lifting my finger,
I weakly pointed to
a few red cedars
standing together,
supporting one another.
—Yes, I think so.
Right over there?

—Just beyond those cedars,
you'll find Sxwayo'klu.
She's got all your friends,
'specially the li'l ones.
She's waist deep, so
you got t' swim on out.

I anxiously turned and
found dear Dori, broken.
It almost broke me.
—We're tired.
We need rest.
We won't make it.

—Don't worry, Kushtakas
will hold you up.
For certain you won't drown.
Li'l Freya didn't drown.
Those Kusktakas
kept her li'l nose 'bove
th' Humptulips an'
delivered her right to
her momma.

Dark and darker,
John Tornow said again
—Hey, you got a mother
to go home to, Bernard?

And Bernard only smiled,
motioning us forward.

I took my dear Dori's hand.
—Remember? You said
we got to rise above.

EXCUSE ME, TSUNAMI HAS SOMETHING TO SAY

Gray Whale,
blessed are you
who are mothers,
who knock out while you calve,
who cling to your young,
who remain in the shallows
far from your deep.
I will roll over you.

Razor Clam,
blessed are you
who are thin-shelled,
who reach beyond the sand,
who risk exposure,
who stretch to taste the air,
your foot not so deep.
I will roll over you.

Candlefish,
blessed are you
who are consumed,
who are Pacific-schooled,
who are now returning,
who burn brightly
anointed deep with oil.
I will roll over you.

Ghost Shrimp,
blessed are you
who are insignificant,
who are soft and transparent.

And Salmon,
blessed are you
who burst with promise,
who hurdle the rapids and falls
deep into the land's immaculate heart.
I will pass over you all.

Kyrie eleison.
Christe eleison.
Kyrie eleison.
Je ne suis plus un créature
de la terre
or the air.
I am a creature
de la mer.

I FELT A MIRACLE

BAIE'S JOURNAL

Entry 74

Beyond farmhouse wreckage,
beyond Wildsisters' strength,
beyond cranberry blessings,
dear Dori and I
heeded Bernard and
obediently waded in:
first to our knees,
then to our thighs,
finally giving up,
laying ourselves out,
thoroughly baptized.

To keep us alive,
a white otter appeared,
leading us forward.
The Kushtakas appeared,
gently supporting
dear Dori and me at
each wrist, at
each ankle.
Praise be the white otter!
Praise be the Kushtakas!
We did not sink below
the floodwaters.
They were heaven-sent!

And praise be
dear Sxwayo'klu:
her head all carved angles,
her body all bear grease,
her basket a sanctuary.
Here, Freya snuggled in
Sesily's own arms.
Here, Aces beamed a grin,
Ruth Ann formed a plan, and
Shasta Lynn saw a future.
Here, Petr was draped in
our Pacific kelp,
his transmitter in
his backpack,
his hand awaiting
mine.

Kyrie eleison.
Christe eleison.
Kyrie eleison.
Tout
est perdre.
Tout
est retrouver.
Now and
here,
wildsisters.

BOOK NINETEEN

AFTER THE BIG ONE

BLINK

Petr felt the earth shaking. He felt the earth drop, a down elevator, the slack instantly gone. Then he felt the earth shoot into the canopy, an up elevator, the jerk wire pulled so fast it was enough to make someone a split ear. But it wasn't the earth, at least not this time. If Petr were a trailer monkey steering some heavy timber, he had come to the end of his ride. He found himself tumbling off the load onto a red cedar platform.

Petr blinked. He felt unsettled. He found no point of reference. He blinked again, blinked a third time, and then, quite deliberately, a fourth, and this time he brought into focus an infant's face, yes, Freya, and his eyes followed an arm to a shoulder, past a neck, up to a woman's face, yes, Sesily, the infant's mother.

Petr blinked and then another woman's face, yes, Ruth Ann, and he blinked again, an additional woman's face, yes, Shasta Lynn, and he blinked once more, and this time a child's face, yes, Aces. Now he had points of reference, dots if you will, but not the sort of dots he could plot on a map, not even a map of his own imagining, his own dreaming, but dots all the same.

And Petr blinked to see more, others, too dark, too stunted, too young, a glint of light in each eye, yes, the children from his ascent into the Olympics; yes, the children from Baie and his tryst among the cranberries; yes, the ones who egged on a child.

THUMP and Petr heard a voice, "Jeez-us Green River Killer Christ!"

THUMP and Petr felt Baie intertwine her fingers with his.

Then Petr felt the red cedar platform shift from center one way and then back, and then he felt himself and all the wildsisters and their children and all Sxwayo'klu's children move through space. He stumbled a bit, his center of gravity continually shifting. He turned his face skyward, blinked, and achieved a new perspective, the sun flooding in.

Petr felt Baie snuggle her head against his shoulder, "Just close your eyes and listen."

Petr did as Baie said, and after he closed his eyes, Baie placed his hand on her belly. What he felt was hard from working her cranberry bog and soft from living her femininity. He understood her gesture. Then he felt her fingers again slip between his and heard her say, "Dip netting rainbow smelt. Gath'ring up sugar kelp. Berries, berries, we all hold hands! Can you imagine it, dearest Petr? Dip netting rainbow smelt. Gath'ring up sugar kelp. Berries, berries, we all hold hands! I know it's silly, but it feels good to say. Dip netting rainbow smelt. Gath'ring up sugar kelp. Berries, berries, we all hold hands!"

Petr liked the sound of Baie's voice. He liked the image her words gifted. He liked the feel of her fingers coupling his.

PORTRAIT OF A SIGNAL AS PIRATE RADIO BROADCAST

You are listening to HOO HOO FM, the station where even your dead father can call in, and now it's time for our Who Told Petr the Basket Woman Story Contest. As you all know, we run this fine and dandy little contest every morning, and you, yes, you listeners, can win a bouquet of wild sugar kelp if you just call in at one, one hundred, one one one, one one one one. Be the fifth caller and answer this question: Who told Petr the Basket Woman story?

"Why, just yesterday, Jessie Slough won a case of Berry Scat. That's right, Berry Scat, brought to you by our friends on Burnt Hill who want you to remember, drink a case of Berry Scat, just to wait your guts to shat.

"Hey, we've got a winner, Harry Pounder of Donkey Creek. He says his mother put on a mattress cover after he wet the bed. You gotta be kidding,

Harry. You're telling us the mattress got sunny and then it got cloudy. That's disgusting!

"Well, as you know, we're running this little Who Told Petr the Basket Woman Story Contest, and you were the fifth caller. So for a bouquet of wild sugar kelp, can you guess who told Petr the Basket Woman story? Can you, Harry Pounder of Donkey Creek?

"You're absolutely right, Harry. The Steam Donkey Academy told Petr the story. Harry Pounder of Donkey Creek, you're our winner, and in honor of your winning answer, we'll just cue up this logger's ditty, so all our listeners can unite."

> Misery sery
> Misery seryppy,
> Misery sery
> Misery misery.

FREYA, WE'RE NOT IN HUMPTULIPS ANYMORE

> bodies tumbled down
> below Anderson Glacier,
> Honeymoon Meadows

BUT I DIGRESS, A WEDDING INVITATION

I know it's only a haiku, but you've got to admit, that's some change of setting, one which could use some explanation. With that in mind, you'll remember we were listening to Petr chat up Hugh Sudderth when the Cascadia Subduction Zone Quake cut loose. Then Sxwayo'klu scooped up Petr and the wildsisters to save them from the tsunami. And now you should know that Sxwayo'klu has taken them all up here to Mount Anderson and dumped them out of her cedar basket onto Honeymoon Meadows. Got West Peak to our left. Got East Peak to our right. And in the foreground we got some bare rock and scree fields, an unnamed burn with its unnamed water-falls, and countless spars of fir, some more black than green, a few bleached like skeletal spines.

So what, you might ask, have I been doing between the time Coyote cut that hole in Jackal's net and me flying up here to be with Petr and Baie?

To answer that question, we need to go back to when Coyote splash-landed in the Pacific. Back then I thought about fishing him out of the swell-ing tsunami and returning him to Mole. After all, she had served me some heavenly beetle grub and salal berry cobbler. I'm not heartless, you know; well, maybe I am sometimes, because truth be told I didn't take Coyote back to his wife. Instead I let him ride that tsunami back to shore, figured it would do him some good, and as for me, I thought it was high time for me to retrieve that light-filled box, the one I'd stashed along the Satsop River.

After returning to the Satsop drainage and locating the correct red cedar root tangle, I took that light-filled box fast and high, and when I reached the apogee, I tucked in my wings, rolled into a supersonic billdive, hit the surface of the Pacific, and dove DOWN, DOWN, DOWN. And as it turned out, I wasn't really prepared for what I found. Instead of the Salmon Village, I found the Ghost Salmon Village, its residents' skin eaten with lesions, ge-latinous, their bodies corrupt. Their eyes were dead-end pearls. Their mouths were box canyon cadavers. Their scales thickened the water into a carrion stew. I moved through vertebrae and eye teeth. I pushed aside rib and jaw bones. And I continued to struggle until I came to Dog Salmon Brother and Silver Salmon Sister's door. Inside I found Dog Salmon Brother dissolute and disillusioned. His voice came from the open barrow of his mouth. "No."

"We need to get you and your sister out."

"This is the way our world ends."

"No, it doesn't. I've brought light to you and your sister."

"We're already forgetting."

"I won't."

"You will."

"And your sister?"

Silence.

I fought the urge to lie next to Silver Salmon Sister, to go full on tragic hero. Instead, I opened that light-filled box, FLASH! and the sun shone so bright that Silver Salmon Sister and her brother were in a better place. And right after that, I flew up here and settled onto this subalpine fir above Petr.

But none of that explains what happens next. Not why the BIG ONE figures into what happens next. Not why a wedding, MY WEDDING! figures into what happens next.

You see, the BIG ONE shook everything up, so much so, in fact, that Silver Salmon Sister, my recently light-filled beloved, my freshly light-filled betrothed, is making her way back up our Dosewallips River in preparation for catching our first thermal.

And, hey, if you're so inclined, you're welcome to be our wing bird!

Kyrie eleison.
Christe eleison.
Kyrie eleison.
Je ne suis plus qu'une créature
of the air
mais aussi une créature
de la mer.

SERMON

A charm of hummingbirds came out of a waterfall and down from the trees. They darted this way. They paused, hovering. They ignored the white Sitka valerian and blue harebells. They tested the blue lupine. They dove. They chirped. They sipped from the red columbine.

Filled with a night's feeding, a far-ranging hawk moth heeded the sun's call. It came to rest on Baie's shoulder.

A family of whisky jacks sat on a subalpine fir, its tortured trunk and branches bowed by the snow weight of years. Shasta Lynn began to speak and taught them, saying:

"Yass, yass, blessed is silence, for it springs between the fissures.

"Blessed is disorder, for it blooms among the paintbrush and lupine.

"Blessed are the nameless, for they ride undetected, free, and without care, eh.

"Blessed is a spirit deranged, for it springs, blooms, and rides the swirlin' currents."

PARABLE

Baie said to Petr, "See these trees bowed by wind and rain? And snow? They are bowed in prayer."

"So?"

"We aren't the only ones beneath the angels, dear Petr. They are, too. When we pass away, they will still be here. World without end. Amen."

SUPPER

Baie and Petr walked out into a clearing of black mountain huckleberry. They knelt and picked a handful of ripe berries. The memory of cranberry picking was in their fingers. They took and ate.

Baie fed the child inside.

HONEYMOON MEADOWS GATHERING

Down from Anderson Pass came White Otter and the Kushtakas. They had the preparations for a wedding feast. White Otter carried a small book. The Kushtaka men balanced poles spitted with blueback salmon smoked in an alder fire. The Kushtaka women brought red cedar-woven baskets lined with sword fern and filled with salal berries and razor clams preserved in candlefish oil. The Kushtaka children carried small red cedar boxes containing delicacies wrapped in kelp: roasted chanterelle, king boletus, and snow morel mushrooms as well as steamed fairy slipper, camas lily, spring-beauty bulbs.

Raven, Silver Salmon Sister, her brother at her side, Petr, and Baie assembled in Honeymoon Meadows, the blue-white of the Anderson Glacier behind. A series of aftershocks rumbled through.

Dori led the wildsisters out of the black huckleberries and over to the wedding. Shasta Lynn stood and scanned this tree line, that rocky ridge, painting in her mind's eye a vision, formulating in her spirit ear a prophecy. Sesily collected Sxwayo'klu's children and found an erratic upon which to sit and nurse Freya. Sxwayo'klu was a totem. Ruth Ann tried on a new smile

Dori tousled her son's hair, and then Aces ran from his mother back into the black huckleberries. There he found Petr's backpack and returned, dragging it back. After searching inside, Aces removed the radio transmitter, checked the wires, extended the antenna, and began to crank the eggbeater. This was the boy's first shift on Radio Free Olympia.

Speaking to those in attendance, White Otter, the one officiating, said:

Dearly Beloved
We are gathered together to
witness two wondrous marriages.
Earth, once cracked and sorely broken,
now reunites in holy courage.

Do you, Raven, take Silver Salmon Sister
to be your aether-wedded wife,
to have now, to hold forever
for the duration of your lives?

For sure.

Do you, Silver Salmon Sister, take Raven
to be your sea-wedded husband,

to have now, to hold forever,
throughout all that events command?

Naturally.

Do you, Petr, take Baie to
to be your spirit-wedded wife,
to have now, to hold forever
for the duration of your lives?

Uh huh.

And do you, Baie, take Petr
to be your fruit-wedded husband,
to have now, to hold forever,
always pledged to holding hands?

Oui, s'il vous plaît.

May goodness and mercy follow
you through all the days of your lives,
and may you remain tuned to our
Olympic frequency and thrive.

When the ceremony was over, a procession of latecomers came down from Anderson Pass. Mole arrived with Coyote, who although he was a bit worse for wear, faithfully carried Mole's cooking pot filled with bubbling Pacific flotsam stew. Sxwayo'klu found her little ones, and she settled them among the scarlet paintbrush, wooly sunflower, and avalanche lily. Bernard approached and sat back on his haunches. He exhaled an alpine fog. John Tornow, unkempt beard twisted, wide eyes unblinking, floated these words on the breeze, "You got a mother to go home to, Bernard?"

Raven and Silver Salmon Sister then began to dance, a lively step out among the cobweb thistle, out among the fan-leaf cinqfoil. Aces and all of Sxwayo'klu's childen ran to join in. White Otter gave out bull kelp ribbons, and the dancers wove this way, then that way.

Baie and Petr returned to the black mountain huckleberries. Baie picked a few of the finest berries and offered them to Petr. He smiled and accepted the round, sweet bodies.

Petr took Baie by the hand. She had found him, and now he waited to do what he did best, listen.

Baie then took Petr by the other hand, the two making a circle. She began to sing a song. The song was her gift to the newly united. The song was her hymn to a new time.

Kyrie eleison.
Christe eleison.
Kyrie eleison.
Tout
est perdre.
Tout
est retrouver.
Now and
here,
wildsisters.

GLOSSARY

TIMBER TERMS

barber chair a stump where a portion of the tree trunk remains extending upward

bean can a lunch bucket

bitch a bad deal

blew up the engine had a wild time in town

brush ape a logger

buck for grade cut logs into various lengths in order to produce the greatest quantity of high-quality material

bucking removing limbs from cut timber and cutting logs into lengths

bull line cable main line of a high cable system for pulling cut timber to the landing or collection area

bull stick a steel bar that punches holes under stumps so that the holes can be filled with dynamite

butt rot blowdown decay at the bottom of tree that causes a tree to fall in a windstorm

calk boots (also caulk or cork) boots or shoes with steel spikes for traction

chippy trick bad luck

chokebores fancy pants that no logger respects

choke setter a logger who passes a short steel cable from the choker hook around a log and back again.

choker cable short steel cable that is circled around one or more logs and cinched tight

conky (from blind conk) rotten, specifically from wood-rot fungus, which is a mushroom shaped like a conch shell

crosscut saw a handsaw for falling and bucking timber

crummy a railcar, truck, or bus for transporting loggers

cull timber not worth cutting

donkey engine a small engine used to haul logs to the landing or collection area

donkey puncher an operator of a small engine or donkey

donkey whistle the sound device that signals commands (a certain number of toots) to workers in the timber

ferrocerium rod metal alloy used to spark fires when struck with harder material

flume a wooden structure that carries water with logs

four-four four long and four short blasts blown on a steam donkey whistle when a logger is injured

gopher hole a hole dug for either a choker or blasting powder

guttersnipe a bum or vagrant

grain fed filly a well-endowed woman, possibly a prostitute

green bucker a logger new to removing limbs from cut timber and cutting logs into lengths

gyppo small-time logging companies that make a living cutting timber larger companies won't

hard rub bad luck

hickory shirt cotton work shirt preferred by loggers

high-water pants pants cut off above the ankle and preferred by loggers because they won't interfere with working on logs or in water

hog at the cookhouse door pig fed on table scraps from the logging camp cookhouse

hooktender a logger in charge of a logging site

jacklight a portable light for night hunting or fishing

jerk wire a wire that when pulled activated the donkey whistle

landing central location where logs are collected and loaded for shipment

load a unit of work (collection of logs for shipment) on a work site

misery whip a two-man crosscut saw with a handle at each end

one-match burn a fire started on a day so dry it takes little effort (one match)

outlaw tree a tree that is dangerous to cut down

rigging the equipment used in cable logging systems

saddle blanket a tough pancake

saw oil lubricant, usually kerosene, put on a saw blade to dissolve pitch

sawyer a logger whose job it is to cut timber

scrub timber not worth cutting

sinker log timber on the bottom of a lake or stream

skidder a large engine used to pull in logs for collection

slash the remaining branches, treetops, and other leftovers after the logs have been taken to the mill

snus tobacco snuff

spitter a short, hand-fired fuse with a notch in the casing that allows fire to shoot out

split ear a mean horse or man

splitting maul a wedge-shaped axe used for splitting fire wood

spraint otter dung

springboard a strong wooden plank a logger stands on for cutting because the ground is too rough or steep or the tree bottom is too swelled. A notch is cut in the tree and the plank extends from the notch.

steam donkey a small steam engine used to haul logs to the landing or collection area

steam donkey whistle the steam-powered whistle that signals commands (a certain number of toots) to workers in the timber

stinger (trailer) the pole that connects a log truck with its trailer, which is most noticeable when an empty trailer has been pulled up onto the back of the cab for transport

stove up injured or broken

stump farm or ranch a piece of land a timber company sells to a prospective farmer or rancher

timber beast a logger

trailer monkey a logger who rides on and steers the back of a log trailer

turn-too-big-to-handle a wife a logger can't deal with

whipsaw bad luck or a hand saw with a long, narrow blade

whistle punk a young logger whose job it is to yell commands back and forth between the choke setters and the donkey puncher

widowmaker a dangerous loose limb or treetop

yard location where logs are collected; or to pull logs into a central location for shipment out

yarding cable steel line used to pull logs into a central location

LABOR LINGO

I.W.W. Industrial Workers of the World, a union that aims to unite all workers in the struggle against employers

scab someone hired to take the job of a worker who is on strike

scissorbill a worker opposed to joining a union

Wobbly slang term for a member of the I.W.W.

SEWING SLANG

beading (needle) long thin needle for stringing beads

beggar's block quilt a quilt pieced together from nine 5-inch-square blocks. Eight of the blocks are pieced together from rectangles and triangles (pieced together into squares). The one center block is a solid piece of fabric. The name refers to the begging that takes place to collect scraps of fabric.

between (needle) short needle for quilting

bodkin (needle) blunt needle for threading ribbon or cord

chenille (needle) sharp needle with large eye for heavier thread

charm block quilt a quilt made up of square pieces of many different fabrics

crazy quilt a quilt made up of pieces of many different fabrics in many different shapes

curved (needle) sewing needle that is bent so that it can sew items that are not flat or fit into a sewing machine

darning (needle) large, blunt needle with a large eye for yarn or embroidery floss

embroidery (needle) large needle for doing embroidery

family album quilt a quilt constructed of blocks, each block having been appliquéd with a different design, that in their entirety represent a theme, in this case a particular family

frogging taking out completed stitches

glovers (needle) heavy triangular needle for sewing hides

quilting (needle) either a between for piecework or sharps needle for appliqué

sailmakers (needle) heavy triangular needle for sewing sails

sharps (needle) general sewing needle

tapestry (needle) blunt needle used for woven and knit fabrics

tink back knitting backward to take out completed stitches

ACKNOWLEDGMENTS

Huck Finn once said, "If I'd a knowed what a trouble it was to make a book I wouldn't a tackled it," which in my case, isn't exactly true, but it is true that *Radio Free Olympia* required "a whole lotta love" from friends and family.

So in the spirit of Baie, let me thank my dear magical wife Jamie Shepherd, my dear wild first child Wilson Shepherd, and my dear precious second child Beck Shepherd, without whom I would not have traveled to and experienced the Olympic Peninsula. They are the family, my family, that Petr and Baie yearn for and begin to form.

Let me thank dear Maurrie Aukland, dear Charles Boyer, and dear Deanne Woita, a most memorable troika of Elma High School English teachers past. When I came to the Olympic Peninsula, you did not know who you were welcoming nor what would be the result. I hope you approve.

Let me thank my dear friend Bob Fouratt, who has watched and supported me from early high school through the present and beyond. You read the early first draft of *Radio Free Olympia*, and like our friendship, *RFO* has come a long way.

Let me thank dear Tim McConnehey and dear Sam Bass of Izzard Ink Publishing for picking up *Radio Free Olympia*'s development and marketing. Books like this, complicated ones, idiosyncratic ones, ones that hold hands with the modernist tradition, need champions without which they die a manuscript's death. Yes, you have been *RFO*'s champions and more.

Let me thank dear Skye Loyd of Edit Guru for acting as developmental editor. You put *Radio Free Olympia*'s body on a diet while protecting its soul. You made *RFO* a healthier book.

Let me thank dear Andrea Ho for her brilliant cover design. I asked for something eye-catching and unexpected, maybe even iconoclastic, and you surprised me.

Let me thank dear Daniel Lagin of Daniel Lagin Graphic Design for his remarkable interior design. I imagined something enhancing but not distracting, and you did my imagination one better.

Let me thank dear Michelle Argyle of Melissa Williams Design. You were the first to take the trouble.

Let me thank Britain's dear Jeff Scott of Platypus PR for early support. Your kind words kept me plugging.

Let me thank dear Dan Hewitt, the once inimitable general manager of WARC FM, Allegheny College Radio, Meadville, PA. You generously opened the doorway through which all of *Radio Free Olympia* walked. Going through radio's door was a good time then and continues to feed me now.

Let me thank dear Professor Colin MacCabe for opening my mind to writers such as James Joyce and to the intersection between realism and culture studies. It is true that I never became the academic you trained me to be, but I know that your heart beats more for artists than critics. I hope you find in *Radio Free Olympia* some of the magical berries that have sprouted from your labors.

Let me thank the late, dear Professor Richard Tobias for nurturing my skill and passion for deep cultural research. Because of you I have become a successful hunter of cultural quarry: watching, listening, smelling, tasting, and feeling for signs, following historical trails, reading cultural ecosystems.

Let me thank the dear Reverend Bebb Wheeler Stone for opening up spiritual space within my Presbyterian tradition. Your example has given me license to follow all the spirituality that I experienced on the Olympic Peninsula and later explored in *Radio Free Olympia*.

And most importantly let me thank my dear Olympic Peninsula for introducing me not only to its plants, animals, topography, geology, and weather but also to Bernard "John" Huelsdonk, John Tornow, Hugh Sudderth, Joseph P. O'Neil, O'wota, Sxwayo'klu, and the Kushtakas (hardly all-inclusive). Experiencing the Olympic Peninsula is where I learned that a place is not a place but a living, breathing, changing idea. Like Raven says,

"After all, a mountain is merely its immense interior, its water and windswept exterior, a bedazzled sight one moment, a muted maw the next—not at all a mountain. A glacier is merely its fickle interior, its faceted exterior, a blind-struck sight one moment, a haunted shroud the next—not at all a glacier. A pass is merely its singular infinity—not at all a pass." Thanks, my dear Raven, I couldn't have said it better!